Bed Table Door

Csilla Toldy

Bed Table Door
Csilla Toldy

ISBN 978-1-903110-98-0

First published in this edition 2023 by Wrecking Ball Press

Book design: humandesign.co.uk

Supported using public funding by
ARTS COUNCIL ENGLAND
LOTTERY FUNDED

Prologue

The rain served him well. Nobody cared. The good citizens of the state were rushing under umbrellas, trying to avoid the deep puddles at every kerb on the road and the occasional spray from heavy trucks. Samu entered the public toilets of the Southern Railway Station. Pop music roared from Radio Kossuth. The suspicious attendant searched his face from behind the *People's Freedom*, his eyes zapped like mosquitoes. Averting the attendant's scrutiny, Samu smiled back at a hopeful Brezhnev on the front page. He could not find enough money in his pockets and the attendant, getting bored, waved him to go in.

Once inside the cubicle he got down to work. He unfolded the rope tied tightly around his body under his Mackintosh. He lifted the seat and stood on the edge of the toilet bowl. He reached up and managed to tie the rope onto the pipe well enough. Then he slid his head into the noose. Now he had to jump and, hopefully, be found in time – before he choked. He put one foot on the door handle to be able to kick it open, if necessary. He had designed each step of this show precisely, nevertheless, he was nervous. Anything could go wrong. Just when thinking this, his foot on the bowl slipped and, instead of jumping, he fell. The rope strangled his neck uncomfortably, but he held onto it, trying to swing from side to side to make a noise; not able to shout, or even breathe, for that matter. When he kicked the air, his bum banged into the wall of the cubicle, but not loud enough to drown out the twelve o'clock bells on the radio. Another swing – no result. He could feel the blood rising in his head, feeling less and less confident about the whole business, when, at last, the pipe broke. Samu fell on the ground, breaking down the door. Finally, he could breathe.

The attendant ran to him.

'Fuck it!' he shouted, slipping on the wet tiles.

Samu stood up slowly, gasping for air. He looked at the attendant pleadingly.

'Get away from here,' the attendant shouted.

'No, you have to call the emergency services,' said Samu, according to his own design.

'No, I don't want the fucking police. It's just a pipe break, nothing special. And you, vanish!'

Samu, still clinging to his plan, repeated, 'you have to call the emergency services. I've tried to kill myself. I might try it again.'

'You can try it as often as you like, but not here. I'm not your father, you chicken, shall I smack you, or what?' He started to push Samu towards the door. 'Go. I'll call the railway management to fix this pipe and you go and do what you want. I have had enough of you stupid hooligans. Breaking the pipes that's all you can do. Bloody chickens.'

Samu, defeated, and still with the rope around his neck, scurried out of the public toilets into the streets of rain-soaked Budapest. He threw the rope into a waste bin and walked on. A number four bus stopped, and Samu managed to jump on. He sat down and let the bus rock him into quiet retrospection. They took the tunnel under the castle, and then beneath the grey-green Danube, whirling under the stone lions of the Chain Bridge. In Pest the sycamore trees that lined up on both sides of the People's Republic Street seemed naked, with their arms hanging down lifelessly. Only the wide space of Heroes' Square cheered him up and he reminded himself to go and see the travelling exhibition of Van Gogh's works in the Museum of Fine Arts before it left the country again. A huge billboard with a Van Gogh painting plastered the side wall of the building; the only source of vibrant colours, sunshine, and life. Samu glared at it, bemoaning his meek existence, where it was raining inside, too.

The Bed

Chapter 1

Under the window, the number four tram noisily jerked into motion, shaking Sofie out of sleep. She turned on her other side, the silk of her long hair tickling her face.

Don't rush, it's Saturday.

For Sofie the bed represented the best and safest living area, the place of birth, dreams and...sex? She loved the fluid space between sleep and awake and she tried to expand it. Part of her sleeping self recognised, from the eerie silence, that she had the flat to herself. She could slip back into the zone at her heart's content.

Even awake, she often became disconnected from her body when she was on her own in the flat. She wandered around like a ghost, often shocked by the apparition in the mirror: *an absolute stranger.*

Another yellow tram rattled by and she was floating over her home place, Angel Land, the oldest worker district of Budapest; famous for its steel works and train wagon plant; notorious for its gipsy shanties. Even in the People's Republic, District XIII, or Angel Land, carried the label of violence and low class.

Further on, following the yellow tram and passing Heroes' Square, she saw Uncle Lenin. He stood there, unmoved, lifting his right fist into the sky, looking ahead with stern eyes.

As a small child, still sitting in her mother's lap, she had travelled to the kindergarten on the yellow tram and a dark red trolleybus every day, passing him.

'Mum, who's that bald man?' she would ask her mother and their conversation became a game with the whole tram as their audience.

'That's Uncle Lenin, Sofie.'

'What's he doing there?'

'He is greeting Communism. And you know what? I saw him with my own eyes in Moscow in the Mausoleum.'

'What was he like?'

'He looked pretty much the same as this statue.'

Seeing Sofie's disappointed face, Mum would quickly add a grisly fact. 'His beard is still growing, you see. He has special barbers coming to groom him from time to time.'

Sofie could picture the powerful man lying on his white silk pillows being served by hairdressers and manicurists in his glass coffin in the snow-covered Mausoleum in Moscow, almost like Snow White.

The marches beneath Uncle Lenin's feet on May Days were often jolly occasions. Carried on her grandfather's shoulders, waving her flag, or floating a balloon, she had enjoyed looking down at the drunken faces and listening to jokes.

Floating above it all, she looked down on her Nan's house and her first school where she felt liberated. After school her grandmother had looked after her, respecting her space ... Nan taught her the 'Our Lord' prayer: a real lady, who wore her wavy white hair like a crown. She made sure that Sofie did her homework and mingled with the right children. With a hawk's eye, she watched over her affairs and friendships from her high place of dignity.

'Sofie, I don't think you should play with that girl.'

'Why?' she would ask dreamily.

'She has cracks in the corners of her mouth, she must come from a bad family.'

Nan's real stories were a thousand times more useful than anything Sofie could have learnt at school.

'What do you recall from '56, Nan?'

'The fear for my son and my daughter. Your mother had to stand up against the wall for keeping books by Marx and Engels, and your uncle fought for something he believed in.'

'Uncle George?'

'Well, we called him Gyuri then. Our reckless hothead. They thought they could change everything, but they were betrayed by their own man, who is now our party leader.'

'And you had to say goodbye to your son. Do you think Uncle George is happy in Manchester?'

'He must be homesick, that's why he comes so often.'

'Well, at least he can come and go as he likes.'

Sofie was growing up in their tiny apartment in a long block of flats in Peace Street in Angel Land. A huge red star was fixed onto the top of the house, exactly over her bedroom. Two beds, a wardrobe, and a tiny desk with a bookshelf built over it crowded the miniature room. It took only one step to get to the desk from her bed and another to the door that opened to her parents' bedroom. She barricaded the door with an armchair, making the space even smaller. Her only exit route led through the bathroom into the kitchen, then to the hall, and finally to the open corridor. She loved her bed, the place of birth, dreams and—

Another tram shook the pane and Sofie opened her eyes. Oh yes, it was the long weekend of the 7th November. Her parents must have gone to the market, one of their favourite pastimes. She cautiously put her feet on the cool wooden floor, stood up, and opened the window. The cold November air rushed in like a dragon, bringing the smoky scent of autumnal Budapest. She looked at her clothes cast on the parquet and flashes of the previous night started to bubble up to the still surface of her mind.

She had accompanied Attila, a boy she used to go out with for a while, to a party at the other end of the city. Having agreed that they had no chance of getting on as a couple, they remained good friends, nevertheless. This seemed to be her lot: boys were good to her within the framework of brotherhood or friendship, but not as lovers. In the matters of the heart, she was powerless.

Looking back, the villa under the frazzled, rainswept chestnut trees seemed more like a tomb, but at first sight the mysterious old building had impressed her.

On the way there Attila briefed her in an all too hush-hush manner. 'It's a sad story. Susan is lonely. Her parents died when she was very young, her grandmother brought her up, but she died last year as well. She has that huge villa all to herself. She has parties every night to escape her loneliness. We should be nice to her.'

Susan opened the heavy front door in a drunken stupor: a wavering shadow behind the oversized glasses. She beamed hostility towards Sofie, but hugged Attila.

'This is my ex, Sofie.'

This benign introduction seemed to soften Susan for a moment. They went into a large living room that had a piano in the corner. Dark velvet curtains hung on the high windows over bare dark brown wooden floor. Antique furniture cast around in disarray. Bottles here and there on the floor, a chaise long and a settee. Sofie found that in the small group of six she and the hostess were the only females. Attila settled down at the piano and Susan pulled Sofie down onto the settee to sit with her and talk like old friends. Sofie listened to a litany of grief. It was a hard job to decode the meaning of each half-pronounced word, but the underlying feelings were clear. Susan knew in her guts that most of the guys, even Attila, were just using her, even the bald guy in the Western boots, who pretended to be her boyfriend. After a few more bottles of wine she broke down crying on Sofie's shoulder.

When Susan crashed out the mood in the room visibly lightened, but Sofie could not bear the atmosphere. The boyfriend-pretender, called Olli, started to dance on the coffee table. His western boots were sure to scratch the surface of that beautiful antique piece. Sofie tried to play Susan's advocate. 'Stop! Get off there.'

But Olli only laughed.

Sofie became angry. 'You're her boyfriend. You should look after her things, her property.'

'Fuck property,' said Attila from behind the black concert piano, with a cigarette hanging in the corner of his mouth. Sofie attacked him, too:

'You're just using her like the rest.'

'No, I'm here to play her my songs. She loves art. My singing helps to heal her heart.'

The boys laughed. Sofie was not sure whom they found so funny; Attila, Susan or herself. The guy lying on a dark green baroque chaise lounge in a sleeping bag, joined their duel. 'And why are you here, Sofie? Did you come to listen to her misery, or did you come to have a good time? I think you are selfish,' he said with a grin, turning to the wall.

She tried to brush away the aftertaste of cigarettes and wine, but mainly the sense of guilt lingering in the pit of her stomach. No, she did not need to meet Susan who seemed to be a sack of unexplored emotions. Sofie understood her too well, she knew that Susan suffered for having inherited so much by surviving her loved ones. A black hole in her soul sucked up all the light. If life was a mathematical equation, only another black hole could have tipped her emptiness into balance; *healing could only come through fire and more suffering,* she thought, *through an equal kind of Purgatory experience.* Worthlessness and depression were the two feelings that still echoed in Sofie and she had to fight herself out of this dark hole with force.

Was this a metaphor, or pure religion? Saint Sofia, please help us. She inherited the religious imagery from Sándor, her last boyfriend and his friends. They attended one of the very few Catholic faith schools near Budapest. Taught by Franciscan monks, they were so bright and knowledgeable, while Sofie knew nothing about the church and its liturgies. Her mother was an atheist and Communist. Sofie found intellectual pleasure in these boys' fascinating discussions about Abraham, the father that killed his own son for God, and other cruel stories from the Bible. While they painted the portrait of a dreadful God, Jesus, the son, offered everything you could dream of, asking for nothing in return. Without the need for much persuasion, she was instinctively drawn to the suffering of Jesus.

While she had got over Attila easily, she was still brooding about Sándor. Catholic and deeply religious, Sándor danced on the thin line between the passionate urges of the body and his spiritual commitment to God. He had dubbed her *Saint Sofia.* She had no idea who Saint Sofia was, but Sándor had assured her that Sofia of Rome had been a good woman, the mother of Faith, Hope and Charity. Naming the nameless, Sofie found it often annoying that her father's first name was Sándor, too. Nan found this rather funny, for the two men were the least bit alike. Sofie's father could not be bothered with religion, even though he had been brought up in the Catholic tradition. Accordingly, Nan approved of Sándor, the boyfriend, although she did not value his looks, calling him a horse-face. Whenever he phoned, she sensed him like a distant soul-mate, but enquired about the caller as usual, looking up from her knitting, 'Who's that?'

'It was my Sándor. You know the boy that kissed your hand.'

'Oh, yes, I remember him. He has good manners.'

'He is very special, too.'

'Is it serious then?'

'Yes. He doesn't seem to notice, though. Perhaps, I should tell him.'

'That's the last thing to do. Didn't your mother teach you anything useful? In our days we made men crawl at our feet, my dear.'

'Good to know. You forgot to teach this to your daughter. My mother crawls at my father's feet. Anyway, being cool doesn't work anymore, Nan.'

'Not, if you are weak. Just wearing trousers doesn't make you stronger. The only time I wore trousers I did it as a disguise during the war, and I didn't enjoy it, you can believe me. We made ourselves ugly so that the Russians wouldn't rape us.'

Sándor was full of light and, of course, the Almighty won the battle. Sofie did not know how to seduce him, herself an innocent in the kingdom of carnal pleasures. Drawn to each other, groping, mainly in the darkness, never reaching climax, her virginity became an unbearable burden. In the end it was a relief to be dumped by him.

After a long hot shower and breakfast, prepared with slow devotion, Saturday started to promise joy. 'So, here we are, Saint Sofia,' she said to her reflection in the mirror, although she started to hate this nickname, after all.

Chapter 2

It was the long weekend of 7th November. While the country
leaders celebrated the Great October Socialist Revolution, at least
the factory workers had a holiday. As every year, the television was
to broadcast the military tattoo from the Red Square in Moscow all
morning and school children had their compulsory dos. As it was
a Friday, the whole country was looking forward to some rest later
on, when all the boring theatre was over.

Samu woke up groggy. Meli was shaking him and Samu could
have punched the bloody maniac in the face, he was so cross.

'What do you want?'

Meli just grinned and said in a low voice, 'Come on, the horses
are waiting.'

Then he remembered where he was. They had arrived late last
night and even though he was sleeping at a new place, he slept well
in this country house. His sleeping bag was warm, and the air was
so clear here. He had promised to his housemate, Meli to come and
ride with him over the weekend. On the way here, while travelling
on the bus, Meli had explained to him that the horses needed to be
ridden. Their health depended on it. Man and horse were made for
each other.

'Fine, we'll do it,' Samu had promised, although he had never
ridden a horse before.

Meli was crazy for horses. He loved them more than girls. Unlike
Samu, who loved girls or better to say girls loved him. Whatever,
they were there, the two of them and the two horses at dawn. The
winter mornings were dark and he did not like them. Getting up
every day at six, going to work with Meli and his mother. She got the
job for them at the shoe factory and as it was to be with any good
Samaritan, theirs was better than hers. She was working on the
assembly line, like all the other women, preparing the upper coat
of the shoe for the glueing machine. Every five seconds there was
a new shoe in front of her. She was part of the machinery, as a cog
in the wheel. *Inhuman*, Samu thought. The women were moaning

all day about backache and headache and whatever ache and on top of that, they had to beg the foreman to give them a break. Samu and Meli had much better positions. Their job was to make huge cardboard boxes, albeit all day. Although the foreman bullied him for his long hair and ponytail, which he had to hide under a black felt beret anyway, as it was part of the worker uniform, all they could really complain about was the stink that one could smell as far as from a kilometre away from the shoe factory. Was it the glue or the leather, they were never sure. The only way to stop it was to smoke during the breaks, but Meli did not smoke. He'd rather crack jokes.

'Samu, what've you done again, you filthy fart box. Can't you control your hole?'

Or he cracked cobbler jokes that he had made up himself.

'What did the devil say to the communist cobbler?

Sell me your sole!

What did the communist cobbler say to the devil?

You have to ask the factory management, sir.'

Now the smell of hay mixed with manure was a perfume to his nose. Entering the stable the horses nodded to them as if to say 'good morning'. Their nostrils fumed in the cold air. Meli led him to the smaller of the two, a brown mare that looked at him with its huge inquisitive eyes.

'You'll ride this one. Her name is Lilly. She's old and she'll cope with your inexperience. She'll teach you how to ride her, just feel her rhythm.'

Samu tapped the horse's nape and looked up at it. *Gosh, I've never thought horses were so tall.* Yet, he managed to climb up on it with Meli's help.

'The fastest we'll go is gallop.'

'OK. Just go slowly.'

So they rode off and Samu was soon able to take up the horse's rhythm and hold onto the saddle with his thighs. They rode around the edge of a forest and soon they found a path into the thick of it. He knew his bum would hurt the next day and Meli had warned him of that, but he enjoyed it. After the gallop, which he managed just as well, Meli excused himself and rode off, much faster. Samu was left alone with Lilly, to explore the landscape. Today, he had a chance to enjoy the sunrise. First, it was just that the darkness turned lilac then the slow shimmering on the horizon crept forwards onto the frost-covered grass. The dark silhouettes of the bare trees took up rounded forms. The two dimensions of the night changed into three with depth and height. The air became moister, it was no longer the biting cold, but soft and misty. He listened to the noises, how the field started to rise, the noises of animals, the wind in the trees, the slow tapping of Lilly's hooves, her tail swishing from side to side. He had not been so near to nature for a long time. *Meli, my friend, thank you,* he thought. Yes, man and horse were made for each other.

They had to come back to Budapest the same night. In the afternoon, when they were having their bacon and bread, Meli's friend, the forester arrived in a jeep. 'Sorry, mate you'll have to leave now, but thanks for riding in the horses.'

It turned out that the horses would be ridden the next morning by some Bulgarian visitors that were coming to see the agricultural co-op and they would need the cottage, anyway. Samu did not mind, for his bum was already hurting. When they arrived back to Pest he decided to go to the jazz club in Petofi Street and have some fun. His favourite band, the Binder Quartet, was playing and this was the perfect crowning of an unusual seventh November, after a day spent in the company of a rather beautifully smelling Lilly. He hoped that he would meet up with some friends, and perhaps with his latest pursuit, Cleo. The girl had taste. She wore long dresses that hugged her body and she was extremely tactile, lovable even. He knew that anything would be possible with her, if he wanted. She was strong and he suspected, very talented. The only problem was that she studied in Warsaw. She was soon to go back and Samu had only a very slight chance to get her into bed with him before she left. On the other hand, this was just as well. He always enjoyed the chase more than the actual contact. But boy, she'd told him fantastic things about Warsaw! There, in the student hostel the showers were collectively used by both sexes. There was a sign everyone knew and you had to hang up a towel on your shower door, if you did not want anyone to come in with you. *Imagine that.* Cleo, like some Greek nymph, kind of lured him to the jazz club. She had said that although Warsaw had the legendary *Aquarium*, she wanted to hear a bit of *real* jazz before she returned.

Meli didn't join him. He was into different music and anyway, you don't want to be with your housemate all the time. Meli went to the ice-rink instead. Samu knew that his friend would be racing himself into oblivion, drinking in the whiteness of the ice, getting drunk on his own speed and the deafening music out in the cold. He was much more physical than Samu.

Although he couldn't find Cleo anywhere in the crowd, he had a good time. He just loved the Saxophonist. His bushy head with its wild curls, bobbing up and down with the melody, like a boat on the ocean surface. When he left, full drunken with music, he saw another, being questioned by the police in the street just outside the cinema. The girl had amazingly long brown hair, down to her bottom. In leaving she threw a coquettish smile at one of the policemen, *man, these girls are going crazy they are just full of themselves.*

Chapter 3

The jazz club in Petőfi Sándor Street had a full house.

Sofie had grown out of pop by the age of seventeen. Pop concerts attracted too big crowds, too much alcohol and even more police and she learnt to be frightened of the violence that needed no excuse. Free jazz, on the other hand, provided some freedom in the literal sense of the word, or the illusion of it. Music without words seemed like a jungle without a compass. Her mind and body followed the rhythm, which grew like an organism, far out into space, while stirring the hot soup of nameless emotions in her. Even though she was dragged away on a wild trip, at the same time, there was structure; a sure end to the journey that offered relief and satisfaction.

Her favourite jazz band, the Binder Quartet, were playing. The club was in a huge flat on the first floor of an old town building in Petőfi Street and the queue ended half a floor lower. She stood about, searching for familiar faces. Through the gap of the frequently opening door, she had a glimpse of Sándor and his new girlfriend. They both seemed very tall and alike, stuck together like clingfilm. Sofie shuddered: *So this is it. It's sex, nothing else. You either do it or you are forgotten.*

She laughed when a guy talked his way into the club pretending to be the lead singer of the Omega band. When the second guy tried the same trick, the middle-aged doorman finally got the message and had to admit how little he knew the Hungarian pop world.

Still laughing, Sofie left. Coming out onto the street, the smoke of the city grabbed her by the throat and her eyes started to burn. In the corners of her tearful eyes the Elisabeth Bridge was gleaming white near by and she took a left to stroll. There was a cinema on the next corner, they showed a film *Monsieur Klein*, with Alain Delon. Always a good choice. She sunk into the red plush seat with a pretzel and soon she was taken to France and forty years back in time. *Monsieur Klein* was a Catholic, yet through a strange twist of fate he was deported to Auschwitz. *Monsieur Klein*'s tragedy emanated from his mistaken identity. He was not a Jew, he should not have been on that train. She cried at the end over this absurd but possible scenario, shocked by the idea that life could turn so cruel on someone.

With the mix-up of identities, the director, Joseph Losey, presented a mirror to the bourgeoisie, for the bourgeoisie had allowed the Holocaust to happen. At the beginning of the film, Mr Klein profited from the cheap deals that Jews were forced to make to survive. The film resonated with Sofie's own contempt for the bourgeoisie. Her mother had implanted the seed of this ignorance by calling any social climber 'Little Bourgeois', but in Sofie's philosophy, this communist morale grew into contempt for any opportunist that used their contacts or protection to achieve anything in the socialist society. And slowly but surely she discovered that it meant nearly everyone. On the other hand, she loved the Jews. She did not know many Jews, but she took it on herself to protect them. She found it appalling that even now, thirty-five years after the Second World War, anti-Semitism survived in her country. Anytime she heard somebody abusing the Jews verbally, her stomach turned. She convinced herself that anti-Semitism in Hungary was based on envy and narrow-mindedness, for Jewish people did well, but they also dared to keep their small trade shops against the pressure of the communist nationalisation process in the fifties, when people were deported and killed for keeping profits. She admired their resilience, thinking that, although they were abused, accused, and hunted, the Jews were genetically equipped to survive in the face of persecution.

When Sofie left the cinema she bumped into two policemen outside. *Saint Sofia, help us.*

'Identity card,' hissed the bigger one of the two.

Her innards squeezed, and she associated her angst with *Monsieur Klein*'s in the film. Her fear, infused by her parents and the whole society she had to contend with, had no grounds. Nobody could send her to the gas chambers, those times were gone; she had a fixed address and she attended grammar school. She gave the man her card and looked away, waiting patiently. She could not escape the smaller one's gaze, who seemed to fancy her, looking at her bottom-long hair. Sofie knew the effect of it on people, but to be fancied by a policeman? This annoyed her. The powerful had sex on their side, or was sex on her side?

'It's too late and you're underage, go home, immediately,' boomed the hulk.

Sofie scrutinised his stiff, grey fake leather coat that made him look like an enormous walking rubbish bin. Rushing away she gave the smaller guy a contemptuous smile, wondering why she felt being watched and smiled about. She looked around but saw no one.

From about the age of thirteen, Sofie had become aware of how socialist education had estranged her, not only from her parents but from her whole world. She hated the notion of the socialist community and she refused to be part of it. She wanted to be a free individual, whatever that meant. Her father, with his anti-socialist thinking, nurtured this fire in her, while her mother tried to dampen it with fears. But she most detested people that had no compassion, like her neighbour, the army officer, who caught her sneaking through the gates late one night and tore her bead necklace, or her first schoolteacher, who humiliated a boy that wet himself in class, or the ones that shot the Jews into the river. The people that followed orders blindly, themselves being directed and manipulated by fear. Instead of saying goodbye, 'Take your ID', were the last words she heard when leaving the flat, for they knew that she could be checked around the next corner. Nevertheless, she laughed in the face of the fear that her mother and father tried to infuse into her.

On Sunday she had lunch with her parents without much enjoyment. She did not talk, for she knew that anything that she would say could be used against her. Her father, with his conservative upbringing, wanted to keep her in a cage of his moral values: virginity and vanity. Her mother, with her liberal upbringing, let her follow her own path within looser limits. Sex and rock and roll were fine, drugs not, but she defended her daughter, no matter what the accusation. During Sunday lunch Sofie sat in their focus, answering questions about school, talking about art and other neutral subjects. Her father keenly supported her artistic endeavours, while her mother happily avoided the issue of sex and boyfriends. Sofie swallowed the bitter pill, accepting it as her job to protect her parents with lies, if necessary, so that they could live their life in illusion. She managed to survive this Sunday lunch, too, and joyfully escaped to Janos.

They had known each other for two years. He had grown into her friend, the man she never wanted to have sex with, and he showed her so much joy: the joy of art and poetry and philosophy. They used to read to each other the wonderful poems by Endre Ady, Attila Jozsef, and Antal Szerb.

For her sixteenth birthday, Janos gave her a story he had written about her in the future, living with her man in her castle, celebrating her birthday. Janos was not present, but she could perceive him around them, like a ghost. When she dropped a glass, it somehow landed on the table unharmed. The fire flamed up just when she felt chilly. A light breeze touched her brows and she could recall a pleasant memory.

Nothing in life could surpass the beauty of this friendship. Janos taught her that even the worst atrocities of life were bearable if you could just turn your perception upside down and tried to laugh.

Chapter 4

The Academy of Fine Art had a gloomy facade. You could only guess whether the walls were black due to the pollution from old lorries and the Trabants and Ladas stopping and going in front of the building, or some war or revolutionary fire in the distant past. This was one of the oldest palaces on The People's Republic Street, the long avenue connecting the Hero's Square with Bajcsy-Zsilinszky Road. Wide steps led up to the huge front doors, and inside, after passing the portiere's cubicle, undulated worn marble steps led up to the ateliers. *I'll definitely slide down the bannister on my way out,* Samu promised himself, as soon as he entered the building on the first day. The ceilings were incredibly high in the studios. Glass top windows let in the light from the North. In the mornings the rooms were flooded with a soft light that together with the dust in the air gave every object an otherworldly shimmer around the edges. *Heaven is art, art is heaven.*

Samu was pleased with his new life. He got the job in an instant, all he had to do was to say to the administrator that he was prepared to do it. Although it seemed to distance him from his true friend, Meli, who rather despised the idea of doing nothing but posing for eager art students, it opened up countless opportunities and many more new connections in the art world and the modelling community. The latter was a mixture of two generations. The youngsters – a group of ten was made up of a couple, and many boys and men. They belonged to an underworld of counterculture and knew each other from the small circle of concerts and clubs. There was a huge gap and absolutely no connection between the younger models and the older models, who were alcoholics or homeless men and women trying to survive on a small pension. Nobody seemed to notice the parallels between these two groups: the fact that many of them had no homes and stayed all over Budapest with friends, wherever they could. The crucial difference was that the young people always had some place to go, for they created the widest circle of friends. Both groups were dropouts of socialist society, but the young ones distanced themselves voluntarily as an act of resistance, while the old ones were where they were because of a life they had given up a long time before.

One of the younger guys, Victor, became Samu's new friend. He had longer hair than any girl he knew, down to his bottom, and he was an ideologist of the movement. He was said to have a special relationship with Jesus Christ based on his claim that Jesus had actually appeared to him in a bathroom and instructed him what to do. He had *The Making of a Counter Culture* privately translated and circulated as an ideological basis for everybody. He himself was working on *The Criticism of Dialectic Materialism*, a pamphlet that he hoped to get published one day, to change the system.

Unlike Meli, Samu did not see nakedness as humiliation; the whole act of modelling involved some privacy. Indeed, he could undress behind a privacy screen, and step forward naked. He was proud of his lean body and had no reason to be ashamed of the size of his penis. Only his first session was extremely hard: he had to take tranquillisers because he was so worried about having an erection; but after this initial fear of arousal, he was clear that he could control himself in any situation, no matter how long a girl stared at him.

The company of Victor and the other guys from the underground movement was highly rewarding. It did not matter to him that he only worked part time and earned much less money than in the factory. Meli's mum was cross, seeing that he wasted half the day with doing nothing, but as long as he paid the rent she could not say a word against him. *She is not my mother, after all.* He knew that Meli and his mother looked down on his new profession. They thought it was not a "manly" thing to do, standing naked all day, but they had no idea of "manliness". Samu, on the other hand, knew too well the extremes of male power. Deep in his loins, he remembered the brutality his father had applied to make a *man* out of him. When he escaped his clutches and his father had no more means to try to educate him, his old man swore to make sure that somebody in the army would finish his work. Two years of military service was compulsory for every healthy young man in the country; by the age of twenty-one he was likely to get his papers. Samu did not intend to become a soldier. But his father was wrong in assuming that he was not a man. In fact, with the beatings he suffered as a child, Samu became indifferent to physical pain: he was fearless.

He had to become unfit for military service. He was healthy and he knew that he could not fake an illness, but faking mental instability was still an option to try. In the underworld, where he now belonged, many guys became psychiatric patients for the same reason. Samu decided to fake a few suicide attempts in public places to get on the list of the mentally unstable.

Chapter 5

In the café one Friday afternoon Sofie saw a boy and she knew immediately that she would be having a relationship with him. His forehead shone over his brown eyes, framed by long brown hair, tied together in a ponytail at the back. He seemed to be intelligent, yet somewhat wild. Then she tried to forget him, for he obviously fancied someone else: a girl in a very tight knitted dress. She looked like a slinky cat in that dress, very warm and languid.

Sofie preferred to keep her body hidden in long wide robes or loose trousers that not only concealed but caressed her body. She dyed her own clothes and she managed to create wonderful lively colours: blue-green, carmine-purple, mauve and lilac. Mostly made of cotton and snugly to wear, they complemented her waist-long chestnut brown hair perfectly. Nevertheless, she envied the girl for the special attention she got from the boy while noting in her mind that she could not and would not want to be like her.

Her nature did not allow her to let anyone know that she desired them. She must have inherited sexual repression from her father, she thought. He was brought up as a Catholic and passed onto her a refusal to yield. On top of that hairs on male bodies terrified her. They represented something animalistic, dark yet powerful. She refused to look like prey; she wanted to preserve her freedom of choice and she could only do this by remaining incognito. As far as her body was concerned, it had to be hidden.

Did jealousy really illuminate the impossibility of certain desires? *Am I jealous because I feel insufficient? Or is it just that I detest the fact that I am so limited?* She brushed away the girl and boy, not wanting to linger on a feeling she did not like.

She loved walking in the city, even in winter; her body nearly floating on air, every step massaging the asphalt; arms light and being carried by supreme energy. She might have been a ghost, who knows, but she loved the anonymity, being the observer or the outsider. She did not belong. Happy without commitments that she did not have to take part in: the rushing and shoving. The idea of having to grow up scared her. *Most grown-ups have a pitiable existence. Men think of nothing else but prestige and sex, and women are the prisoners of their families.*

One night she got into the jazz club. She saw Sandor smiling good-naturedly at her over his shoulder, his body attached to his new girlfriend's. She noticed that his whole demeanour had changed. He looked like a man, while the girlfriend looked like a 'big woman': strong and experienced.

When she got closer to them, Sandor introduced the girl, 'this is my girlfriend, Sofie.'

Help me, Saint Sofia. Numb and speechless for a moment, 'hi, nice to meet you,' she mumbled at last. The crowd pushed her away from them towards the music and she was grateful for that. She could see, bewildered, that she had just greeted her own projection in the future: the 'big woman' she would become one day. Then she smiled, helplessly, suspecting with a touch of melancholy that such a projection could only be an illusion.

She immersed herself in the music for a while, willing to be washed away. Then she went to the bar to catch up with two of her friends, Mercedes and Susan: a funny couple building such a strong unit that no boys or girls could interfere with. They greeted her with big smiles.

'Hi Sofie, we're going to Pecs to see the market. There is a great guy, Tibi, we can all stay with. You have to hitch-hike down, but I got somebody to go with you. He would be going alone as well. His name is Samu.'

Mercedes pointed to the bar and there he stood. *Long brown hair, brown eyes, and high forehead. The boy from the café.* Sofie uttered a sigh of surrender. He came closer.

'See-a, I'm Samu.'

'Sofie.' She could not say more than that.

'Well, we're going together then?'

'OK.'

'What about leaving on Thursday?'

'I can only leave on Friday after school.' She enjoyed saying no to him for a moment, hoping that this would mean the end of something that had not started yet.

'Fine. Friday then. I meet you at Liberation Square in the subway, at the elevators of the metro. All right?'

'Three o'clock sharp.' She heard herself sounding like a matron.

Samu looked into her eyes deeply, surprised, but also inquisitive. She was not prepared for this closeness.

'My father is an army officer,' she lied, quickly, to explain her harshness and to build a wall between them.

'I'm so sorry to hear that.'

This was too much, they had to laugh. Then Sofie escaped into free jazz and tried to forget his hurt demeanour that seemed to follow her like a cat eager to be caressed.

Chapter 6

On Sunday afternoon Sofie paid a visit – *the usual pilgrimage* – to Janos. They read some poetry, giggled a lot, and played chess. Sofie won for the first time ever and Janos threw the chessboard on her in his anger. She regarded this as a fantastic victory, especially because he lost his temper.

Overfilled with confidence she finally asked Janos, 'would you come with me to Pecs at the weekend?'

'Hitching is not my thing, Sofie. And anyway, Anna-Maria is coming.'

'Good that she has a double name, you get two for the price of one,' she said bitterly. She could not avoid going with Samu, as it seemed, but, of course, she could have decided not to go at all. She preferred to postpone any decision about it until Friday, when she found herself on the side of the road, hitch-hiking with Samu.

They had arrived at the exit of the metro at Liberation Square at the same time. She was coming down the stairs and he was coming up on the elevator. The rhythm of their meeting was reassuring and beautiful, Sofie observed. They took a bus to the outskirts, where the motorway to the city of Pecs started. It was fortuitous to have Samu with her, for she had never tried to hitch on her own: it was too dangerous for a girl. She would have taken the train or not gone. In a way, his presence seemed useful; they were chatting all the way. Samu kept mentioning his friend Meli with whom he shared a place, acting very mysteriously.

'Meli is a boy, but everyone thinks that Meli stands for Melinda.'

'Well, I didn't think of a girl for a millisecond, although I have two cousins called Melinda and we nickname them Meli, too.'

'How come?'

'I don't think too much. I rather feel. And this Meli feels like a boy.'

'Great. I'll tell him. He'll love you for it.'

They laughed. She did not know what to think. He worked very hard to impress her, but without success.

It took only two cars to put the hundred and ninety kilometres behind them, which was an achievement. They arrived at their shelter in the middle of the night. People were preparing to go to sleep at Tibi's flat, but they were welcome. Sofie did not know half of the people, but this had never been a problem for her. Tibi liked her and she liked him, too. Mercedes and Susan introduced them and gave her a sleeping bag. She laid it out next to a sleeping body, alongside the wall. It was a relief to be able to crash out without seeming to be impolite or too selfish. It was late. Six of them were sleeping on the floor, claustrophobically close for a few moments. The next minute she left into the land of dreams without noticing.

On Saturday she managed to stay away from Samu, hiding in the crowd, recognising friends from the city. Orpheus, a flamboyant music student, came too. She had not known him for long, yet, she had known him for aeons. She even took it upon herself to protect him, many times. The girls seemed to fall in love with him the minute they saw him, while Sofie did not understand the reason for this craze. Again, she was the observer and her position gave her power. *I am the only person on the planet who understands Orpheus.* Perhaps, Mercedes did too, but none of the silly girls that fell for him did. Clearly, they wanted to be hurt, for Orpheus moved on very quickly, like a bee, from flower to flower. He was wooing a dark sweetie even now and they seemed to be 'in love', whatever that meant.

The centre of attention was a guy from Budapest, with nearly as long hair as herself. His name was Victor and everybody knew him, except her. He was a leader of some kind, always benevolently smiling at Sofie and she found herself drifting towards him. He asked her many questions and seemed to beam love all over. Sofie found herself talking about a play she wanted to write, which would have a child as the main character. The child would be sitting on a ladder in the middle of the stage, narrating.

'Great idea,' Victor agreed.

'You look like Jesus Christ, has anyone told you that?' Sofie asked.

'Well, it's just as right I tell you that I met Jesus Christ.'

'Where?'

'In a bathroom, after my girlfriend died in an accident. He came to me and we talked.'

Sofie was amazed, but there was no time to ask more questions. Tibi, their host came and walked on her side.

'I had an epiphany, too. A friend of mine taught me philosophy. He is a lecturer at university.'

'Great.'

'I love all the antiques, the sophists, indeed.'

'The sophists?'

'Yes, Protagoras, for instance. He said, "Man is the measure of all things" this is the opening sentence of his great work "Truth".'

'How fascinating, I wish, we would be taught the truth. I learn nothing but lies at school.'

'Learn philosophy. Nobody can tamper with that. I love it, even some of the moderns, like Kant, but I got bogged down by Kierkegaard.'

'I know nothing about him, tell me.' Sofie said.

'Kierkegaard wrote a book called *Either/Or*, in which he says that you have to make a choice in your life. You can live a life of beauty or you can live for moral responsibility.'

'It sounds like the artist and the bourgeois. I suppose we live for beauty.'

'Not exactly. The minute you get a paid job you are on the ethical path. According to Kierkegaard, you can choose either path, the outcome is the same, namely decay. This was too cruel for me.'

'He might be wrong.'

'No, the truth is that everybody is right. No matter which philosopher you read, they are all right. And this is maddening.'

'You seem quite happy, though.'

'Since my breakdown I have been getting psychotherapy and I've begun to like myself for the first time in my life.'

'How old are you?'

'Twenty-five.'

'Yeah. It's time. Well, I like you already,' she said, with charm, but he shook his head disbelieving.

In the evening they played *Hot Seat*. Tibi, being the host, suggested it, but Victor was the lead, explaining the rules. 'You are allowed to ask a question from anyone in the group and they have to reply honestly.'

This seemed simple enough. Only, there was a boy called Zed who openly fancied her. He got his name, obviously after his tattoo on the neck, a sign of thunder. It reminded Sofie of the sign of Zorro, in fact. *Zorro was here,* she thought teasingly, but she did not dare to say it aloud. Zed had his eyes fixed on Sofie, all the time, which she found very unpleasant. When Samu had to sit on the 'hot seat' Zed asked him whether he was Sofie's boyfriend. *Saint Sofia, help me.* Victor noticed Sofie's displeasure about the topic and stopped Zed, reminding him that the ground rule was to avoid intimate questions. While Sofie was grateful to Victor, she grew to dislike Zed, who had a self-pitying demeanour she could not stand. It was obvious that Zed knew he had no chance with her. *Then, why did he have to force it?*

In the middle of this game Orpheus arrived with the new girl and laughingly announced that they banged the parish door wildly until they managed to get a priest out into the street. They begged him so much that he finally agreed to wed them, and they were married in front of God. *Grow up, Orpheus.* It sounded too romantic. It was clear that they had made it all up.

The city of Pecs seemed to liberate the rest of the party, too. There were no police checks in the streets, in fact, they did not see a single policeman. Carried by the crowd of young faces she only half knew, was strange and sweet. She belonged to this community.

That night she was woken by caresses. *Saint Sofia, help.* She pretended to be sleeping and turned away with a groan and, luckily, Zed stopped.

On Sunday they went to the market. It was a real country market, with animals and cars mixed together; farmers selling strange artefacts, tools of some kind that Sofie knew from museums, but these were newly made. *Surely, nobody used mangles and mangling boards anymore?* The whole place seemed surreal. The farmers, dressed in folkloristic clothing, were sitting on wooden benches with long pipes in their hands, like in the novels of Mikszath set around the turn of the twentieth century. They were making eyes at her, piercing through narrow slit eyes, naughtily hiding their smiles behind thick moustaches. She saw some beautiful *shubas*, sheepskin worn as a gown, and some fur coats that she did not dare to touch. She did not have a *forint* to spend, she was just browsing. Most sellers saw it immediately, weighing her spending power with one well-trained glimpse and then gazing back at her with indifferent eyes. Zed kept following her everywhere. Trying to escape his attention, she ran straight into Samu's arms, making it clear that she fancied him.

They started hitching back at lunchtime. In the beginning, Zed stayed with them, spoiling their chance to get a lift. They soon separated. The weather turned chilly and it took them hours and four cars to get half of the way behind them. It was already night-time; the temperature below zero. Sofie's toes were dead and she guessed that her nose was frozen. They were standing under a streetlight on the outskirts of yet another town. Samu suggested that they jumped around to heat up their bodies. Sofie was jumping around Samu and moving her arms up and down, like an impatient bird that could not fly away for it was tied to a stick.

'I lied to you about my father,' she said, as if literally wanting to break the ice. 'He is not an army officer.'

'You liar,' he said, teasing, through his chattering teeth.

'My mother is a communist sheep, as my father calls her, for he is the descendent of a noble family and a real anti-communist. He did not join the party.'

'That's an interesting concoction. Do they quarrel a lot?'

'They kill and love each other day by day.'

'I'm surprised you haven't gone mad yet.'

'Oh, I'm glad it's not so obvious.'

'Well, I'll tell you something funny. My father is an officer. He is a regiment captain.' Sofie stopped in front of Samu. *Is he playing a game?*

'What? I can't believe it.'

'It's true. I'm not a liar. But luckily, I don't have to live with him anymore. He put me into a boarding college when I was fourteen and that probably saved my life.'

'Why?'

'He is brutal. He used to beat me a lot. He said it would make me harder. I've never lived at home since then. I kept moving and moving till I ended up at Meli's.'

This confession stunned her. She could not say a word, she just gazed at him with tears in her eyes. Then he stepped closer and kissed her nose.

'Your nose is frozen.'

'Thank you,' she whispered.

A car stopped at last and they were grateful for the warmth inside. The driver introduced himself as the luckiest man in Hungary, for he had won the lottery twice and he even won the car they were sitting in. This jovial Jolly Joker, full of his own luck, saved them from frostbite. Sofie stared into the starry night. *Luck at first sight.*

She got home exhausted and too late. She tried to sneak in without waking the family, but as always, her mother was waiting for her, only half asleep. Mum stumbled into the kitchen, whispering, so that her father would not wake up and create a scene. She was protecting Sofie, for which she was grateful. Mum quickly scurried back to bed, murmuring words of relief: '*Jó éjszakát,*[1] at least you're back safe'.

Sofie took a hot shower and slipped under the duvet, praying that her giddy heart would leave her alone.

---

1 Good night.

Chapter 7

The next time they met at Liberation Square Samu greeted her with a kiss on the lips and immediately declared himself.

'Sofie, I profess polygamy.'

What? Saint Sofia, help. She laughed. She knew the term, but she was yet to meet a professor of the trade.

'What?'

'I cannot be faithful to anybody. I can only exist in an open relationship.'

'OK?' she was quiet for a while.

'What're you thinking about?' he asked at last.

'This can only work, I think, if we are both totally honest with each other,' she said pretending lightness, kissing him back. *With me you will change. I'm special.*

As if reading her thoughts, he reinforced his special request. 'Listen, Sofie. I want to have freedom and I feel that I can have that with you. No restrictions, no jealousy.'

'No restrictions, no jealousy,' she repeated like a parrot, remembering the first time she saw him in the café, chatting up a girl in a knitted dress.

They started to go out together. Samu worked as a part-time model at the Academy of Fine Art, which was near Sofie's school. So, they could spend most afternoons together, strolling in the city, sitting for hours over a cup of espresso or a coke. Nearly every café had a pianist, so they listened to the old pre-war, wartime, and post-war songs of Hungary, full of desire, suppressed passion, wistful love. These songs were completely forgotten: they were never played on the radio, for they were contrary to the socialist ideal. Their decadence, sleazy sexiness, their nostalgic mood coming from the mouth of an old lady were something else.

To begin with, she was not sure whether she wanted to be with him, she was just drifting along. But, she was intrigued. He seemed very brave and provocative, at the same time inquisitive.

He doubted everything. He discussed everything. There was nothing that his mind would not attack in one way or the other.

One day they heard that Janos was interpreting for a travelling yogi in someone's flat near the Danube. This was amazing news, given the atheist socialist culture, and their exploration of beat poetry. One translation of a volume by American beat poets was circulating from hand to hand and Sofie had read Salinger's *Clap of one hand*, too, who was a real Buddhist, she thought. The chance to meet a representative of oriental culture excited them both.

The seminar was set up in one of those huge downtown flats in one of the old nineteenth-century buildings. The rooms were spacious with four-metre high ceilings. This one seemed to have hardly any furniture. The yogi and Janos on his side were sitting in the middle on the carpet, young people surrounded them in a circle, on the floor. The yogi, who asked to be called '*Swamiji*', wore a bright orange robe. He was dark-skinned, had black bushy hair and beard, his face was round and he smiled constantly. Sofie had only seen pictures of very skinny Indians so far in old issues of National Geographic that were sent to her by her uncle George from Manchester. This yogi was quite the opposite, he had a round big belly. He greeted all of them with *Hari Om*. He chanted OM three times and started his talk. Sofie understood some of the English, but not all, and even Janos's translation did not make much sense to her. All her energy seemed to focus on Samu. He was in his element. The yogi was talking about freedom and transformation and a strange name - Mahaprabu Ji, was repeated many times. Sofie did not understand the freedom he was talking about. When he opened the session for questions, Samu was first to ask, 'What do you mean by freedom?'

'You can only achieve freedom inside you.'

'And what about human liberties, which are not granted to us in this country?'

'There is no need to resist the government or any superior power. Freedom is not external, but internal.'

'I thought India fought for independence. Is that not freedom?'

'Come to me when we finished, Samu,' Swamiji said.

Sofie could sense Samu's excitement. When the discussion was over, he went to Swamiji as asked.

'You are a bright man, Samu, but the mind is not all you need to understand,' Swamiji said to Samu kindly, while pushing a thumb into the middle of his chest. Samu cringed with pain.

'You'll stop asking questions one day,' Swamiji said smiling.

Janos nodded knowingly, and Samu leapt away from them laughing, trying to hide his nervousness. 'Sure, I will. Hari Om.'

For days after this, he kept going back to the experience. His opinions fluctuated between saying that the yogi had no other argument but to hurt him and wondering whether the yogi had actually pushed a button in his heart that would make it sure that he stopped arguing.

When Sofie discussed the incident with Janos, he thought that the yogi, most probably manually opened Samu's heart centre, but Sofie kept this from Samu. She was waiting to see whether it was true. For a polygamist, surely, love meant something else and she needed to be sure.

Chapter 8

When Sofie exited the metro at Liberation Square she recognised Samu and Victor in a group of youngsters. Victor was older than anyone she knew in these circles; he must have been approaching thirty. He also had longer hair than Sofie, who was herself proud of her long mane. Victor wore a pair of baggy trousers, a tight-fitting felt jacket and a long striped Bay City Rollers style scarf around his neck. By now Sofie knew that he slept in other people's houses; he did not have a fixed abode, although he must have had a registered address on his identity card otherwise the police might have put him into a workers' hostel. Victor worked as a life model at the Academy with Samu. Until she met Victor, Sofie did not know that the so-called 'work–avoiders' were put into a forced labour camp for a few months as a punishment. The Academy served as a refuge for people that did not want to work full-time, as it provided a workplace registered on their ID cards. Victor had been incarcerated in the Baracska camp for three months and he did not make a secret out of it.

'Why?'

'Because I did not have a job in my ID card.'

'How was that camp?'

Victor laughed. 'They saw that I was not made for stone mining, so they put me in the library. I became a librarian, but they only had books by Lenin and Marx, so I started to write my critical pamphlet there.'

'Of what?'

'The Criticism of Dialectic Materialism. You see, I don't believe that we have no soul, so the whole concept is based on false assumptions.'

Victor had a large group of followers. Some followed him physically; they were runaways, fallen out with parents, in search of a temporary sleeping place. It became necessary that, wherever they went, there would be a party, not so much with music or drinks, as Victor never took drugs or alcohol, but rather a kind of seminar where they talked and discussed whatever came up, but mainly the insufficiencies of the regime.

They kissed on both cheeks to say hello and Sofie immersed herself in Victor's endlessly blue eyes, enjoying the soft rub of facial hair caressing her face. *He looks like Jesus, no doubt.*

'Hello, Sofie,' he boomed, emanating warmth and love, so that she immediately accepted and understood all the fuss about him being a leader.

Samu wanted to kiss her on the lips, but she turned her face to be kissed on the cheeks as well, for Samu was standing with a boy she had never seen before. He stared at her as if he wanted to undress her. He had fair hair and brown eyes, a strange combination, but then she noticed the roots were brown, which meant that he must have dyed his hair. Nervously, he kept looking around to check the area for any police presence, which was very likely when many of them were gathering in a public place. In any moment they could be asked for their ID cards.

Samu introduced him. 'This is Zoli, my blood brother.'

Zoli grinned and kissed Sofie full on the mouth. His cigarette tasting lips were faster than Samu's and greedier.

She pushed him away. 'What an animal,' she said.

Zoli just grinned.

'It doesn't mean you can share everything.' Sofie pushed the guy away, wiping her mouth disgusted.

Zoli muttered a half-hearted 'sorry'.

Samu laughed. 'It was just a joke. But Zoli, remember: this one is taboo.'

Zoli playfully bowed to her and she forced a smile, although feeling uneasy. She looked around and saw another young 'veteran', nicknamed Brezhnev. He had long black hair down to his bottom, like an indigenous Indian. His face was completely shaved, including the eyebrows. He wore an old blazer, fully decorated with red stars and golden hammers and sickles, the ones old people got for their service to the state or to the army. He looked funny, but also like a walking provocation. Sofie wondered whether the police ever made him take all his decorations off.

Victor urged them, 'guys, we have to go. Adam is waiting for us.'

They moved on in the direction of the university. The traffic was noisy and the fumes of the buses prickled her nose. She dug her hands into her pockets, not feeling free to snuggle up to Samu, who was too preoccupied with the presence of his blood brother. She was listening to their incomprehensible teasing and messing, coded memories, feeling, no doubt, they did not want to talk to her about them. Instead of being all ears and wearying herself with the jealousy of some indiscriminate past, she rather let herself get carried away by her senses, with the breeze from the Danube that made her eyes water. She used to like the special effects this created when the scenery was slightly blurred, floating away on her retina. She heard a melody replaying in her mind, '*Do love me do*', as if the record player's needle had stuck, playing the same tune again and again. It helped to shut out the hilarious chatter streaming from the two boys on her left, so enamoured were they with each other.

They entered the huge university building and she could smell the mustiness of museums, books, history. She did not know what component made it smell so good, but she loved it. She hoped to be admitted as a student to this sacred place in the future, but she knew that the selection process was rigorously brutal: only one out of six hundred would be admitted each year. He greeted the guy called Adam with awe. He seemed like a giant, a temple servant of this holy place. He was waiting for them in the hall, then he ushered them up the stairs, clearly smuggling them in.

They entered a lecture hall. The room was so packed she could not believe it, she could only sit down on the floor together with many others: squeezed like herrings in a can. It seemed that they were the last ones to arrive; not one more soul could have been crammed in there. The murmur of the crowd died down when the door behind the high lecturing platform opened and a lecturer of the English department, Istvan Eorsi, a translator of beat poetry, walked in with Allen Ginsberg, Orlovsky, and a young guy with a guitar who was at least one generation younger than the others in the group. He wore old-fashioned glasses and seemed very nervous. Orlovsky had long grey hair bound in a ponytail; Ginsberg was partly bald with a long beard, black button eyes peeping from behind black-rimmed glasses. He unpacked his harmonium slowly, then he sat cross-legged on top of the counter. He boomed, 'Tiger, tiger burning bright,' and the crowd joined him, 'in the forests of the night which eternal hand or might create your fearful symmetry.'

Ginsberg smiled. 'Good morning, Budapest.'

Sofie subsided into a trance. Her English was hopeless, but she listened to the harmonium and to Ginsberg's deep velvety voice when he was singing, and she floated with the mesmerising chant he exuded.

Sofie and Samu spent the rest of the day wandering about in the city and ended up at a concert of the Hobo Blues Band, no longer her favourite, but she accompanied Samu, who was in a nostalgic mood. She drank coffee with rum, like Kerouac in *On the Road*, still lingering on the experience of seeing Ginsberg in real life. When Zoli appeared in the club, Samu excused himself and disappeared with him for a long time.

When they returned Sofie asked him, 'where have you been? You missed the best songs.' When she looked into his eyes his pupils were twice as big as usual. 'Did you take anything?'

Samu laughed. 'No, he just sucked my blood.'

'What?' She turned to him to see what he meant, but he was on the dance floor already, in with the groupies, dancing in front of the band. Sofie, confused and feeling dumped, took her coat and left for home.

A few days later she had a date with Adam. On the way to his place, he filled her in with the gossip about Ginsberg's tour.

'Do you remember the boy with the guitar? He is a Hungarian student from the university. He has been with them for the last three days.'

'Do you envy him?'

'How could I? They are all men if you hadn't noticed.'

'Now I see why he seemed so green and embarrassed. Because all of you guys think that he had sex with either or both. But I envy him, he is with one of the greatest poets of this century.'

'I would be embarrassed if that was the price.'

'Perhaps, if there was any sex; he was gay, anyway,' she said dreamily.

'Homosexuality is not a natural state for us humans,' said Adam.

'So, you cannot imagine anyone being gay from birth?'

'No. I think it's a psychological disorder, which manifests itself in actions. No wonder the age of consent for homosexuals is eighteen.'

'Oh, I didn't know it was illegal under the age of eighteen when between girls and boys it's just fourteen. Does that make it bad for them, if it's illegal? I mean, sex is sex.'

'Of course, it's worse. Physiologically, it's disgusting. But it can happen that someone's first experience is homosexual and then they are doomed for life, for they don't want any women.'

'No, I was just talking theoretically. There are many books that are illegal, like *Doctor Zhivago* or *Animal Farm*. Does this mean that they are bad for us?'

'Now you think you have won, but you cannot compare sex with literature. You could not bring it up in any serious argument, anyway.'

Sofie knew that she was just as rubbish at discussions as at chess. She always lost in arguments and usually became quite emotional.

Adam lived in one of the high prefab houses near the Slaughter House in the district VIII, which had been a white spot on the map for Sofie; just another unexplored, industrial territory at the other end of the city. They had to take two buses after the metro, deep into alien country.

She walked up and down, from wall to wall, in his tiny bedroom, feeling trapped. She always trusted her own instincts and was never frightened once she had decided to trust someone, but now she could not fathom her own carelessness. The penny dropped that, although she admired him, she did not know this guy at all. From the window on the fifth floor, she could partly see the Danube; the view was blocked by a high chimney of the Slaughter House or some other factory, she was not sure. On the wall, between the window and above his desk, were five life-size outlines of profiles, pinned one on top of the other, reminding her of a Native Indian Totem pole. Although it was hard to say for sure, they all looked feminine.

'Who are they?'

'Past girlfriends.'

He moved closer. Goosebumps broke out on her arms. She pulled away from him, towards the wall, her head nearly touching the silhouettes of the others. *Saint Sofia, help! He is a trophy hunter; I don't want to end up in his collection.*

'The only reason I'm here is that I would like to find out how you got into the university,' she blurted out at last. Adam got the hint at once.

'I studied,' he spat.

To her, this sounded like a blatant lie. Nobody could get in just by studying!

Adam sensed her change of mood and, with renewed vigour, he tried to impress her by telling her about his journeys to London.

Sofie began to feel contempt for the boy that could not accept that he had no chance. She could smell the mummy's boy who always got what he asked for.

Soon, to confirm this feeling, Adam's mother returned from work. She fussed about in the hallway, then sneaked a look at Sofie half curiously, half worried, through the gap in the open bedroom door, meeting Sofie's eyes. There must have been a rule that she would not disturb her son if he had guests. Having thought this through in the flash of a second, Sofie did not wait even to be introduced but stormed out of their flat with a feeling of great relief.

Chapter 9

Sofie met Meli and had a look at the boys' room in the green belt of the city. The boys had a separate house in the garden, often called 'summer kitchen', in the Hungarian countryside. Samu and Meli lived in the small shed, independently from Meli's parents. The room had a washbasin and a toilet and its walls were plastered with newspaper cut-outs and posters. They slept on bunk beds: Samu at the bottom, Meli up top. Together they had a remarkably large collection of records. Samu was a fan of King Crimson, Meli loved Jethro Tull. Sofie had little knowledge of these bands. She collected records of Emerson, Lake & Palmer, and the Beatles.

'Only girls love the Beatles. Yeah, love, love, love,' Meli said, and laughed.

'Love moves the universe. There is nothing more important,' retorted Sofie.

Although they seemed to be very close friends, the boys were completely different. Meli loved horses and whips, like a cowboy, and he wanted to live in the country. He planned to volunteer in the army to get better treatment during the break-in time of compulsory service. He was looking forward to the fun he would have in the army. Samu was adamant that he would never touch a gun and wanted to escape the service at all costs. Since meeting Sofie, he became a vegetarian, which caused many conflicts in both of their families, even with Meli, who prepared meat sandwiches in front of them, just to tease them.

'Oh, I forgot, no meat for you two. Now I have to eat it all myself.'

The shock of John Lennon's death shook Sofie terribly at the beginning of December. She kept humming *Imagine* to herself, trying to heal the wound and rebel against reality. Samu took her mind off her grief. They often went to the cinema, where they watched French films, Italian films, American films many times over. They watched *Easy Rider* nearly every week, fumbling each other in the last row. Sofie started to drink espresso with rum, like Kerouac. The hot coffee, doubled with the alcohol, gave her a rush in the head like nothing before. She enjoyed the self-inflicted madness, till one day she had a panic attack during a film. It was a film she knew by Bertolucci, but she could not concentrate, grabbed by the overwhelming fear of death by asphyxiation. Her heart pumped the blood into her head out of control, like in the films the wheels of steam engines rolling and rolling faster. She could fall under the wheels any moment, getting run over by a power she could not keep up with. They had to leave the cinema and she took some time to come to, gasping for air. She was not sure what made her more upset, the fear of death or the fear of having to die as a virgin. She clung to Samu in the hope that he would be the answer to all the secrets she wanted to find out about men and women. But was he worthy of her love? Was he the one? Was it time for her to take a plunge and stop asking questions?

The first snow fell. Sofie loved this time of the year, the time before Christmas, when nights became longer, and the days shorter. The annual Christmas preparations excited her even more than ever, for she had to dream up a present for Samu, too. Something that would express all her personality and her love for him. She started to make the materials for a gown, hand-dyed and painted motifs of birds in a landscape. When the painting had dried she started to embroider the cloth, each stitch a confession, a badge of desire.

By the middle of December, she was unbearably engrossed in love. They were regarded as a beautiful couple. Robi, a flamboyant artist friend, asked them to model for a few shots that he needed for a photographic exhibition. Sofie stood over Budapest, on Castle Hill, watching the twilight. As the streetlights went on one by one, spreading a chain of neon shimmer among the houses, she posed for a young man she hardly knew, harbouring the feeling that it was inevitable she would make love with this soul she knew as Samu.

One evening near Christmas, Samu dropped the news that Meli was not going to come home that night. While it was heavily snowing outside, Sofie and Samu went to his place. The room was cold, only heated by an electric heater. Samu put on a desk light and the radio, which was badly tuned to Free Europe. To the crackling sound of the news, they undressed each other quickly. 'Referring to the SALT II conference in Vienna, Mr Carter, the President of the United States of America, avoided the subject of Human Rights in Eastern bloc countries. Mr Carter's previous attempts to come to an agreement with the soviet leaders appears to have been temporarily removed from the agenda—' The radio changed to music and they jumped under the covers on the lower bunk bed, giggling.

Samu had the skin of a baby, *no hairs at all.* She enjoyed caressing him, feeling his body trying to find its way into hers. They kissed and kissed and he kissed her all over. Although she was scared she would not show it. All she could say was:

'Samu, Samu, Samu.'

She enjoyed his excitement, his wanting her.

'I love you. I never wanted a girl as much as I want you,' he said.

But she could not tell him that she was a virgin. He did not ask her either, confirming her suspicion that he was not such a great professor in the trade of polygamy, after all. At some point she passed out, gone beyond. Perhaps, they fell asleep. Later, when she came to herself she could not decide what was stronger the pleasure or the pain, yet her mind was triumphant.

When they put on the light, Sofie secretly searched the bedsheet for some bloodstains, but could not see any. *Saint Sofia, I've never been a virgin at all!* Hugging Samu and kissing him again with joy, her finger touched a huge scar on his back.

'What is this?'

'My perfect father's last attempt to make a man out of me,' he said and his jaws tightened.

Sofie caressed the scar and kissed him again, but he did not kiss her back.

'You don't want to hear the story?'

Sofie shook her head. 'It's too sad.'

'It was a victory, in fact. I left home soon after.'

'And now you have the whole army at your back.'

'Yeah. Life is hard on us boys.'

Sofie clasped her hands and started to pray.

'My God, are you praying?'

'For love and peace.'

'I love you.'

'Amen.'

Sofie spent the whole night in a haze. Her soul was wandering on a different planet. The next morning she went to school from Meli's. She was sore all day, but it was a sweet soreness, it reminded her that she was reborn as a 'big woman'. She told her friend Eva, who shared her happiness, and they sneaked out of school to celebrate. They went to the cinema and saw *Help!* for the fifth time, screaming with the crowd in the film when the Beatles boys appeared in public.

She went home late that evening, just remembering that her parents did not have any news about her whereabouts for more than twenty-four hours. Her mother opened the door, on her face the signs of exhaustion from a night spent awake. Her father pushed Samu out of the way and dragged Sofie into the hall with unbelievable force, starting to slap her face. Her head was blown apart, dangling from side to side, but she was so stunned that she could not utter a word. She looked at the scene from above. She heard her mother screaming and she could see her own blood spraying on the walls.

Eventually, her mother pulled her father away and she was booing like a baby while her mother pushed her head under a cold shower to stop the nosebleed. Sofie was hysterical and wanted to leave them immediately, but her dad took her coat and identity card to make sure that she could not go very far. She ran out into the winter night in a jersey, cooling her swollen face in the icy wind. She was stupefied with the shock and humiliation, for her father had never ever hit her before. She was floating between ice blocks on the Arctic sea, Samu acting as the Northern Lights, silently shimmering on her horizon. He did not say much, and her ears were still ringing, so she could not have heard him either.

They rang the door at Janos's and he let them in. Sofie could not understand what Samu and Janos were talking about, but eventually, he advised her to go home. Sofie was led from one place to the other again. It started to snow. Samu wrapped his coat around her, 'Even if you moved in with me they'd come after you. You're underage.'

She did not want to go home but had to. She felt thoroughly "beaten". She thought *how cunning of him, he locked Samu out so that he couldn't protect me.*

The following morning when she awoke she was a changed person. *Well, this is the end of me being the good girl.* She decided not to talk to her father ever again, except for the necessary formalities. She said 'good morning' when she saw her parents in the kitchen, but that was all. At breakfast her father apologised for slapping her.

'I didn't want to hurt you, Sofie, I'm sorry. I just lost my nerves. We were too worried about you.'

She did not reply. *You might apologise as you like, but I know that you were just trying to stop me from becoming me, from becoming a woman.* She knew that she needed her parents' support to survive until she finished her Matura. She had roughly seven more months to endure. In July the following year, she would be eighteen and free to leave. She would move in with Samu and they would live for their studies and art. *I will be his muse and model. We will work in the same room where we sleep; our whole lives will be filled with art and freedom.* She even found a place, a basement nearby, which she thought they could get somehow, even though she knew that housing was in crisis and finding rented accommodation was a nightmare in Budapest.

Chapter 10

It was great that he was allowed into the studios early in the mornings. It was warm and he enjoyed being alone analysing the students' works and comparing them with his own. Samu soon worked out that he could draw just as well as the art students. This gave him a certain satisfaction. He was hoping to show his drawings to the professor, although he knew that he would never be admitted to the Academy. It was partly because of the limited places: some people tried for six to seven years to get in, and partly because he dropped out of school and never finished his Matura. He was surprised and delighted when the professor approached him first, after a morning session, while he was putting on his clothes. 'Am I right you're called Samu?'

'Yes. Samu Horvath.'

'Has anyone told you yet that you have a very aesthetic body? Would you like a second job and earn more than here?'

'It depends.'

'I pay twice as much as the Academy to the models that come to stand for me in my studio.'

'That sounds great. Where and when?'

The professor smiled and they arranged to have a session at his studio the next evening.

When he told Sofie that he had other plans for that evening, she seemed saddened, but accepted that survival was quite a big issue.

Samu went to the professor's house in the Buda Hills, near the castle. This was the poshest and oldest part of the city, kept for tourists. The automatic gate gave in to his push with a buzz and he stepped into the courtyard. While the building kept its old facade, here he discovered glass and wood, modern features. The professor opened the door dressed in his painting gown. His skin was tanned, which seemed unusual, as it was just the end of winter. Greying chest hair seemed to bubble out from the white material under his chin. He had very short greying hair on either side of a shiny bald patch in the middle of his head. He might have been older than

Samu's father, probably far over fifty, but, except for the bald patch, there was nothing old about him. He had a strong muscular figure and brilliant blue eyes.

He smiled, asking him to step in with a broad gesture. 'Come in, Samu. I'm very glad you could make it.'

Samu entered shyly. *Gosh, art is heaven, heaven is art.* He had never been in an artist's private studio before, nor in such an extremely luxurious house. The professor was one of the leading artists in the country: his works were hanging in the Parliament and all the government buildings and sent to international exhibitions. One was hanging opposite the entrance: a huge modern canvas with a naked man wrapped in a red flag, seemingly dead. *Wow.*

'Is this your latest work?' Samu asked.

The professor smiled again. 'Yes. It's my last attempt to paint social realism.' He laughed.

'Wouldn't you lose your job if somebody from the ministry saw it?'

'They have seen it. I have parties here every week. They can see it, but they cannot see it. They think that it is a scene from the October Revolution. In fact, that's what I called it. October Revolution.'

'Wow,' exclaimed Samu, 'and in fact it looks like the end of it.'

'You can do anything in this country if you play your cards right.'

'Yes, I know.'

Samu had to think of his father who openly admitted to having been a revolutionary as a young man in 1956. When the Russians broke down the Revolution, being a minor, he was lifted out from prison and he was offered education in the army. He traded in his rebellious self for his life; a life in the army. During his twenties and thirties, he slowly crept up the ranks, which meant moving around the country with his family. With every move, he got a higher rank till he became a captain of the Hungarian Army.

Samu stood model for the professor for two hours. The professor put some music on and Samu was pleased to be able to recognise Vivaldi's *The Four Seasons*. The music really suited the professor. Samu was getting tired and annoyed with himself for not having the courage to ask for a break when the professor seemed to have run out of speed and he finally stopped.

'You seem to be shivering.'

Indeed, he was very cold.

'Can I give you a brandy?'

'Yes, please.'

He put on his trousers and they sank into the huge cream leather sofas each with a brandy glass in their hands. Samu started to summon his courage to talk to the professor about his own drawings, but the professor spoke first.

'Samu, I must confess something to you. I am not like every other man.'

Samu nearly dropped his glass, but there was so much light in the old man's eyes, that he had to trust him. 'Are you gay?'

'Yes, and I would pay you three times your wages if you let me play with your body.'

'I've never thought about making love to a man.'

'Well, there is always a first time,' the professor said and laughed. 'But you know what, you can walk out of here tonight and we will forget this whole conversation. It doesn't have to be.'

They did another session for an hour and it was getting late. Samu was thinking hard what to do. He had immense opportunities here and he was intrigued. He was always of the opinion that one should try everything at least once in life. He knew that there was no force in this situation; even if he said no, the painter would never retaliate. *Man, it's clear that he is a gentleman.* Samu played such a minimal part in the Academy to mean any threat to his job, and anyway, his sexual orientation was nobody's business.

'A penny for your thoughts.' The professor was amused, passionately moving his paintbrush over the canvas. 'This will be a very good one, I think,' he said, pointing to the picture. 'I'm inspired.'

So, I inspire you, the Big Artist. Samu's tension gave. 'OK. I'll do it, but not for the money,' he spurted it out. 'I'll do it for the experience,' he heard himself saying.

'Well, then I'd better wrap this up for tonight.'

Samu had a look at the painting. He was amazed. It showed a totally different version of him than he had ever seen in the mirror.

The young man in the painting looked much wiser, but much softer as well; somewhat androgynous, not like a girl, but not like a man, either.

'I'll call it Angel,' the professor said, turning towards Samu and kissing him fully on the mouth.

Something happened. The world started to spin around Samu and all of a sudden he knew that he had no control over anything in that room anymore.

He slept at the professor's house. In the morning, the professor gave him a lift to the Academy, but this intimacy was too much to bear. Nothing that happened the night before could have hurt him more than the short trip through the city in his car, for he had to face the world beside this middle-aged man.

He spent the day miserably at his workplace, terribly exposed. No matter how much he smoked he could not cover up his bruises inside and out. He was dreading the moment when he would meet Sofie's eyes and curious scrutiny, and he had actually worked up a fever by the time she arrived.

She was all-cheers, wanting to see the money he'd earned.

'Sofie, I'm not well today. I must have got a cold last night. It was a big mistake to go there.'

'Why? Didn't he pay you?'

'Ah,' he said, searching in his pockets for a tissue. This was the moment when he found the bundle of money in his inner pocket. The painter must have smuggled it in when, after the hours of passionate sex, he crept into the guest bedroom to sleep. He pulled it out and it was indeed three times the agreed fee.

'Good Gracious,' Sofie squealed, but Samu could not bear it any longer; he had to run to the lavatory to vomit.

When he returned Sofie was all over herself to help him, but he refused her company. 'I just need to go home and lie in bed.'

Although a bit surprised, Sofie accepted his wish and he was released to go home to Meli's and sleep.

The next day when he went to work he could not look into the professor's eyes. Samu purposefully avoided him and made sure that they had no reason to talk to each other. The professor did not push himself upon him, and he was grateful, but at the same time, thinking bitterly, that the professor must have a whole line of young models to seduce. He did not dream about showing his drawings to the great man anymore; he actually gave up on the idea of drawing, for the time being, turning his attention to his flute that he had been playing since his tenth birthday. He would rather play flute serenades under Sofie's window.

Samu just wanted to make it so that nothing had happened and to go back into the safety of the love affair with Sofie. Their sex life intensified and they had sex whenever and wherever it was possible. He had a great hunger for her body and she gave it freely. It was true that he loved her more than anybody ever before, but also, their love life made them grow into each other with invisible roots and branches, strongly intertwined, sometimes scarily, incredibly chaotic, so that he could not see back or ahead: the world was made of Sofie. At these moments he needed to escape back into the world of boys, mates, blood brothers. That world meant a constant challenge, he had to find and defend his place in it all the time, while in Sofie's world he was perfect and fairly, boring.

Chapter 11

Sofie lost interest in Christmas. Although she made him a very special present, a dark red magician's gown, Samu was spending Christmas at home, with his parents. So, she went to a pub and got pretty drunk with Janos. This was one of those typical drinking establishments that you could smell just by passing in the street and a place she would never have entered on her own. Sofie never knew that pubs were open on Christmas Eve, the holiest of days in Hungary, but the people that stood there were all loners. They obviously did not have a loving family to share this evening with, just like her. People could only drink standing, there were no chairs, only high tables with ashtrays full of butts and you could have cut the cigarette smoke in the air. After the second pint she understood that this was a safety measure. As soon as the drunks started to show signs of imbalance on their feet, they were not served any more booze.

'Your father will never hurt you again,' Janos promised her.

'How do you know?'

'I phoned him and told him that I have some very good friends in the underworld that would be happy to beat him up for a few rounds in the pub.'

This was so out of character that Sofie did not know whether to believe it. When she arrived home for the traditional dinner at six her parents were ready, and this was the first time ever that she had not helped with the preparations. They ate the roasted carp in silence. It was obvious that Sofie did not need to drink any wine, so she was left out of a little ceremony of clicking glasses that used to be her privilege in the preceding years. They gave each other presents. Sofie did not really look at them, but rather automatically thanked them. She just wanted to get away and go to bed early, crying over baby Jesus who was born to bring love but could not bring any to this cold household. In Samu's absence she was alone with her worries about baby Jesus and other babies.

When she arrived to her first date of the New Year, at the 7th November Square one night in early January, while getting off the bus Sofie realised that she forgot to bring the present, the beautiful magical gown for Samu. She was overwhelmed with worries. The four weeks following her birth into womanhood had become a nightmare.

The afternoon was turning into evening, the neon lights lit the street. The square was crowded with people watching their steps. The traffic was slow, due to the big heaps of cleared-away snow that barricaded the sides of the pavements. They were very cold, so Samu invited her to the Abbazia Restaurant to have some food and wine, for he was loaded, still with his Christmas money. When they settled and she managed to push down a few bites of a tired looking breaded mushroom and rice, she finally summoned the courage to inform the father of her phantom baby:

'Samu, I did not get my menstruation.'

'When was it due?'

'A week ago.'

'Don't worry. It'll come. You're not pregnant.'

'It's easy for you to say that.'

Sofie found it difficult to enjoy herself and she drank more than usual. After the wine, they had rum with cola and no matter how she tried to explain her feelings, Samu did not seem to share her anxieties and more and more she started to resent his selfishness. For an agonising week, she actually learnt to hate him and blame him for everything they had done together, until she decided to take the matter into her own hands.

She went to see a doctor, but the pregnancy test was negative. Being a minor, she needed permission from a parent to take the pill. She went to her mother's workplace with the permission slip. At first, her mother was shocked, but signed it without comment. Thus, her mother became her confidant and there were no more limitations to sex and love. With a *God Bless you, Saint Sofia*, Sofie finally became the 'big woman' she had yearned to be.

Chapter 12

Sofie stretched out on Janos's bed, half reclining, looking up at him seated at his desk, gazing into the air. She remembered that this was the position in which people talked their souls away in Woody Allen films. In their topsy-turvy world, she had the power over the dreamer. It seemed that her underlying position presented her with a rare opportunity and Janos would spill out his innermost feelings to her.

'Have you been a soldier?' she asked Janos abruptly.

He seemed disturbed for a moment and surprised by her question. 'No.'

'How did you manage to avoid it?'

'With high blood pressure,' he said, and gave her a wry smile.

'Really?'

'I paid a doctor but, of course, was called in many times for these check-ups. I have a friend that knows a lot about herbs and drugs and he told me which herb to take in excess before my conscription examinations. My blood pressure was 170 for hours, they could not enlist me.'

'What is that herb?'

'I won't tell you. It's too dangerous.'

'Typical. Are you my father?'

'No, but I'm conscientious.'

'Can't you be a conscientious objector, by the way?'

'You know, you can be a conscientious objector, but then they put you into prison for twice the length of the time you would serve in the army. I would not have done that.'

'Yes. I heard a story that someone refused to go in due to religious grounds, saying that his religion forbade him from touching a gun. Then they put a rifle into his cell and he could only reach the food if he used it as a tool. After a few days, he did touch a gun.'

'I heard this story, too. That's why I went for the drug. But if I had not succeeded, I would have gone in. It's not so bad; many think the army is a fun place.'

'My father said that the new ones are always tortured till they break.'

'Well, if it's done to each and everyone, it doesn't matter so much. Humiliation and bullying is easier to bear if you are in a group.'

'Hating the sergeant forges community spirit, but how would that work in a war situation?' Sofie said, sounding upset.

'By then they love the sergeant. Remember that the bullying is only a means of hardening.'

'Glad that I don't have to be a soldier. I probably would not cope. Anyway, the army is just a cheap workforce. The poor guys have to build the railways.'

'Why, wouldn't you be proud to say "I built this bit of railway?"'

Sofie laughed. 'I'm more worried about my loss of individuality and having to kill on order.'

'To kill or to be killed, this is the question.'

Sofie shuddered. 'We are owned by the state.'

'Yes, even with my so-called high blood pressure I am a reserve and they can call me in for paperwork if they want.'

Sofie remained silent. She had no more to say about this futile subject. She was a pacifist, and she knew that if all people refused to become soldiers, the world could be changed. Since the liberation in 1945, she thought, the biggest threat to her country was the Soviet Union, but they were the so-called friends and protectors. Neither the revolution in 1956, nor the Prague Spring of 68 could change that. The Czech were defeated by the Hungarians. Her father told her how ashamed he was because of that. The Russians made sure that the two nations now hated each other. Resistance could only be non-violent.

'Janos, Samu needs our help. Can you?'

'Your polygamous friend needs my help?'

'This has nothing to do with our open relationship; he should never be a soldier.'

'I think, you're mad to have agreed to it. I can see that you're suffering. Have you lost your sense of dignity, Sofie? And anyway, you are so much more evolved than he is.'

'I'm not doing anything I don't want to.'

'Well, you're my friend, even if you're mad enough to be with him. If you ask me, I'll help.'

***

One sunny afternoon near the end of winter, Sofie and Janos were sitting in the window of the Bajkal Russian teahouse near Astoria Square. Samu got off the number seven bus and headed towards them. Sofie laughed, but Samu could see her nervousness. Janos kept looking intently at his watch, sipping his tea with no enjoyment. As agreed beforehand, Samu walked in, passed them without a sound of greeting, pretending not to know them, and went down the stairs to the toilet.

The extractors were humming with the rush of blood in his head and behind the noise, coming from upstairs, he could hear the balalaika and the Russian choir of men humming the *Volga* folk song he hated so much. They sounded like a congregation of emotional wrecks: men who were born to be old and oppressed, with bushy greying eyebrows and moustaches. The song was a major theme in every Soviet film about the war or the glorious October Revolution or the suffering of the peasants.

He went into a cubicle and took out the scalpel he had bought for a series of Lino etchings he planned to create. He took a big breath, aiming the blade at the soft bit under his left wrist where doctors take the pulse, but he could not stab into it. He blamed the stupid music. Then he looked at his watch. He had only about seven minutes left before Janos would come down to save him. He took off his watch and put it into his back pocket.

He had to think of something. It did not help to think about the beatings he got from his father; he became immune to them in the end and indifference was his last memory. Then he remembered the fear when he heard his father coming home, his heavy army boots hitting the stairs, which was much worse than the beatings. With this memory, he became even more paralysed and started to shake, powerless. Then the professor's features jumped into his mind. As he remembered them from underneath, reflecting in the professor's bedroom mirror the image of sexual pleasure mixed with the rage of power, Samu's face pulled into a grimace as he slashed deep into his left wrist. Then he passed out.

What happened next was later conveyed to him and he had to piece it together from Janos's and Sofie's stories. When Janos entered the male lavatory, a puddle of blood was seeping through the gap under the door of the cubicle, and he could not open the door, for Samu had locked it, forgetting their agreement. Janos had to run and bring the waiters. They broke the door down and fractured Samu's right collarbone by doing it. Somebody called an ambulance. Meanwhile, Janos tried to stop the bleeding with his bare hands, and the waiter had the sense to tie a kitchen towel over the main artery on Samu's upper arm. When the ambulance arrived some ten minutes later, it turned out that Samu had cut up his tendon so badly that he needed an operation in the hospital.

The police came and took a record with Janos as the witness. Sofie just stood around in the window, sipping cold tea, pretending not to know him and trying to withhold her tears.

'What happened?' she could only ask Janos once the paramedics had rolled Samu onto a stretcher and into the ambulance and the police had left.

'It was terrible. He passed out. I'll never ever do this again.'

'Thank you so much, on behalf of both of us.' Sofie said, but Janos was angry.

'You should not play with life, this is not right.' He showed her his shaking hands. Samu's blood had stained the edges of his cuffs.

'That's gruesome. I'll wash your shirt if you want.'

'Thanks, but I think I will get rid of the shirt.' Then he added, 'let's hope they won't section him yet. He wouldn't enjoy the freedom of thought in an asylum.'

Samu laughed when he heard this from Sofie. It was a joke, after all, even though he was never so stupid as to confuse freedom with anarchy. Freedom granted respect for rights, while anarchy was the disregard of all rights. They did not take him to an asylum, but he had to stay in hospital. A week later, with a bandaged left wrist and tied-up shoulders that inhibited his movement, he was ready for work.

He was advised to go to see a psychiatrist at his registered address: the same as his parents'. He could not possibly do that, but at least he could be sure that a file got opened on him, and somewhere in the ministry of the interiors they had a record saying that he had mental problems. There was hope that he would be exempted from military service.

Chapter 13

It was a sunny afternoon in early spring and Sofie strolled the streets after school. She only had a hunting bag on her shoulder that she had bought from her wages after working through last summer. The bag had enough compartments for her notebooks, pens and pencils and one or two books for the day. She kept tampons in the holes meant for rifle bullets, they fitted neatly. She loved walking without much to carry and wore flat shoes for this purpose. She even sewed off the heels to make them feel bare foot.

She walked along The Road of the People's Republic, leading from Hero's Square to Deak Square under bare plane trees, their bark peeling away in irregular patches. The sun warmed her back and she took off her winter coat, laying it over her shoulder. She patiently waited for the little green men to let her cross the avenue and strolled into the square, where old men were feeding pigeons and people rushed by her. At Rozsavolgyi music shop, she searched for records and listened to music, knowing all too well that she could not afford to buy anything.

At Liberation Square she stopped to look for familiar faces. Peeping in through the glass window of the Omnia Café, she glimpsed Victor. He sat at the tiny round table with a big bag between his legs, talking animatedly to an older woman, who seemed his age. Sofie waited to be noticed, not sure whether to disturb them. Then she mentally admonished herself, *how can you be so conditioned*, forgetting that in their circles there were no social boundaries. She walked in on dancing legs.

Indeed, Victor greeted her with a broad smile and said in English, 'Hi Sofie, this is Margaret.'

Although she had learned English at school, this was the first time Sofie had an opportunity to speak the language with an English person. She could barely say hello, but Margaret was very kind and soon she was babbling away. Margaret had pale white skin, and blue eyes behind the glasses; her hair was light brown. Up close she looked very English. Her spectacles tended to slip down and she kept pushing them up on her nose. Sofie was fascinated to discover that they were large and round, like John Lennon's, and she remembered having read in *The Beatles Bible* that these glasses were given away free by the National Health Service in England and John Lennon wore them out of solidarity with his Liverpool working-class roots. Margaret did not seem to be rich, but then she said that her father was a minister, which confused Sofie again. Margaret said that she worked for the Red Cross in England and her visit to Hungary was semi-official. Victor was talking about the pamphlet he wrote in Hungarian, but he did not have the English words for it. Sofie became his interpreter, 'Something like the "Criticism of the Dialectic Materialism".'

'Tell her, I've been writing it for the past six months, since I had the vision of Jesus.'

Sofie looked at Margaret anxiously, but translating Victor's words was easy. She enjoyed her role of the neutral middleman, helping both parties to understand each other. Margaret was not put off when she heard this statement.

'Great. Can I read it?'

'It's in Hungarian,' said Victor, looking at Sofie, who immediately volunteered.

'I can translate it for you.'

'You know, I could help you to get it published in England. My father is a minister and we know people that print pamphlets.' She added, laughingly, that it was a tradition in her family to work for free.

This confused Sofie even more: she knew that ministers in the Hungarian government earned huge amounts of money. 'The problem is,' she interrupted, 'the Police intercept the post, so I doubt we could send it to you that way.'

'We will find a way,' Victor assured them and they left it there; his words had authority, as if Jesus had said it himself.

Sofie took the manuscript and promised to translate it as soon as possible.

When they left the café they saw a big commotion in the square. Two policemen were holding down a boy from both sides.

'That's Miki,' Victor said agitatedly. 'He was coming to meet me.'

Sofie recognised the boy with the slim frame and long blond hair hanging over his face. He was one of Victor's steady companions, a runaway. The last time she asked him about his parents, he said that he just did not like to go home. Sofie knew that as he was underage his parents could have called the police to get him home. Victor ran to him, trying to help. They asked him for his papers and Sofie, paralysed with fear, watched them push him into the police car together with Miki, immediately after looking at his ID card.

Sofie could barely stand, her legs were so soft with nerves.

'Are you all right?'

'You can't imagine how lucky he is that he did not have the manuscript on him. They could put him into prison for that pamphlet.'

'But why did they take him, too?'

'As far as I know, Miki's mother is a psychiatrist and she can't accept that he refuses to live with them. She treats her son like a patient. Victor has a reputation as a maniac of some sort, when in reality he is looking after their child. His parents might have given his name to the police, although I'm sure there is a thick file on him already, anyway.'

'Sofie, my visa will expire soon, I have to go home tomorrow. But please do tell Victor, when you see him next time, that he is always welcome in my house in London.'

'I just hope they won't beat him up too much.'

'Jesus will give him strength, believe that,' said Margaret and hugged Sofie to her chest.

Sofie was surprised by it, as it took much longer than the usual tap with the lips on both cheeks she was used to. Margaret took her into her arms, gathered her onto her heart, and even kept her there for a moment; their chests stuck together as if by magnetic force. Awkward for a moment, but oh so good at the same time; she did not want to leave the warmth of that place. This might have been the first hug she ever got in her life and that from a stranger. *Wow*, she thought, *perhaps peace and love are not just slogans, but tangible entities that really exist in the universe. You just have to put up your hand and ask for it?* They exchanged phone numbers, promising to meet again sometime in the future.

That night Sofie saw the whole incident with the police again in her dream. This time she levitated out of it, looking down on Miki and Victor being taken away. She flew up like a sky walker, swimming in the air, enjoying the feeling that she could master gravity. She looked down at the globe, at Europe, and she laughed when she discovered the boot of Italy. The boot seemed to be dancing to the music of 'Amore Mio', then the music mixed with some wild rock from England. Then she could hear Ginsberg's harmonium mixed with the sound of someone coughing. She looked towards America, which looked like a blanket covering a big body, someone coughing vehemently under it. She heard Ginsberg's voice reciting *Howl*: 'America is coughing under the blanket.' This ended the dream, for her father's coughing in the next room woke her.

Chapter 14

On the same day he met Uncle George, Samu attempted his last suicide in public. By now he had become a legend in the underworld. Everybody knew that he had tried to kill himself in public lavatories many times. In any other ordinary citizen one or two of these attempts would have been enough to be prescribed psychiatric treatment, but not in his case. He knew that his father's hands could reach very far and was convinced that his father had arranged it so that he was still eligible to be enlisted. In fact, he had had his last mustering examination in his hometown just a few weeks before and nobody seemed to be aware of his mental instability. Samu suspected that he might have to do something outrageous, but he had not yet decided. For his present performance, he had found the thick rope in the Academy's prop collection: a dark and musty smelling side room where they kept all these treasures, funny objects to make life drawings. When he collected the rope, he smiled at the flash of memory: making love with Sofie in the corner, pushing her up against the wall in the semi-darkness. He wore his long Macintosh that day, which hid the rope underneath perfectly, and went to the Western Rail Station. He walked down to the underground toilets and paid the compulsory fifty-*forint* fee for using the toilet. The attendant was listening to the radio, too preoccupied with the news of the strikes in Poland to react to him.

Finally inside the cubicle, he made sure not to lock the light blue varnished door. He took out the rope, fixed it onto the rusty looking heating pipe that ran around the top of the wall just under the ceiling, and slid his head into the noose. With a big sigh, he jumped off the toilet seat and dangled and dangled. When he started to choke, he kicked into the door, trying to force it open, making noise, hoping that the attendant would hear him. Then, with a huge bang, he broke the water pipe. Samu landed on the black and white tiles in a flood of shitty water.

At last, the attendant ran to him, pulling him up by his legs, roughly shouting abuse.

'Fuck, the Pipe-Breaker. I've heard about you. What are you doing, are you mad?'

Samu tried to stand up, but could not move very well, being in shock. He did not have to pretend to be out of balance.

The attendant pulled him up roaring even louder. 'Get away from here, or I call the police and tell them that you are doing this to avoid the army!'

Samu panicked, seeing that this would not take him anywhere near a hospital. 'I wanted to kill myself.'

'And I'll kill you if you don't vanish. You chicken.'

The attendant slapped his face and punched him in the side. Samu gasped for air.

'Go away, you queer, did you hear me?'

Being called a queer shocked him twice as much as the fear of death. His eyes brimming with tears, he walked away, maddened by the ineffectuality of his endeavours. He knew that if he were called in to the army, his father would make sure that his first year was a nightmare.

When he phoned Sofie she was too excited to talk to him as her uncle from England had arrived to their house and was concluding his short visit, saying goodbye to her family. Samu couldn't go back to the Academy anymore. He went to the Szechenyi public bath, only for men, hoping that his clothes would dry while he was soaking in the hot thermal water.

He let his body sink into the pool, watching the foul egg-smelling steams evaporating in the thin spring sunshine. Older men were sitting in the water, playing chess, talking in whispers to each other. They did not look too old to be retired, yet they were here, having a good time in the early afternoon. Samu tried to guess who they were, what role they could be playing in the socialist mechanism, but as they were all naked, except for a thin plastic apron covering their dicks, it did not matter what uniform they wore during the day. He was wondering how they could enjoy life in this dark smelly asshole of the world, but the warm soak softened his joints and made him relax.

From further away, a well-tanned man in his fifties stared at

Samu's young taut body greedily, openly enjoying the view.

Just you watch, old cunt, Samu thought to himself. He grinned. He enjoyed mentally teasing him, thinking that he was paying it back to the professor, but then the old man got braver and started to drift towards him with a big winning smile on his face.

'Enjoying the soak?' he asked.

All the anger about his weakness and submission broke up to the surface like a thermal spring: foul-smelling and full of poisonous gases. 'I do, you dickless idiot,' Samu spat back at him.

The man turned very quickly, pretending he did not hear, floating away in another direction.

Frustration squeezed Samu's chest again. He was just so fed up with the men in his world: his father that would do anything to humiliate him; the professor that thought money could buy anyone; this old gay that thought him being there gave him permission to make advances. All his male friends abandoned him; even his blood brother only came to see him when he needed something, like the other night when he came to ask for his passport. Zoli had got into trouble, what kind he did not say, and needed to leave the country. Of course, Samu had no problem helping him; Zoli was like his brother, perhaps more than a brother could ever be; they shared so many important memories in his hometown.

Zoli had been there when he lost his virginity with a whore, and helped him to sort out the ticks he got from the woman. Zoli helped him when he was kicked out of the hostel where his father had sent him. He could stay at his house, with Zoli's lonely mother; all he had to do was pay rent, which his father, after the compulsory punishment beating, had agreed to pay, anyway. Samu would never say no to Zoli, who needed his help in this instance; although, he could not imagine how Zoli might forge the picture in the passport so easily, but he muttered something about peeling away the top layer of the black and white picture and manufacturing his own on the top. Samu did not believe it would work, but let him have it anyway; he would never say no to a friend in need. But now he had to go back home to get a new red passport, only for the Eastern bloc, of course, as he could not get one for the West before serving his military service. He would have to say that he had lost it. This meant facing his father again. Then the thought of introducing Sofie to his sister came up and he thought that a good pretext to go home. Sofie might soften the atmosphere at home. This thought cheered him up. He was ready to face the world, and his clothes had dried. He decided to go and meet the famous Uncle George.

Chapter 15

A dark blue Jaguar with a yellow GB number plate was parked amongst the heap of pale-coloured made in GDR Trabants and USSR-produced Ladas in front of Sofie's block. Samu had phoned Sofie in advance to warn her, for this would have been his first proper introduction to her parents, too. Since he had beaten her up, Sofie's father tried everything to win her back. Clearly, the cold shoulder treatment Sofie applied to him, worked. Sofie's mother had invited Samu for Sunday lunch 'any Sunday he had time', but Sofie always found an excuse to keep her family and Samu apart. Her trust in her father had been completely destroyed and all she wanted was to punish him. Samu sensed the proverbial wrath of a woman and thought he would not like to cross this one's path. This time, however, she wanted Samu to meet the famous Englishman-uncle, she adored so much. She came running down the staircase to meet him and flew into his arms, but smelling his wet clothes, she recoiled.

'Is this your best suit to show your respect to my dear parents?' she asked mischievously.

'Sorry, you know the pipe broke. I'll take my coat off quickly and then it might just go; I smell lovely underneath.'

Sofie pushed her face under his shirt and rubbed it onto his chest, arousing him. She laughed, feeling him shudder.

'I see.'

They took the steps two at a time up to the second floor. Sofie slowed down and stopped giggling at the top.

'I only care whether my uncle and Nan will like you. My parents can be very nervous when he's here, but you'll see it for yourself. I cannot promise much fun.'

'You can always move in with me and leave them to sort it out between themselves,' he said seriously.

As she had foretold, the background noise of a loud discussion greeted them when they opened the front door. Nan rushed to it, saying, 'come in children, look who's here'; overjoyed at being able to introduce her prodigal son. Sofie's father rushed in between them to meet Samu, shaking his hand and saying, 'sorry to be rude, but this is strictly a family gathering.' Sofie, immediately hurt, turned up the volume of her voice, becoming a tone shriller, 'Dad, Mum, Uncle George, this is Samu, my boyfriend.'

Her mother and Uncle George shook hands with him, while her father gazed, senselessly. Then he woke up from the shock and became the well-mannered gentleman, giving him a drink of whiskey, brought by Uncle George, no doubt, and ushering him to take off his dirty Mackintosh and inviting him to join the table. Nan had obviously been preparing a meal, for there was enough Cordon Bleu for everyone, together with the compulsory mashed potatoes and gherkins on the side. She had made baked cheese for Sofie, who, some years previously, to the annoyance of them all, had become a vegetarian. She offered Samu *csalamade*, pickled tomatoes, hot chilli, and cabbage: George's favourite, as they found out. Nobody knew how it came about, but after ten minutes they were already discussing the Revolution. It was so important for George that he had named his pub in Manchester after it.

'We were young and foolish then,' declared Sandor Benedek, Sofie's father.

George became agitated by the memory, 'better than old and silly. Sofie, imagine, your father found the guns for us.'

'Yes? Did you really, Dad?'

'Shush. Not so loud, the walls have ears in these new blocks.'

Samu noticed him looking at George angrily, visibly at the end of his tether.

'Leave my daughter out of this, George. You talk easy; you left. We had to stay here and deal with the aftermath.'

Samu interrupted, 'I admire you for that.' For a moment, nobody knew whom he meant. 'I admire both of you for fighting for what you believed in.'

'Nothing to admire,' retorted Benedek. 'We wasted our energy and lots of lives. One of our classmates, Kovacs Feri, was caught with a gun in his hand. They kept him in prison for two years until he turned eighteen, then they hanged him. I'll never forgive myself for that.'

'That was surely, the government's doing, not yours.' Nobody reacted to this bold comment, only Uncle George nodded pensively. Samu had to think of his own father. How did he get away without any punishment just by signing up to the army? It all seemed miraculous now, sitting at the table with two '56 veterans: one who had never been found out and had lived in constant fear ever since and another that had been forced to leave the country.

Uncle George's voice was emotionless, 'I see Kovacs Feri as a sacrifice. But you cannot deny how exuberant we were and how proud of ourselves, because we had the courage to stand up and try to change the world.'

'But we didn't,' Sofie's father spoke low, 'and the West gave a damn. That's the point. Sofie wants to go to university. I don't want to spoil her future. The fact that you keep coming here can jeopardise her admittance.'

'No bother, I can keep away from your house, if you so wish.'

Sofie took flight at her father. 'Dad, how can you be so rude? Using me, as well? Please, Uncle, don't think people are so mean. And who cares? I'll study, and they'll take me.'

They spent the rest of the dinner in near silence, and Benedek seemed to be sorry for his over-protectiveness, for he kept filling up the glasses, trying to infuse some frivolity into the atmosphere. Sofie's Nan reigned the table and she made sure that they even laughed about some childhood stuff that occurred between George and Sofie's mother.

After dinner Uncle George took them on a ride in his Jaguar. Samu admired him, for he did not show any sign of drunkenness. Transported into another world, Samu was impressed by the soft leather seats and the air of luxury the car emanated; the effect of excellent workmanship and lavish use of material that he had never seen before.

'What if they stop you and do a breath test?' Samu asked, but Uncle George just waved his hand. 'Nothing that a few thousand forints couldn't sort out.'

They were sitting on the back seats, holding hands, floating in silence through the streets towards the Danube, coolly observing the early 1940s blocks of flats that dominated this part of the city, through small estates with tiny gardens, finally driving down Vaci Street and onto the quayside by the Danube. Samu rolled down the window and smelled the river air, looking over to Margit Island to the sporadic neon lights that speckled the dark wood. A yellow tram snaked over the brightly lit bridge. On the roof of a building, neon lights advertised Tungsram. For a moment, he closed his eyes to a slit, taking in its orange shimmer.

When they turned back towards the Western Station on Lenin Avenue, Sofie started to interrogate Uncle George about life in England, a subject that had seemed taboo at the parental dinner table. She tried to cram as much as possible into the conversation, becoming, as always, very intense.

'Is it true that in England no one starts work before nine o'clock in the morning?'

'You ask the most important things, don't you,' said Samu, but Sofie squeezed his hand to remain silent.

'Pretty true,' said Uncle George, 'I don't open the pub until eleven.'

Samu, to show her who the man was here, carried on, 'that would suit me. Are the English girls as beautiful as the Hungarians?' He squeezed Sofie's hand now and leaned in to her face with the intention of pressing a kiss on it, but she pulled away. Uncle George grinned at him in the rear-view mirror.

'Yes, and they're notorious for their loose morals.'

'And what about English politicians?' asked Sofie not noticing the grin, or not wanting to see it.

Uncle George, now being reminded of his past, became morose. 'There is no morality in politics, but girls can do a lot of damage. We had an MP lately that had to resign because of an affair with an escort.'

Samu could only guess what an escort was, but did not want to ask for confirmation. Sofie did not ask either, even though she led the conversation. She pretended to know, but she was sulking, obviously. The cobbles under the car became too bumpy for the Jaguar and Uncle George had to slow down and navigate big potholes; a sign that they were approaching the outskirts. Soon, they were back at Sofie's house, and pulled up to the kerb.

'Thanks for the ride. It's a pity I have school tomorrow and I cannot spend more time with you,' said Sofie.

Samu did not have to go into the Academy until nine; *wow, I have the freedom of an Englishman,* he thought laughing at the absurdity of the very idea.

'It was short, but I understand. It's great that you want to study. I keep telling Sally how proud I am of you. Look after your grandmother. She has aged so much since my last visit.'

'I will. Goodbye, Uncle, have a good journey home.'

'I'll be back soon. Take care and good luck with your university entrance.'

'Thanks. Luck, I'll need it.'

'You'll make it, I'm sure.'

Samu clambered out of the car to give her a hug. She was tense, but eventually melted into his arms.

'*Jó éjszakát* "darling",' he said grinning and she kissed him back.

Chapter 16

After delivering Sofie home, Uncle George invited Samu for a few more drinks in his hotel. The restaurant of the Hotel Astoria was packed with people. This was the first time Samu had gained entry, owing to his poor status, and clothes. The doorman looked him up and down three times, but Uncle George's demeanour allowed Samu in. To his surprise he recognised a few faces from the Hungarian art world: a writer, and film director, and his hero, Cseh Tamas, the singer-song writer. They were sitting together at a table with a group of foreigners, probably at a business meeting. While taking in the dark wood-panelled walls, the gallery and the chandeliers, he relaxed and thought that he would enjoy this night.

While they settled down, Samu noticed Uncle George eyeing up the waitress. She must have been over thirty, too old, really, but the tight black skirt emphasised her curves. In the dark shadows under her eyes she wore the strains of the job, but they were large, brown, beaming warmth and kindness. Uncle George seemed to be falling in love with her, following her with his eyes. He did not even have to sign to her – she appeared with a broad smile on her face – but Samu understood her speed to be evidence of the quality of service, as they were in a four star hotel. They ordered a bottle of Tokaji Muscat, demi-sec, Samu's favourite; Uncle George let him choose the wine. Out of politeness, as it was a restaurant, they had to eat as well. George ordered goose liver pâté to start with, until they decided on their main course. Samu did not feel like eating, but George insisted, so finally he agreed to have bone marrow soup, to give him strength.

'You're far too thin, Samu,' was Uncle's argument.

Samu tried to query him about life in England, but George only wanted to talk about the Revolution, as if that had been the only time he was happy in his life. Samu kept looking around, checking whether anybody listened, but this place was teeming with foreigners. Uncle lowered his voice when the waitress approached them, otherwise, his slogans moulded into the cacophony of international jumble and the gipsy musicians' efforts reached them from the far corner of the room.

'They killed the industry. Did you know, for instance, that before the war, there was a Hungarian car industry in place? With all the resources we had here, and the amazing agriculture, Hungary could have become totally independent from everybody else. Like another Switzerland. The Switzerland of the East.'

'Yes, and my father and Sofie's father and all that stayed here bought into this system. I am ashamed to say that my father used to be involved, a revolutionary, as well, but he was luckier than your friend who was hanged. He signed his life over to the army and now he is a high-ranking captain. It's really disgusting.'

'Look at me, my Jaguar, my freedom to travel, my existence. The world belongs to the brave ones. But I had to work hard for it. I worked on an oil rig for six years. Imagine that, no women for six months in a row. How would you cope with that?'

Samu could not but trust this man. He knew that he would never be able to tell it to anyone else, and Uncle George would be gone tomorrow. He could let him have his secret. Perhaps, if he knew it, he could take it away from him.

'Did you ever get anywhere close to having sex with a man?'

Uncle George did not seem to hear him, for he looked at the cow-eyed waitress trotting up to them, swinging her padded hips with careless motion.

'Would you like to order something else?'

'Oh yes, miss. Let us have another bottle. What is your name, if I might ask?'

'Marika,' she chirped.

'Marika, isn't that wonderful? This melody! It's worth travelling a thousand miles for it. Thank you.' He kissed her hand, which the waitress seemed to enjoy; yet she looked around to see whether the chief waiter had seen it. The *Ober* was further away talking to the leader of the gipsy band.

She pulled her hand away with a smile and added, '*Igenis*, another bottle of the Szamorodni. I'll bring it straight away.'

She carried her lively hips away, which George fixed on for a moment, then he focused his eyes on Samu's face. His voice was shockingly cool. 'I know that in Hungary everyone thinks that all sailors are homosexuals, but the answer is no.'

Now Samu was frightened that George had misunderstood and probably thought Samu wanted to have sex with him. 'I didn't mean that, either. I just heard that England is teaming with bisexuals.'

'Well, homosexuality was a punishable criminal offence until lately, just like here. If there are bisexuals, they do it in secret.'

The subject seemed to have been exhausted. Marika brought the *Tokaji* and after a while the gipsy concertmaster came to their table to play George's song into his ears.

Uncle George shouted '*De szomorú a muzsikátok!*' and the *prímás* immediately knew that this was the title of his song. He grinned and nodded subserviently, acknowledging the hundred-*forint* note that George slid into his pocket. The *prímás* pulled the song about the lost love of a woman. George sang.

On shaky legs, Samu escaped to the toilet. His forsakenness hit him hard in the chest. In the cubicle he burst out crying. He did not know why exactly, but for a moment he felt so lonely on this planet. When he tried to urinate he surmised the extent of his drunkenness, for he could not aim at the toilet. The screen of alcohol darkened his vision in front of his nose, while giving him eyes on the top of his head that made him perceive the neon lights like the flashing blade of an axe. He recalled a dream in which he entered a urinal in the middle of the city for a piss and when he came out he was naked from the waist down. He took good care to zip up his trousers, which took him a while. He washed his face with cold water and grinned at his idiotic mirror image, trying to put on a mask of joyous indifference, which could have been true, after all; the axe did not matter.

On his return he found George and Marika wooing each other. He took it as his cue to leave. George waved him close and gave him money for his taxi home.

'See you soon,' he winked at him, 'see you in England.'

Chapter 17

Sofie's hatred of the system and the treatment she suffered from the pestering police force could only be matched by her love of the pamphlet she was translating for Victor. For the first time in her life she had valuable work to do, but most importantly, helping Victor made her happy. With every page she developed more and more respect and admiration for him. She discovered that he had been deported to a forced labour camp for being a "dangerous work avoider, and enemy of the people". Although he had only been there for three months, the longest you could get for not having a job registered in your ID card, the experience hardened him. He worked in a stone mine, for no payment, getting an education in Dialectic Materialism on Sundays. His personal history, prior to being imprisoned for not working, was just as interesting. His girlfriend, the love of his life, had died in a freak accident. After this Victor was unable to work or study; his family looked after him. He was lingering on the verge of madness, harbouring suicidal thoughts, until he had a vision of Jesus. His concerned parents wanted to get him psychiatric care, which he refused. He broke off his relationship with them and started his life on the streets, living with friends, moving from place to place and not working. Because of his convincing stories about Jesus, and for not asking for anything, he was passed on like a legend, which meant that young people offered him shelter and fed him. He did not need much, and often they had to beg him to eat. He was very thin, but the long hair and beard covered his bony structure and made his mesmerising blue eyes even more impressive. His work, *The Critique of the Dialectic Materialism*, simply quoted all his visions: the apparitions, the talks with Jesus, who said that the system could not survive too long as it was based on the lie of atheism. Materialism had no grounds, for matter needed the spirit to become animate, therefore the whole system was fake.

Sofie became the prophet's advocate, talking about the manuscript to everyone worthy to hear about it, but not to her parents, of course. Her mother was a communist, after all. For her, religion was the opium of the people, as Marx had said. Although she was open-minded. Acknowledging that religion was part of world heritage, she gave Sofie the Bible to read when she was around fifteen. Her father was too weak to protest. He lived for his work. As long as he could work, he was happy. Sofie chose to talk about Victor's ideas to Nan.

'Sometimes, I doubt that there is a God. I knew it even less during the war.'

'They say that man has freedom to decide which way to go and badness is only a consequence of bad choices.'

'Carrying a dead baby in your arms for miles makes you question the purpose of it all. Were we really so bad? Did we really have to be punished so badly?'

'And the Jews? Why so many? When they were God's people? Is God so cruel to his own people?'

'We'll only find out how good He is, when we die. Sofie, you won't believe it but carrying the baby to the cemetery I prayed all the way long. I prayed to God to take back that soul and prayed that He did not send any more to my sister, who was so fertile. She lost all her girls; it must have been something genetic, but they died before reaching six months. She had seven babies and only two boys were left alive. The boys left for Canada in '56 and she followed them later. She would do anything for her sons. But I always trusted God.'

'And Jesus?'

'Not so much Jesus. He was only a prophet himself, after all.'

'Nan. I met a guy that says that he saw Jesus with his own eyes.'

'Really? Isn't he mad? Be careful, Sofie, choose your friends wisely.'

'He is so trustworthy. He could be a saint in another era.'

'I'm a reformed believer, we're down-to-earth people, we don't believe in saints.'

Sofie accepted that Victor's visions were real and that Jesus chose him to spread his message. It was simple: *There is more to life than matter, we all have a soul.* She believed it to be true. How could she have butterflies in her stomach or dreams that came true?

Her enthusiasm for the text she was translating infected Samu and they became the promoters of Victor's work. She typed a copy and carried the manuscript with her everywhere she went. It was Victor's spirit that she carried with her, while in reality they had no idea what had happened to him. It was now two weeks since the incident with the police, when he was taken away, and nobody had heard or seen of him. There were rumours about him being imprisoned, but no one could imagine on what grounds, as by now he had a job on his ID card: he was one of the models at the Academy.

Apparently, Susan and Mercedes went to the police station and enquired about him, but they were just jeered at. Only relatives were entitled to get information. But Victor could not be forgotten, and Sofie and Samu made sure that copies of his work were circulated. Sofie typed a copy of the manuscript on her mother's typewriter and she asked anyone that wanted to borrow it to do the same on their typewriters. Some of them did, so there were already five copies in circulation, without the author's name; but everyone knew that it was written by Victor.

Compared to her translation work, her Matura exams seemed like a game of pretend and soon enough a day came when she found the mystery of Victor's writing most comforting.

In the morning of that day Sofie cut her index finger very badly. Since childhood she'd been superstitious about hurting herself; any cuts or the sight of her own blood filled her with foreboding. At the age of six, on the day of her initiation into the communist community when she was made into a *Little Drummer*, she ran through a glass door in the hall and almost died. At the time this was caused by sheer excitement, childish joy, but later Sofie concluded that it meant it was the beginning of the end. Soon enough she became disenchanted with the communist community and anyway, blood reminded her of violence and violence reminded her of Jesus, and Jesus reminded her of futile sacrifice and the cruelty of the masses, and the cruelty of the masses reminded her of the October Revolution. The glorified version of it had been hammered into her head since early childhood. November the 7th was the date when the whole school went to the cinema to watch yet another Soviet film about the Second World War. Hungarian Television had special programmes during school holidays. After the 7th of November, winter became the time of darkness, when she watched the silent film, *Ivan the Terrible*, by Eisenstein, on television. This was the first film she could remember seeing; she started watching it at six and watched it every winter and it became part of her psyche. She was mesmerised by the hateful death of the Tzar. He seemed to be a true sacrifice. The intricacies of the court, the deceitfulness of women, the fear and hate of the boyars and the boyarinas expressed in silent acting and black and white images of fear and foreboding, long and lingering shadows, sudden moves: how a single move could express so much, she did not know, but the artistry captured her imagination. There was something about blood, the sight of it, even in black and white. Drama, the foreboding of the end, just as it occurred when her father hit her and she saw her own blood on the wall.

Sofie was celebrating her Matura results with her parents. Her finger had a huge bandage and she was too clumsy to cut her cake. Mum had to feed her and they laughed about it, but excused her from doing the dishes later.

'There is something good in every bad,' Sofie recounted the adage of her childhood with relish. The telephone rang in the hall. Gabi was on the line, hysterical, asking whether she had heard about Orpheus.

'They say that a motorbike knocked him down last night. The last thing I heard was that he died.'

'That's impossible,' was her reaction. 'Do you know which hospital he was taken to?'

'Yes, the Army Hospital.'

'I'll go in the morning and I'll find out.'

'OK, I'll come with you.'

When she told her parents, her mother screamed, 'not tonight!' as if it was Orpheus's fault that he was dying when they were celebrating. For her mother it was inconsiderate of him to spoil Sofie's joy. Sofie did not sleep very well, partly her throbbing finger kept her awake, along with the fear that Orpheus might have really died. She had not seen him for a long time, perhaps for three weeks.

Depression had spread like an epidemic that spring. The very reason Sofie and Samu left the city was because they wanted to avoid getting dragged down. They were fed up with the whole mood of Budapest. They escaped and stayed in a tent near a brook in a forest for a week, collecting mushrooms and wild berries and living on the conserved food they took with them. They washed in the brook and spent most of the day naked, completely safe. As Samu reassured her, it was military territory, nobody was allowed to come in there. Nevertheless, one morning they were woken by a guard, but Samu told him his father's name and the man was gone in a flash.

There it happened that they had the same dream. They dreamt about living together in a strange country, in a simple room, where there was a chair, a table, a bed, all in vibrant colour. It might have been a recollection, Sofie thought of a painting by Van Gogh they saw together, but having the same dream during the same night, was something extraordinary. This in Sofie's mind confirmed that they were indeed very close, but unlike Orpheus, she had no worries about that. She was rather amazed, thinking that this was a magical relationship.

The last time Sofie had seen Orpheus was shortly before this joint trip. Although she and Samu were going away, Orpheus waved to them and said, 'I'll disappear for a while.' It was funny, but now it seemed prophetic, so typical of Orpheus. He had to be on top of everything, all the time. Orpheus was always on the go, never settled with anyone, always searching for some new girl. He walked on hearts, but his abusive behaviour originated in a fear of being hurt. A few years before she got to know him, a girl had committed suicide because of Orpheus, which he could never allow to happen again. In a way, this was his repentance. So when he started to fall in love, he walked away. The girls, on the other hand, fell in love with the idea of him being unattainable. Orpheus hated to see how deeply she gave herself to Samu. He asked her many times, aware of her suffering, why she had agreed to have an open relationship with Samu. She just smiled back at him, sadly, and waved. Freedom was not just an ideal to her, it had to be acted upon.

Early in the morning, with a still throbbing finger, she dressed with difficulty. She couldn't eat anything for breakfast. Gabi was waiting for her at the bus stop and the sun shone with five thousand watts. It was a cruel sunshine. They travelled to the hospital without too many words exchanged between them: both too nervous and frightened.

Sofie took on herself the task to go in, but as she was no relative, they sent her away without any information. Luckily, she knew Orpheus's real name, so she sneaked up to a nurse that seemed to have just finished her shift.

'Please, please tell me, did you have an eighteen-year-old boy called Frigyes Alfred here last night?' From the look of the nurse, she could see that she was not the first young person to ask this today.

'He had multiple fractures. His hip bones broke, too. He did not survive the night.'

'Thank you,' said Sofie and stumbled away. She fell into Gabi's arms. They hugged and cried. She had to think of Orpheus's protruding hip bones and the tight, coloured chinos he liked to wear, always tone on tone. He had his blue phase, his red phase, and the last phase was cream. She could remember the fragility of his hip bones, the fragility of his fingers that played the clarinet so well. Only his hair was big as a tent on his head – untamable.

Sofie and Samu could not accept his death. 'He didn't die,' they kept telling each other. They did not go to the funeral. Gabi told Sofie about it. Mercedes was the only one who took a glimpse at him lying in the coffin; the rest of them did not dare. Her face revealed the bleak truth. It was indeed Orpheus. After the funeral he became a legend. Every girl wanted to have known him. He was every girl's lover. Some were even pregnant by him.

Victor's absence made this darkness even more unbearable. It would have been good to hear what he had to say about Orpheus's futile death. All that Sofie could do was to spread the word that the soul exists and if Orpheus died his leaving must have had a reason.

Chapter 18

Sofie stopped going to school in May when she started her exam holidays. Temperatures were already soaring, promising a hot summer. She did her best and studied early in the mornings, when it was still cool enough to concentrate. At the weekend they planned to go to the country to meet Samu's parents. Hitching was easy in summer.

The minute they left Budapest the strangeness of the Hungarian countryside hit her in the face and sat on her shoulder like a banshee. She liked it and hated it at the same time. Country people looked and talked differently and in their eyes Sofie and Samu were the folks from 'Pest': the aliens. Sofie often wondered how a country could have only one city, the rest of it just plateau, planes, villages, and farmers who seemed to be at least fifty if not a hundred years behind. Although she spent part of her childhood summers in a small town near the Yugoslavian border, her grandparents were civil servants. Her grandfather was a customs officer before taking a stroke, and her grandmother led a kitchen in a school. Although she saw pigs and chickens in their garden and they had an orchard and a vegetable patch, she had never met real country people. Walking through the villages, with only main streets and exactly the same square-shaped houses everywhere, she saw that Hungary was dull and faceless.

They had to stop at the end of a village and hitch. From somewhere behind them, a pack of dogs ran out of an open gate. She started to run, but Samu turned to face them. He howled at them and stamped his foot on the ground. The dogs stopped and shied away. Sofie was amazed by so much human power. She would not have known what to do; on her own she would have been chewed up into bits.

They had to pass Lake Balaton. Even though she had no swimming costume they went down to the beach. She swam in her knickers, using a scarf to cover her breasts as she ran into the water. It was sunset and she enjoyed the feeling of the last rays of the sun drying her body. She pulled a Fruit of the Loom top from her satchel and changed in the changing room. She always travelled light, with a spare pair of knickers, a toothbrush, and a spoon in her satchel. Of course, she had Victor's manuscript with her, too, in case she had the chance to show it to somebody. They had an invitation to a party at Lake Balaton in Keszthely.

It was dark when they arrived; everybody was around the bonfire in the garden. The boy, Gabor, was Samu's friend from the first boarding school he had attended. Gabor was a bit tipsy and extremely happy to see them. The party was to celebrate him getting a place at university. Sofie had never seen such a happy family before. His mother was his best supporter: his confidante and best friend. He told this to everyone. 'This golden woman is my best friend,' said Gabor to Sofie to introduce his mother. 'I would never have been able to do it without her.'

'Congrats to getting a place. What will you study?'

'He'll study ornithology,' his mother was keen to speak for him.

'I didn't get into medicine, as I wanted, but at least it is a place!' Gabor said, wobbling around, using Sofie's shoulder as crutches.

He can't stand on his own feet, for sure, she thought. Gabor seemed to be bursting with libido. One of the girls he fancied was a runaway from an orphanage. His slurred speech became louder when he told his mother about it. 'Poor Ida has to live in that horrible place. She should never go back there.'

'I believe the opposite is true. She'll be caught very quickly. If not today, then tomorrow. It would be better to face the consequences of running away than having to be taken back by the police,' she said, but Gabor was tipsy; he resisted his mother's reasoning. 'She'll be eighteen next week. If we helped her to hide until then she might never have to go back there.'

More than anything, Sofie could sense his mother's fear for her son's position. She did not seem honest; there was something very wrong about her. Sofie could not tell why, but she doubted she would ever trust this woman with her life.

When Gabor crashed out, the party was over. Everybody had to go, including the girl from the borstal. The mother superior took over and cleared away the mess, making sure that nothing stood in the way of her son's future. Samu suggested that they took a train to Kaposvar, where his parents lived.

At the railway station they found out that the next train was leaving at four in the morning. They had two hours to kill, but all the pubs were closed. They sat down on the wooden slatted bench in the dark waiting room.

'Do you regret that you did not stay in that boarding school?' Sofie asked Samu. 'You could go to university by now, perhaps, like Gabor.'

'He tried for two years to get into medicine and now he will be an ornithologist. I don't think so. I am for all or nothing.'

Sofie put her head onto Samu's shoulder and fell asleep.

Gabor's glasses twinkled in the night. He pushed them back up his sweaty nose. He had a bird in his left hand, which he ringed on the leg, numbered, and registered. Then he let the bird fly away. It drew a black silhouette onto the clear blue sky. Men were cutting reed on the frozen lake. The stems were swaying in the wind with a tinkling sound. Topped with brown cigars, dried into yellow sticks that would make such wonderful thatching for the houses. She loved the thatched houses. They were so different from the square-shaped modern blocks she had seen on the way.

'Give me a cigar,' she said, laughingly, to the reed cutter. He was a man she knew from the bus stop in Budapest. He wore dreadlocks. He looked like a lion, walked like a lion, and moved like a lion.

'Give me a cigar,' she repeated, but the man gave her a kiss full on the mouth instead. She lost her balance and looked down, just to discover that her feet were frozen into the lake. Just like the reed, she could only sway. The man was going to cut her down and take her or leave her. She did not know which one she preferred. When she opened her eyes, she registered the freezing cold on her sandalled feet. She tried to roll into a ball, to make herself smaller, but the bench was too hard. The wooden slats had cut stripes into her thighs. Samu was already up, walking up and down, jumping around to warm himself up.

The train rolled in at three forty-five and they carried on sleeping inside the wagon. After two hours travel they arrived at Kaposvar, just in time for the town's awakening. Kaposvar surprised her with its old-town style. She actually loved it. It had some pretty old streets, and more newly built ready-made house blocks, but she even liked those, for they were much lower than the ten storey blocks she knew from Budapest. These blocks, although made of the same prefab panels, were modest and still humanly bearable.

Chapter 19

With her apprehension mixed with excitement, Sofie bravely faced meeting Samu's parents. The family atmosphere, however, was worse than she could have imagined. His mother did not speak at all: his father ruled the table and the house. Samu introduced her and they smiled at her, but did not seem to like her. His father was literally the head of the family, nobody else was allowed to think. Keenly intelligent, whatever he said was right. The fear of the others was tangible. Samu had a younger sister, Brigitta. She was thirteen, just as subdued as his mother.

The whole family watched Sofie's struggle when she bumbled into a discussion about vegetarianism with Mr Horvath.

'I don't think that we humans have the right to kill animals. We do not need meat for our survival.'

'Killing is often necessary. We have to control the animal population, otherwise there would be too many,' Mr Horvath said.

'Killing is not right. They would die of natural causes.'

'They would kill each other and spread diseases. It is better to kill them while they are still healthy.'

'The hunt is unfair, as men have much better guns than animals.'

Samu took the opportunity to interfere. 'Sofie, you should see Dad when he is hunting with his mates, comrades and party leaders. They speed around in army jeeps and shoot deer and boars with Kalashnikovs.'

'How awful.' She regretted saying it immediately and Mrs Horvath was obviously scared by her blunder. She stood up quickly and started to clear the table. As his father had no words to retort with, just a purple face, Sofie stood up as well to help her. They went to the kitchen. She could see Mrs Horvath's hands trembling. She turned away with tears in her eyes. 'I'm sorry,' she said.

Sofie did not understand why she said that, but did not dare to ask.

Samu and Sofie were not allowed to sleep in the same room, therefore, they went out for a long walk in town. They ended up drinking coke with brandy in a bar and became quite tipsy.

'My mum left my dad once,' Samu explained, 'but after a year apart they got together again. She has been like this ever since.'

'Why did she come back?'

'For the family's sake, according to her.'

'I doubt that it is better for the family,' Sofie said.

'A better life promised, perhaps. Sometimes, when he was beating me, I thought he might not be my father. Which would explain why he hated me so much.'

Samu paid the bill and they stumbled into the street and started walking. The town was dark and quiet, but peaceful. Neon lights lit the road, but there were no cars. It seemed to be devoid of life, or perhaps it was too late. Sofie was not sure anymore.

'Why did you end up in this godforsaken town?' she asked Samu.

'Sofie, don't be so posh. There are other places apart from Budapest. In fact, this can be a nice place. It has a theatre, as well.'

'Sorry, I know. I'm just...'

'Forgiven. The reason why we moved so many times, is that my father only cares about his rank. If he accepts a new position in a new village or town, he usually gets a higher rank. This is how we never settled anywhere.'

'Do you think your parents like me?'

'I think my mum likes you.'

'I might have hurt her. She was crying in the kitchen.'

'When I was a little boy I dreamt about taking her away once I grew up. But now I'm sure she wouldn't come with me. She feels responsible for him.'

'Or guilty. He definitely has power over her.'

'He keeps a gun at home and I am sure he would be capable of using it, even on my mum. Would you like to see it?'

'No thanks. I hate guns, as you know.' She stopped to look at him in the yellow sulphuric light. He was swaying from side to side, like a willow tree in the wind. 'Samu, I think you've drunk too much.'

'And you,' he said. He pulled her into a side street. Darkness as wide as space between the stars surrounded them and Sofie could feel herself drifting away from Samu. She followed him, hand in hand, but his world with the violence at home and the gun in a drawer in the prefabricated house were just unbelievably cold compared to the safe, yet mad nest she grew up in. Perhaps, Samu sensed her moving away from him. He stopped, pulled her to himself and kissed her full on the mouth. She responded, or only her body did. Yet, it was good to be anchored in the physical world, where at least she could be with him.

'Let's go for a swim,' Samu said folding her in his arms.

'Where?' Sofie asked amazed.

'Behind this wall, there is a swimming pool. You'll love it.'

They climbed over the metal gates with ease. Within minutes, they were swimming, naked, in the dark waters, with the black sky overhead. They made love on Samu's clothes in the grass. Lying on her back, with the starry sky like a blanket, listening to the bubbling, womb-like, noises of the swimming pool, Sofie imagined being a huge baby, arm-in-arm with her twin brother, floating in the ancient amniotic fluid of the world.

They scattered homewards through the hot streets, listening to the cicadas. Perhaps it was the soothing effect of the alcohol, but for the first time since Orpheus's death, Sofie allowed herself to relax into being, even though it seemed that her very essence conflicted with the Horvath family.

When they arrived back in the parental home, furtively, on tiptoes, Sofie could not find her satchel with her wash bag inside, but on the spare bed that was made up for her in Samu's sister's room, she found a freshly ironed nightgown and a new toothbrush. Samu's mother had tidied up everything and gone to bed. Brigitta was already asleep. Sofie sneaked into bed as quietly as she could. She lay listening to the sounds in the next room, trying to feel Samu's presence. She fell into a deep dreamless sleep within seconds.

In the morning they left early. They had been standing on the roadside half asleep, gazing at the mirage in the distance over the tarmac, when, suddenly awakened, Sofie had the feeling something was not right. She did not know what it was for a while, but then she became aware that her satchel, hanging on her shoulder, was suspiciously light. Something was missing from it. Sofie could not feel the familiar weight of Victor's manuscript. They rushed back to the house.

Mr Horvath opened the door wearing glasses on his nose. He looked at Sofie dispassionately.

Stunned and chilled, she could only stammer: 'Sorry, I left my history papers for the university entry examination. Did you see them anywhere lying around?' She knew, she was a bad liar, but sometimes you had to lie, even if it did not agree with Saint Sofia.

Mr Horvath smiled and went back into the living room. He returned with the pages in his hand. 'Are you looking for this?'

'Yes.'

'Sorry, I couldn't resist it. It's a fascinating read.'

'Thank you,' she mumbled, shocked and frightened, snatching the bundle out of his hand, and rushing to leave.

She ran to the road, where Samu had just stopped a car: a Cadillac with a Viennese registration plate. When they popped in, with all the gismos, ashtrays, and leather armrests, the car's inside was like the cockpit of a boat, and when it pulled off it slid like a boat, shaking gently. Within minutes they were gliding on the road. The driver spoke Hungarian with a very strong foreign accent, or whatever was wrong with him, Sofie did not know.

'I left in '56 to America. Homesickness brought me back to Europe. Austria is wonderful to me.'

Sofie was only half-listening to the conversation between Samu and the driver. She had a lingering worry about the manuscript; Samu's father had seemed too malicious. What if he told the police? What could happen to her? He might think that she wrote the paper. Knowing what a fanatic collaborator he had become he could easily call the police on her. That would mean the end of her fancy plans. Sofie could see herself persecuted and imprisoned for a manuscript she did not write, then ending up at the Academy, as well, spending her days as a naked model.

The rocking of the boat-like car had its effect and she fell asleep. When she awoke, they were already rolling into Budapest. The Elisabeth Bridge with its white crown and white cables greeted them like the queen of modern Hungary. Sofie had been at its opening in '64. At home, a black and white photo documented it: she was dressed in a white anorak catsuit, a baby. The bridge connected the Saint Gellert waterfalls with the inner city parish church on the Pest side. The first bridge was built in 1904 and named after Sissi, the assassinated Queen Elisabeth, and the new system never changed the name, it remained Elisabeth forever. The Germans blew up the bridge when they were fleeing from the Russians and the new Hungarian regime took twenty years to become affluent enough to build a new bridge on the foundation of the old one. Legend said that when they rebuilt the bridge, apparently, the whole old church had to be moved to the left about a metre, to perfect the design and to give way for the traffic. It was a cable suspension bridge. The whole endeavour became a triumph of the new over the old and when they moved the bridge, they discovered Roman ruins under the church, now covered with a thick glass panel as a tourist attraction. Layers of history were presented in that small spot of Budapest, where now the car stopped to spill them out onto the melting tarmac on the pavement.

'I'll see you in the Casino, then,' she heard the owner of the Cadillac say to Samu. This was his last word. When they started walking on the road towards Liberation Square, Sofie asked Samu over her shoulder, 'since when have you money to gamble?'

'I definitely don't have any money to gamble, but he might.'

'You'll need a suit, as well.'

'Shit, I forgot. Well, no gambling for me then.'

'Perhaps you can borrow one from Meli.'

'Haven't you noticed how much taller I am?'

'Well. Then no gambling for Samu,' she said with a feigned sigh. She did not want him to go, anyway, but she could not tell him that. Samu had his own independent life during the nights that she had no knowledge of. She was only annoyed that she could not go with him, due to her living with her parents and her dream of studying at university.

She had to work very hard for it. Her parents had no connections to help her to get a place and she had not joined the Young Communist

Association, which would have meant a point as well. Her father, the nobleman, was too proud to ask anyone for help, even though he worked at Hungarian Television. He promised that he would never get her a job there either, calling it a 'whore house'. He had nightmares about Sofie being ruined morally, and her mother was always dismissive of people that used their connections to get on. No help from the parents, no help from the teachers. She had a chance to get a place at the English-Hungarian department of the university if she won a national competition in translating, but not with Victor's work, of course. She had collected the papers from her English teacher, who pointed out that she was not allowed to help. She had to translate a short story by W. Somerset Maugham, but none of the available dictionaries in her local library had the words she needed.

She had to go to the library of the British Embassy. Some of her friends were going there already, playing a dangerous game. Contact with the imperialist enemy was not advised for the young members of socialist community. Towards the end of her schooldays a policeman had come to school to warn them about the tricks the intelligence services of western countries might use to turn innocent tourists into spies. The embassy was guarded by two policemen, one at each end of the street, who stayed inside a grey wooden cubicle with mirrored glass peepholes. She knew that every person that entered the embassy got their pictures taken. Sooner or later her school might find out, in which case, she might be expelled. She had to time it well so that her visits came close to her final Matura examinations when it did not matter anymore. She enjoyed the translation work; although some of it was so alien to anything she knew that she had to make it all up, she was progressing well. She finished her translation in time and handed it in. She had to wait to hear and now she had nothing else to do other than translate Victor's work and send it to England.

Chapter 20

Sofie said goodbye to Samu at Liberation Square. Thinking about her weekend, on her way home, she felt sick. Now she knew how Samu had to grow up and she had to carry the baggage of his father as well, and this was too much. It was all right to feel sorry for his childhood, but knowing the man changed everything. How coldly his eyes had pierced her when he had opened the door for her. Samu's lame mother was the exact opposite of her own feisty mother who did not shrink back from screaming and shouting if necessary. Even though Sofie hated her mother's outbursts, there was emotion in there, life itself. In Samu's home everything was ordered and tidy but buried under fear, and now she'd caught it, too. She could already see the power of that dreadful man on herself. She had intended to go to the British Embassy, and did not dare to go in, but passed the main entrance. The policeman in the box looked at her amazed, then put on his usual ignorant face. *No snapshot today.*

At home, as she was sitting with her parents at the dinner table discussing her weekend, Sofie was still under the spell of that encounter.

'I've never seen a man like him before. One minute he was nice and jovial, the next minute he was cold like a rock.'

'Well, we don't have to communicate with him, thank God,' her mother said and her father finished the sentence, adding to the clarification, 'as it's not a really serious relationship. Samu didn't ask you to marry him, did he?'

Sofie was wondering whether *Saint Sofia* had changed sides and joined her father's party. 'Of course not, and I would not want to get married at eighteen, thank you.'

'Why do you worry so much, then?'

'I had a manuscript with me, *The Critique of the Dialectic Materialism*, which I am translating into English. He read it.'

'What? Have you gone mad?' her mother jumped in. 'What's got into you?'

'Whose work is it?' asked her father with real interest. Sofie knew that she would have to lecture him about it within minutes but, luckily, the telephone rang.

Her father answered it.

'Benedek ... halloo ... halloo. The line is very bad. Halloo, can I help you?'

Both Sofie and her mother became very agitated listening to him trying to speak English.

'Yes, there is a Sofie here, just a moment.' He turned to her, 'there is Margaret, from England. Gosh, she sounds really happy.'

Sofie snatched the phone out of her father's hand, squeezing the black Bakelite receiver onto her ear. 'Hi, Margaret. This is Sofie.'

'Hi Sofie, I'm phoning from London. Can you hear me well?'

'Yes, it is a bit noisy, but I can hear you.' She heard loud traffic around Margaret and was sure that she was phoning from the street. She could see her in her imagination, in a red phone box, with Big Ben in the background, red buses, and happy people swirling around her.

'Sofie, Victor has made it. He is standing here next to me. He's made the big jump.'

'Did he really? But how? We were extremely worried about him.'

'Yes, I pass you on.'

Then she heard Victor's wonderfully soothing deep voice. He beamed love, even from a thousand miles away.

'Hi, Sofie. I just wanted to let you know that I am here and I am safe.'

'Oh, Victor, this is wonderful. How is it there?'

'You won't believe it, but the sun is still shining. It's pretty amazing.'

Sofie looked out through the window of their kitchen. The sky was pitch dark, at 8 p.m.; she could not imagine that it could be any other way anywhere else in Europe.

'Are you happy, Victor?'

'I can breathe, Sofie, I can breathe. Could you send me my manuscript? The address is 110 Bayswater Road London W2 3HJ.' She scribbled it down quickly. Then the line became distorted and she lost him. She could hear a click in the line though, as if a magnetic head had snapped shut, or some electric circuit in a tape recorder had switched to reverse. She put the phone down quickly. Her parents looked at her questioningly.

'The author of the manuscript I mentioned. He is in London.' After uttering these unbelievable words, Sofie could not suppress a happy scream.

Her father released a big deep sigh and her mother started to do the dishes. She opened the tap to fill up the sink with water and started to collect the plates. The knives and forks made an aggressive noise, as if quarrelling with each other. Then her father went to the window and closed it. He lowered his voice to say, 'is he there for good?' Sofie just nodded soundlessly with a suppressed grin on her face.

'I'm sure he's safer there.' This was all her mother could utter. The poor dishes in her hand got a rigorous wash, as if she wanted to scrub off all the crap she had to listen to during the party meetings. Sofie could not decide whether her mother was an opportunist or a real believer. Nan could never forget the disappearance of her brother-in-law during the Stalin terror of the fifties for openly criticising the system on a tram. He was slightly drunk when he was taken from the tram, nevertheless he managed to tell an onlooker, asking him quickly to go to his wife and let her know. Disappeared without a trace, in the depths of the big black cars that took people away to be tortured and to be killed, processed into meat, or chopped up and pumped into the Danube. When Sofie's great aunt Margaret went to the police to enquire, she was told to stay put if she did not want more trouble. So she withdrew to her piano to play love songs to Death till He took her, too. Cancer of the womb – the love child her husband sent to her from beyond the grave – a ticket to the other side to join him. The '56 Revolution softened this type of terror, at least. People that belonged to the Secret Police were publicly lynched.

For a short time the rebels were led by Janos Kadar, who was now leading the country. Sofie had found this out during a history class from her young history teacher, who indeed, wanted to teach the truth that they could not find in the history books. He only told them to 'research' which meant going home and asking people that were alive during the Revolution. Sofie was lucky enough to see real evidence of this fact, for one of her classmates brought in a newspaper of the time, with Janos Kadar's face printed on it. He was one of the main critics of the prevailing Stalin terror, but he was a communist. When the fascists of the old system, the Arrow Cross members, appeared during the Revolution, he must have panicked. When he saw that Imre Nagy, the prime minister chosen to represent democratic Hungary, could not get help from the West, Janos Kadar went to the eastern border of Hungary and brought in the Russian Red Army to occupy Hungary and to break down the rebels. Kadar ceased power and gave orders for Imre Nagy's execution, probably dictated by the Soviets. The borders were open for a short while: people could escape. After that all the fighters were either executed or imprisoned for a long time. Uncle George could not return for twenty years, but at least his mother knew that he was safe. After twenty years he started to return and every three years his mother was allowed to visit him in England, which she did happily. She became a fan of the Royals as soon as she entered at Dover, on her first visit. By the seventies there was no resistance in Hungary to speak of, only the Voice of America and Free Europe firing the imagination. The annual 15th of March riots seemed more like a sport of the university students than any possible political movement. The quiet resistance of the churchgoers resulted only in peaceful congregations and in prayers to God, who, even though the National Hymn asked Him to, did not care very much about the Hungarians.

Chapter 21

When Samu heard the news about Victor he was overjoyed.

'I might have to do the same, if all my attempts fail at getting a psychiatric label,' he announced to Sofie, but Sofie was still hoping to get into university. She had studied intently to get good grades at her Matura; and she had to be brilliant at the entrance exams that she had to sit in history and literature at her *one and only* university, the elitist ELTE. *She can't think of leaving Budapest, the poor city girl.*

One day Sofie arrived out of breath at the Academy.

'I've been followed,' she said, out of breath.

Samu did not want to believe it. To take her mind off the paranoia, he pulled her behind the privacy screen, undressing her slowly, then covering her with her own hair. She looked like a majestic bird, covered by its wings: a black swan, ready to take off. He could never get enough of her hair. It was the first thing about her that he was attracted to. He had never seen any other girl with so much hair: the long mane covering her bottom, her pubis just as black and bushy. She kept saying that she had never had a haircut in her life, but that could not be true. *She must prune it sometimes, without admitting it,* as if it was her guilty secret; a perverse addiction of a kind. Samu liked dreaming about perverse addictions, they made her look more interesting and appealing: a Pandora's box that he could never open for fear of death.

He could not really fathom why she fascinated him so much, perhaps because she never said no to any of his requests, like now, lying on the floor behind a screen. They had a lunch break and he had finished for the day, anyway, but anyone could have come in at any moment: the cleaning lady, or a student having left something behind, or even the professor could have returned to sneak a glimpse at him putting on his clothes after the session. *Man, that would be the perfect shock, for him, the bloody pimp.* The slight danger made him want her even more: she risked so much for him. Her heart beat wildly, like a bird's in a human's hands, it made him feel strong. *So different from the sex with the professor.* Although he could not say for sure how it would be with other men, the memory always lingered in his mind: the hunter ready to shoot down the black swan.

Sofie seemed more nervous than usual that night in the jazz club.

'How could they take me off the list? I'm sure I did brilliantly at the university entry examination.'

'Someone must have made an administrative mistake, go into the office and ask them.'

'There are no such mistakes. It's probably something to do with your father or Victor.'

'You're mad.' Samu said. It all seemed so far-fetched. *She is going bonkers, for sure.* Samu watched her queuing for a drink at the bar. Next to her, two men were asking something from the barman. The barman shrugged and pointed around the bar. She must have overheard them, for she started to behave like a robot, totally stiff. She asked for the drinks and fumbled with her purse for ages, then walked back to him leaving the drinks behind. The barman had to shout after her to take them. She stumbled back to Samu.

'Can you see those two older guys at the bar?' she asked him, making sure that her back was turned to the bar.

'Yes, what did they want?'

'They were asking about a girl with very long hair by the name of Sofie. The barman told them: "Have a look around. I can see at least ten girls with long brown hair here."' She clutched the sensual shape of the cola bottle between her fingers, pushing the cold glass on her temple. *Gosh, she looks like a maniac.*

'You must have been hallucinating.' He bit the sentence in half when he saw Sofie's sickly sullen face.

'I must go home. I can't bear this heat and noise,' she said, her voice rising an octave.

'I see you tomorrow then,' he said, but he could see her shocked expression, and he accompanied her to the door. 'What's up?'

'They were looking for me,' she screamed, subdued. 'The police. Your father must have put the police on me.'

'Gosh. That's impossible. He hates me, OK, but he would never do that to you.'

'Why would he not? Don't I represent everything he hates? And on top of that I am a crazy vegetarian!'

Samu laughed, but her face revealed real terror, so he stopped. She started hyperventilating, gasping for air, nearly suffocating, as if she was having another of her panic attacks. They left hurriedly and he waited patiently outside in the street, holding her until the attack was over. He knew that he had to treat her seriously, as if she was ill. He held her hand all the journey back to her home, all the way on the shuffling tram, thinking that she'd gone crazy. She did not say a word all the way, disconcertingly, not at all like her, as if a huge iceberg was building between them: a virulent and deadly accumulation of untold bitter words that could sink their relationship any moment. The lovemaking in the afternoon seemed like centuries before. Society, with its weight, madness with its lightness, all conspired to part them, to pierce their belly of a boat at the most sensitive area of the guts, to kill with its coldness like the one that sunk the Titanic. They parted at her house with a light kiss on the lips. She said goodnight.

'I'll call you,' he said and ran to catch the last tram back to the city, promising himself never to call her again.

The next time they met at Liberation Square it seemed like an accident. Samu was waiting for anything to happen. He was bored. Sofie was with Gabi on a trip to an exhibition. They kissed each other fleetingly and Samu kissed Gabi on the lips, too. He could sense Sofie's annoyance, but he also enjoyed winding her up. Gabi got annoyed, too; she was the most innocent of the three. Yet, Samu did not get the right reaction from Sofie. She was still going on about her entry examination.

She pulled out a list from her satchel and rubbed it under Samu's nose.

He admitted, 'you're right, there is no Benedek on this list.'

'They took me off, you see?'

'I still think it's just an error. You should enquire.'

'There are no such errors. They took me off, for they don't want me. But it's all right, I'll study in England.' She paused for effect. 'Will you come with me?'

Samu looked at Gabi, who was searching his face.

'I don't want to run away like a coward.'

Gabi seemed to approve, but Sofie butted in again, 'they will get you, too.'

'Staying is cowardice,' said Gabi.

Samu looked away from his two inquisitors. Policemen started to approach them from the other side of the square and they drifted apart.

Chapter 22

One morning Sofie woke up in the tiny flat with the clear thought of leaving Hungary. The idea took a few days to crystallise in her mind. She would go and live with Uncle George. There was nothing that could have kept her back, not even Samu. She shivered with the thought of leaving him behind, though. So the next time they met she asked him, 'will you come with me to the West?'

'I thought your aim was to read history, English or whatever at the ELTE.'

'No chance,' she paused, 'but I can study in England.' She searched his face.

Something lit up in his eyes, yet he waited a few moments before spitting it out. 'Yes, I will go with you. But it means going through the Yugoslavian border.'

His words made her happy, but uneasy at the same time. She could not figure out why. 'I heard that the soldiers show you the way to Italy there,' she said to cover up the disconcerting feelings in her guts.

'I heard that they send you back to Hungary if they catch you.'

'Did your father tell you that?'

'No. Some guys that were actually sent back and straight into prison.'

'Well, we mustn't be caught.'

'We mustn't be caught in Italy, either. They put you into a camp for foreigners there and send you on to America, Canada, or Australia. No one can settle in Italy.'

'I don't want to settle there. I want to go to the UK. Apparently, you don't need passports in the West. People just go from country to country without being checked. It's not like here.'

'When do you want to go?'

'After my eighteenth birthday, of course.'

'So, we have two weeks to prepare.'

'Yes.'

They were already fugitives, clinging to each other like partners in crime. For Sofie, personally, the idea of leaving her parents was not as bad as having to lie to them. She could not risk being found out; she did not trust her parents with regards to her personal freedom. They could call the police on her in order to keep her back, or worse, they might destroy her red passport. Therefore, she invented a story about going to Dubrovnik with Samu, where her parents used to go when they were young and in love. She knew that, for her father, this was even more difficult to swallow, as he now had to accept that this was a serious relationship. He did not like Samu.

Sofie was expert in keeping secrets, but she could not lie to her grandmother.

Her Nan's reaction amazed her. 'I always knew this would happen one day. Your uncle will always support you. He had no children, I don't know why, and this will help you with him. He'll look after you, don't you worry.'

Nan gave her two hundred pounds sterling; the money she had saved from each visit when George had come home to see her. 'Keep this money as a safety cushion. Only use this in an emergency.' It was her idea to hide the money rolled up in Sofie's bun. 'Now I can see some use of this bush we had to nurse during the years. Just right for hiding something that nobody should see.'

Sofie could only nod, keeping back her tears.

Nan asked, 'did you talk to your mother?'

Sofie shook her head.

'It will be hard for us, but you don't worry. You have to go on your chosen path. Promise me you will be clever.'

Sofie promised, tearfully, knowing that she might never see her Nan again.

The next three weeks were spent in the frantic chase for money. Sofie sold the golden necklace her parents had given her for her twelfth birthday when they came back from Italy. They bought it on the Bridge of Sighs in Venice, she remembered. It had a moon as a pendant which made her imagine the bridge under the full moon, in another reality. Soon hers, she thought, the real one, no need to cry. The merchant bought it as raw gold and she got a few thousand *forints* for it. She sold her long-playing records; most of them, not the Beatles ones, those had to stay at home. Some huge, heavy books she got for last Christmas: the reproduction of the whole volume of the famous *West Magazine*, for the years 1904–1906, with all the first publications of her favourite poets and the reactions to 'The Dreyfus Affair'. It fetched a good price: more than half her parents must have paid for it a year before. Then, they had to go through the dangerous issue of buying western currency in the streets. They knew that they could be ripped off easily. There were gangs in the streets that dealt, but then pretended that the police were coming and disappeared with the punter's investment or folded the notes so that you ended up with less than was agreed.

It was a difficult thing to do, but Lenin Avenue was speckled with people that changed currency in dark doorways. Samu took on the job himself. Sofie got the role of the watcher, making sure that no police or plainclothes detectives were drifting around in the crowd. Sofie was grateful to Samu who seemed to prove himself a good businessman; the shady characters were even nice to her. Perhaps they looked too over the top with their hippy clothing, but anybody would have noticed them if they had started to panic.

They raked together a hundred dollars for the journey. Once they got over the border between Yugoslavia and Italy they had less to worry about. They analysed the map, found a route, and estimated costs, and decided which currencies were the best for the journey. They planned to go through Italy and France and needed *lire* and *francs*. They could buy the ticket down to Zagreb with *forints* and then they needed Yugoslavian currency for the bus to Rijeka, then Koper, which seemed to be the easiest route to Trieste. They got their sleeping bags and food for the journey. Sofie bought baby food in jars, guessing that it was easy to carry, and it did not go off during the journey. She told her parents that she was going to Yugoslavia with Samu and they were happy for her as it reminded them of their trip together when they were young and foolishly in love. Even Sofie remembered that trip, for they brought back anchovies rolled around capers: two alien culinary delicacies that she fell in love with immediately.

Remembering this journey Mum became sentimental; she wanted to comb Sofie's hair. This was their secret signal. When her mother wanted to touch her hair, Sofie always knew that she could open up to her.

'We went camping, of course, in 1970; our first journey to Yugoslavia.'

'We'll sleep in houses. Apparently, it's very cheap down there.'

'Dad can give you some *Dinars*; I'm sure he still has some notes stuck away.'

The gentle touch of her mother made her weepy, but she could not show her weakness. She knew that she wouldn't be able to see her for a very long time, at least five years, until her dissident status was cleared by the Hungarian authorities. Guilty for lying to her she wanted to provide her with at least a little hint that her mother could look back at later. If she thought about their last chat in the future she would remember and know that she had tried to be honest; only she could not risk involving her parents, for their own sake.

'Mum, would you bake *pogácsa* for me for the road?'

'Like in the fairy tales?' She laughed.

'The youngest son goes on a journey around the world and he is given *pogácsa* by his mother for the road. I will carry it in my satchel and eat it when I rest.'

'Funny you say that. I will make some, of course. I will put all my love into it,' her mother said, dreamily. Then she started to comb Sofie's hair. She seemed to be in a dreamworld of the past with her innocent little girl, while Sofie already resided in the future, being an independent woman that had to lie to tear herself away from the past.

She packed her rucksack with enough clothes for a week's holiday. Although very tempted, she did not take any personal objects or photographs of family members, for she knew that such memorabilia could give them away. She lined the bottom of the rucksack with Victor's manuscript. If anyone searched her bag they might stop sooner, seeing the amount of clothes. The bag was light enough to be carried all along the way. She was ready for the adventure.

They had agreed to meet at the Western Train Station. Samu kept her waiting. Anyway, they had bought their tickets. When at last

Samu turned up he had no luggage with him and his face was dark and broody.

'You have no luggage? What happened?'

'My passport has not arrived.'

'What do you mean? I thought you had one.'

'The truth is that I gave my passport to a friend that needed it more than I did, and I applied for a new one the last time I went home to my parents. But it has not arrived yet.'

'You mean you must go to your parents and get it?'

'My sister promised to watch out for it, so it will be fine; it won't get into my father's hands.'

'Oh gosh, how I hate you,' Sofie said and turned her head away.

'We have to postpone the journey.'

'I'm not postponing anything. I'm going without you.' She spat the words out and saw disbelief in Samu's face, then fear, and then conviction. It seemed to mirror her own feelings, but there was no return.

'You are a girl. You never hitch-hiked alone in your life.'

'I can choose whose car I get into. I'll manage without you.'

'So this is the end.'

'So this is the end,' she repeated and looked at him as hard as she could. He let her down. An intense pain rose into her head and made her light-headed, nearly fainting. Samu led her to a kiosk and ordered a brandy.

'Drink this and have a cigarette.'

'Like a prisoner before execution. Yet, I will be released.'

She swallowed her bitter tears. Samu, avoiding her eyes, took out a small bottle from his jeans pocket.

'Take this. It's Gracidin. You take one when you feel very tired. It will help you to stay awake if you need it.'

Sofie had taken Gracidin before. Some very long time ago she took it and talked through the night with Janos. It was a pill that students took before exams to be able to stay up and study all night. It had done something to her brain, too, for sure. It had given her a beautiful night of confessions with a true friend, whom she now was leaving behind, too. She sighed and took the bottle.

'Thanks.'

'Phone me at Meli's when you are free in Britain.'

Samu managed to push a kiss on her lips and kissed her tears away as well. Sofie stood like a statue, rigid and hard. Suddenly, she was turned into Saint Sofia, the mother of martyrs.

She got on the train, sat down. She did not lean out of the window to wave him goodbye. The train rolled out slowly and she had two hours to worry before they reached the border. She had all her money hidden in her bushy hair, tied in under the rubber band. If the customs officers or border guards searched her, she could even take off her clothes.

The Table

Chapter 23

The compartment was packed and altogether too hot. Sofie tried to open the window, but an old woman, with a face that looked like a crumpled-up newspaper, vehemently objected. The woman wore a black skirt with many layers of white underskirts, with the laces of each layer visible under her, a white linen shirt under a black velvet vest and even a black woollen kerchief on her tiny head, yet she did not seem to suffer from the sunshine seeping through the dirty windows. She seemed to be people and draught-sensitive. As the old woman was guarding the window, Sofie could not open it, just look around, hoping for some support from the other passengers. No words came from the mother with a small child or the young Austrian couple who did not understand the situation. She gave in to the old lady and moved away, towards the door and less sunshine. She opened the compartment door to the corridor and let the air come in from there. This turned out to be another disaster, as the child, called Tommy, about four years old, became too agitated and his mother did not want him to go out. In the end, Sofie asked to swap places with the little boy and sat at the door, holding it a slit apart, letting the draught cool only her own face. By then the young Austrians had figured out the situation and were smiling back at her, encouragingly.

The train stopped near the border on the open rails. Armed Hungarian soldiers mounted the train. They did their routine search in every compartment. One guy tore the door open, looked behind the luggage on the upper compartment and under the seats. He stared up at Sofie through her legs jotted apart; then he left satisfied, but with a morose expression on his face. After a long wait, which seemed to agitate everyone except the Austrians, a customs officer opened the door and asked for passports.

He collected them all in a batch, and looked at them individually. He stamped each passport with great vigour. The Austrians got theirs back first. When he got to Sofie's he searched her face.
Sofie was intensely aware of the two hundred pounds sterling rolled

up, hiding in her hair. She needed to scratch her scalp, but did not dare.

'Just turned eighteen?' asked the man with raised brows.

Sofie forced herself to smile. 'Yes, last week. This trip is my birthday present. My mother signed for the visa, there.' She pointed towards the page, but her finger was shaking, so she pulled back her hand.

The customs officer turned to the visa page and nodded. He pushed a stamp on the next page. 'Have a good time in Yugoslavia.'

'Thank you. I can't wait to see the sea.'

The man pushed his hat back on his forehead and smiled at her. 'It's too salty, but you will like it there, I'm sure.' He gave her the passport and winked, leaving the compartment.

The old woman at the window uttered a big sigh when the custom's officer left. Everybody looked at her and now for the first time during the whole journey she smiled. The Yugoslavian officers did not even stop at the compartments, they simply walked through the corridors, sporadically calling '*Dobar dan*'. Sofie smiled at each of them, a big broad smile.

When the train rolled into motion, the old woman at the window started to chat to everyone. She asked Sofie to lift down her bag from the overhead compartment. She did so. The woman opened it to take out some cookies she had made for the road and to everyone's surprise she revealed a huge collection of Hungarian embroidery. Sofie was reminded of her own creation for Samu, the hand painted and embroidered magician's gown. *Sure, he did not deserve it.*

'I'm bringing them from Transylvania. They are worth a million *dinar*,' the old woman said with a toothless smile.

The child and its mother were very pleased with the cookies, even the Austrians took some, and expressed enjoyment with big gestures, thinking that nobody spoke their language. '*Kosten Sie nun*,' said the old Transylvanian woman to their surprise. '*Ich backte die Stanzen zu Hause.*'[1] After this they were chatting along, all the way into the heart of Yugoslavia. Soon enough the boy called Tommy fell asleep. Sofie closed her eyes. The excitement made them

---

1 'Taste them, I baked the biscuits myself at home.'

both too tired.

The train stopped in Zagreb and everybody got out. Sofie checked the buses going south. She had to wait two hours before the next one left. She got an ice cream and had a rest in the square in front of Central Station. There she bumped into the Austrian couple again, who were wildly gesticulating with the owner of the ice cream stall.

'We're going to the sea, too,' said the girl in English. 'Would you like to join us?'

'Where are you going to?' asked Sofie.

'Koper. It looked wonderful in the guidebook.'

Sofie remembered that Koper was on her planned route, not too far from the Italian border. 'I'm going there, too,' she said, surprised by herself.

They waited for the bus together. For Sofie this gave an opportunity to practise her English, leading to a dishonest conversation, for she could not disclose any of her real plans. It was still early afternoon – they would arrive by evening time. In their company she started to believe that she was a tourist, too, not a defector.

After another hour's sleep on the bus they arrived in Koper. It was a beautiful town with a medieval castle. Hans and Greta had already booked a room in a hotel, but Sofie had no hope of staying there. She told them that she was heading to a camping site. She went down to the seaside, beguiled by the smell of the sea. She remembered Kerouac sleeping on the beach in *On the Road*. This was another wonderful act of freedom. But this beach was stony, not the golden sands she had expected. She walked on, looking for softer ground and away from the town in the hope of finding a quiet place for the night: sand or pebble, it did not matter anymore. The promenade, which was simply a pavement, ended abruptly and only the stones remained underfoot. She struggled on, her sandalled feet kicking shingles and hard ground. Still, the sound of the waves soothed her mind, rocked her sensations. She was playing with the thought of being a mermaid on her way to a nightly abode when she bumped into a boy, about her age. He was sitting alone on the pebbles. He had an open face and a broad smile with crooked white teeth under blue eyes.

'Sunset, pretty.' He pointed and she agreed with him. The sunset was pretty.

Sofie rolled out her sleeping bag and lay down, a bit self-consciously, but the boy became very nervous.

'No sleep, no. Police come.'

Not good news, especially as she was so exhausted.

'Come,' said the boy, and Sofie went with him.

He led her through a thicket of low pine trees and dry undergrowth to a wooden shed that looked like a fisherman's hut. Nets hung on the outside walls of the shed and on sticks pushed into the ground. The pungent smell of the sea was stronger here. It cushioned all her other senses, giving the impression that she was safe. The inside of the shed contained nothing but nets, too. The boy pointed to a dark wooden bed frame that seemed to have straw sacks as a mattress. A table sat beside it. Sofie collapsed onto the bed and crawled into her sleeping bag. Zipping it up slowly, she could only mumble a thank you, before she sunk into a black hole of oblivion. She woke up a few times in the night, every time more aware that the sea was coming nearer and the wind was getting stronger.

She woke up at dawn. The beach had disappeared and the sea was splashing just a metre away from the entrance of the hut. The sky was painted pink and blue with a bright yellow line on the horizon. She extended her limbs in all directions, took most of her clothes off, and ran into the sea. It was very salty, like the customs officer had told her it would be, and very gentle on her legs.

In the hut, she opened a jar of baby food and ate it with the spoon she had brought with her. Then she lay back and did nothing but listen to the waves. The tide must have turned. She could hear birds on the roof, chirping. The rising sun's rays started to creep up to the window, projecting an always-brighter square on the opposite wall, where the nets were hanging. It looked like a golden picture; a second window to the other world. She was ruminating over this vision when she heard the crunching noise of steps on the pebbles, purposefully approaching the hut, getting louder. She sat up, nearly shrieking, and quickly pulled on her jersey. The Croatian boy pushed his smiling face through the door.

Sofie could not believe her eyes. He brought fresh bread and a bottle of milk.

He slapped his own chest and said, 'Karl.'

Sofie returned the gesture, 'Sofie.'

They grinned at each other and started to wolf down the breakfast. Sofie pulled out a map of Yugoslavia from her bag and folded it out on the table. With hands and broken English she explained to the boy that she was headed towards Skofie and the Italian border and showed him the forest on the map that would become her path. On the map there was no sign of the Iron Curtain, it could be a myth, after all, but the boy's reaction confirmed its existence. With a shocked expression on his face, he wildly gesticulated, trying to talk her out of it.

'Never leave home country.' He was very serious about his loyalties.

Sofie sensed that they would never understand each other. She simply brought up a lame excuse, 'my uncle lives in Manchester.'

Strangely, the boy loosened up. 'I have uncle in Munich.'

Sofie could not understand this dichotomy. Leaving your country is bad, but having an uncle in Munich is good. She looked at him, stupefied.

'Uncle work in Munich. Come home all the time.'

So it was OK to work in Munich, but visiting home from time to time was good, too. She added, 'my uncle visits, too. I will visit, too.' Which was very unlikely, for she knew too well that she would be banned from returning to Hungary for who knew how long.

This was the price she had to pay: no return; no physical contact with parents, family, Nan. Her eyes brimmed with tears and she could feel them running down her cheeks. She could see on Karl's face that she scared him, too. *Shit*. The last thing she wanted was looking weak in the eyes of this boy. She quickly wiped her tears away and pointed at the map.

'Show me the way.'

Karl thought that the best way was on the road, by bus to Skofie. If she left at dusk, she would arrive there in the evening and she could get lost quickly in the forest before the soldiers noticed. It sounded like a sensible plan.

Observing her own reflection in the window she looked calm. All the people around her must have thought that she was a visitor, a tourist; a hitch-hiker on the way to Italy. The sun had set already, only a slight shimmer of it remained, and it was getting dark rapidly. By the time they got to the last stop, the bus was slicing the summer night with its front lights. Sofie found it easy to disappear and take her walk towards the woods.

This was her first time ever alone in the woods. The camping week with Samu had prepared her to some extent, and now she remembered a night with Meli and Samu when they had walked out into the forest together, just for the sake of experiencing total darkness outside the city; but then it was winter and snow lay everywhere. She had been amazed how difficult it was to find total darkness, for the snow lit up the night. Here, in the Yugoslavian forest, near the Iron Curtain, as they called it, darkness was a tangible substance. She could not see the moon, if there was one, all she could see in the sky were the stars, the space thickening around them, whirling. The dark silhouettes of trees seemed friendlier than she had expected. This was nothing like the Black Forest of the Grimm fairy tales she grew up with. These trees were kind, soft, mellow. Long tall candle firs and arborvitae, their pointed tips tickling the bottom of the sky, like in Van Gogh's paintings. She walked from tree to tree, touching barks, dry skin with soft fine wrinkles, like old people's arms. *Like Nan's.* She clung to this idea. These trees smelled different, too: firry, citrusy. The crickets chirped crazily, non-stop, but always further and further away, as if they were calling her to go their way, in a different direction. She moved slowly, with ease, looking at the stars for guidance. The Plough lay low, near the tops of the trees and, above them, was the Little Dipper. Remembering her father's interest in the stars, he had told her that the last and shiniest star in the handle of the Little Dipper was showing towards North, she worked out that the Plough's handle would show her the way to the West. She just had to follow in that direction. After a while she arrived at a thicket of brambles or rose bushes that bounced her back. There was no way through them. She did not know where she was, but could not go any further. Exhausted, she lay down, deciding to wait for the first light of the sun. She lay down in her sleeping bag.

When her body became quiet and her heart did not race so much, she could turn her ears to the noise around her. The crickets came closer and seemed to build a canopy of noise around her: a protecting bubble. She was almost asleep when she heard one single bark. It could have been a dog, or a fox wailing. Sofie, although flushed with adrenalin, had to stop herself from moving. She froze on the forest floor, fully alert. Like in a movie, her mind played the worst scenarios: *caught, police station, back to Hungary, prison.* She knew if she moved she would be giving herself away. *So: pretend to be dead.* After a while she must have fallen asleep.

Next thing she knew a thin layer of dew was on her face and the cold was in her limbs. The misty first shimmers of the day drew the outline of what lay ahead of her: a thicket of rose bushes and one single tree fallen over the ditch. She started off balancing on it. The tiny thorns kept catching her arms, clothes, and hair with myriads of tiny claws. She had to tear them off with force, irrespective of the damage they did to her skin, her hair, and palms. She balanced gingerly over the tree trunk till she fell. Then she crawled on all fours, hugging the tree. Each movement a struggle, as if the past wanted to hold her back with force.

When she got to the other end of the valley, she could stand upright, but a tall red brick wall blocked her way. She climbed it, her hands and feet catching on the bumpy surface, falling back a few times to start again. Her feet kept slipping off and some of the roses still clung onto her clothes. She could hardly breathe because of exhaustion and nerves, but at last she did it. The hardest climb of her life so far. On top of the wall she touched dry grass and needled forest floor again. A weather-worn sign with a metal plate said in Italian something about *frontiere verde* and she understood that she had made it: she had entered Italy.

In her heightened state of awareness she could smell the sea again. She started to run like mad in that direction, down a slope, through thickets and shrubs. As soon as she saw the green blue waves she threw her rucksack away and carried on, running with clothes and sandals as she was, straight into the sea. The salt water burnt the wounds on her arms and body and face, but she only laughed.

Chapter 24

She saw Italy and France in a haze. She slept on the train from Trieste to Venice. Got off and sat down in front of the station, looking at the Canal Grande, not understanding what she was doing. The houses seemed like painted scenery in a theatre; they could have dropped down revealing nothing behind. Happy, but not safe. She knew that there were refugee camps in Italy and she did not want to be put up in a camp before reaching the UK. The next train to Milano was jam-packed; she had to stand in the corridor. She was painfully aware of her own body smell, so she hung onto the handrail of the open window, opening her armpits to the wind, and slept. In Torino she crawled under some bushes in a park, for it was the end of the day and the end of the train journey. From there on she had to hitch-hike through the Alps to France. The hitching went well and the first couple that picked her up were Austrians – she was getting the impression that only young Austrians travelled in Europe. They were extremely nice to her, gave her a lift to near the French border, saying that they had to stop for the night in Italy for the motels were cheaper there.

Very helpfully, they dropped her off just a hundred metres before the checkpoint. It was getting cold; the sun had disappeared behind the rocky mountains that were showing some spots of snow at the tops. Sofie was shivering with tiredness and cold. She put on a jersey and walked on resolutely towards the border. Two Italian soldiers stopped the cars randomly and waved them to go on. Sofie, like an innocent walker, moved on, ready to pass them without inviting much intervention, when a tall soldier stopped her.

'*Ferma! Stop! Passaporto, prego.*'

Did he really say passport? Sofie could not believe her ears. *That's me finished*, her eyes were already brimming with tears. She stopped and took out her red passport. The soldier signed her to come to a cubicle.

'*Vieni.*'

She followed him. The young man entered the cubicle with her passport in his hand and moved behind the counter. Sofie was losing her courage. She had enough Italian to understand that the guy knew that her passport was not valid for the West. He compared her face with the faces of young men and women that plastered the wall of the cubicle – all the girls had long hair. Terrorists, she figured. That someone might think that she was a member of the Red Brigade never occurred to her. When her face did not match, the guy made a phone call and checked her name against a list of names somewhere at the other end of the line. At this point her tears were streaming down her face.

'I have to go to England. My family is there, please let me go.'

'You go to camp, near Roma.'

'I cannot stay in Italy. Please, my uncle is waiting for me in Manchester. I have to go on.'

Her tears might have had an effect, for the guy gave back her passport.

'OK. You go up the mountain and walk there. Don't go to the French guys, they won't like your passport. I give you half an hour. In half an hour I will inform my commandant that I have seen someone walking in the mountain.'

Sofie, now relieved, did what she was told. She climbed the mountain, higher and higher, like a goat, till she was completely out of breath but out of sight as well. She lay down panting on the stony ground. The last couple of days' tiredness and undernourishment hit her. Luckily, she had filled her bottle with water that afternoon, before getting into the Austrian couples' car. Now she enjoyed every drop, each sip confirming to her that she was still alive. She thought she might not make it and in half an hour the whole mountain would be full of soldiers looking for her. *Who was the idiot that said that you could walk through borders between western countries?* This was pathetic. Like a real refugee, but now running from the western soldiers!

Then she remembered the clear glass vial with the plastic lid that Samu had given her as a goodbye present. She had some water and a couple of jars of baby food. She swallowed the food and two of the pills.

Within a few minutes, the food and the Gracidin worked their way down into her stomach and soon enough the drug got into her blood and rose into her brain and, with renewed energy, she could walk on. As she did not have anyone to talk to, she talked to herself. She recited every poem she had ever learnt, keeping her head down, for she feared the wolves and foxes lurking at the edge of her perception. Of course, there were no more wolves in the Alps, or so she was told. In the corners of her eyes, she saw lights, it was still twilight for a while; at last, she started to descend towards the lights of a village.

She took very long. She had to stop too many times, gasping for breath, but she made the walk in four hours. By then every step made her cry bitter tears. When she arrived on the other side it was midnight and she could not see any people, only cars drove by sporadically. She wrapped herself up in her sleeping bag and lay down in the woods, under the tallest pine trees she had ever seen. The needles pricked her and by now she was worried about insects and other creatures that might creep into her ears, therefore she stuffed them with tissues. It was much colder here, but at least she knew that she was in France, out of danger. Nobody would try to put her into a camp for foreigners here. She was free at last, absolutely free.

Her sleep was fitful, probably still due to the Gracidin, but at least it gave her body rest.

The next morning she walked into the village and found out that the *lira* she had leftover was worthless. She changed the remaining notes into *francs* and just managed to buy some cheese and bread again, and washed it all down with milk. The hitching began again, further to the West, towards Calais.

From the cars that she hitched a lift with, she gazed at fields of colour not knowing what the plants were: endless, waving sheets of bright yellow, followed by purple and blue fields of lavender. She thought of Vincent and his room in Arles, and she wanted to stay in France forever. She fell asleep in nearly every car. In a truck she got a shock. The driver started to caress her leg. She woke and screamed at him, 'I don't fuck.' The driver dropped her in the middle of Calais at the statues of the Burghers of Calais. Sofie walked around it. The statues seemed to be alive, talking to each other, with the noose around their necks, some distressed others resolute and sad. Saint

Sofia jumped to mind, but she could not care about her anymore. She was not a martyr. She took her fate into her own hands. From a telephone box she phoned her uncle.

'Sofie, I can't believe you are in Calais.'

'How can I get over to you? There seems to be strong control on the boats.'

'Walk up to the immigration officers and give them my phone number. I will sponsor you.'

'Couldn't you come and get me?'

'Sofie, I cannot get away from here at the moment. Trust me. It should be fine. This is a free country.'

Sofie bought her ticket and got on the boat as a walk-on passenger. Nobody asked her for any papers and she calmed down. She sat on the deck for the whole journey, watching the mist, till she could see some shimmering white chalk approaching, becoming larger, and eventually she recognised the White Cliffs of Dover. They soon disembarked and the cars started to drive off the boat. When she got to the exit she noticed that the gangway was a metallic caged corridor attached to the front of the boat. This led to cubicles where people were asked to show their passports. When she got to the customs she tried to smile.

'This passport is invalid and you have no visa for the UK,' the man said in a monotone voice.

'I know. I am a refugee. This is my uncle's number. He is a British citizen. He told me to ask you to call him.'

'Please step to the side.'

Sofie stepped to the side. The man made a phone call, but Sofie heard him saying, 'here is an illegal, could you come and pick her up?'

Sofie stood there, waiting for about two minutes, until two policemen arrived.

'Please come with us.'

She followed them into a huge grey building and into a room where they told her to sit down and wait. She waited for an hour. Then another officer came and called her into another room, where they looked at her passport and asked the same questions again.

They wanted to know where and how she left Hungary; how

did she travel through Yugoslavia; where did she cross the French border, and why did she come to the UK? She kept telling them that her uncle lived in Manchester and he wanted to sponsor her, but they said they could not reach him.

A policewoman wearing black skirt and black tights and black flat shiny shoes led her into a waiting room. On her way, she managed to get a glass of water for Sofie, too.

'Please wait here. We will be with you as soon as we can.' She smiled encouragingly, pushing the paper cup into Sofie's hand.

Sofie tried to be polite and forced a smile.

'Thank you.' In her mind, she was raging, *what for, really?*

The woman slammed the door behind her. She was alone in a room where the doors had no handles on the inside. She could not open them. Her whole being was screaming. Having made this incredibly long journey and so near to her destination these men had pulled out the carpet from under her feet. She was nothing in their eyes. Just an intruder. She could not hold it together anymore. She curled up in a knot in the corner and tried to think, but her brain was numb. After some time, she calmed down and stood up to explore the room that had one high window and two glass panels on both sides. There was a toilet in the corner, but that was all. No pictures, nothing but a grey room with a table and a chair, a recliner, and two doors that had no handles inside. She pulled the chair nearer to the high window, stood on it and, raising up on her tiptoes, she peeped out. She could see other buildings at the back, and behind them, high walls. It dawned on her that she might be in a prison. She became hysterical and started to bang the door with her fists.

When they opened it she said to the policewoman, 'I know that I have the right for a phone call. Please bring me a phone.'

She had seen this in films before. Every criminal had the right to call a lawyer. It worked. They brought her a phone. She dialled Uncle George's number again and he answered. As she expected, her uncle sorted it all out. Within an hour she was sitting on a train to London and then on to Manchester.

Chapter 25

The ten o'clock news came on the BBC. Sally turned down the volume on the television set, not to wake the girl, and sat down in her large dirty white plush settee, watching the news in technicolour. She stretched out her legs and slipped off her house shoes to feel the soft carpet, noticing a broken nail on her right hand. A manicure was badly needed. Mrs Thatcher, the new prime minister (and a woman!), was preaching affluence through the media, which was very well with Sally. Initially, she had thought that this strong woman would put these guys in order, but unemployment rose. Of course, it would not stop people from drinking, the opposite, no wages brought unhappy customers to the pub and riots to the streets. It was high time that she pulled the plug on inflation, as she had promised in her election speech. Although most of the men that visited the pub were members of the Trade Unions, she could not care less if they lost power. There was no trade union for publicans and all she really worried about was the tax on alcohol. The pub was just about doing well: the first themed bar in the area. It was a traditional vault with a snug and lounge, but decorated with images of the Hungarian Revolution, and it gained respect for George with the commoners. He enjoyed telling them about his youth when he fought in the streets against the Russians. He avoided calling them "Communists" just in case there were some sympathisers around. George was wise, for he left the past and politics behind and did not want to take part in any fights anymore. 'I'm just the beer-man,' he used to say when they tried to get his opinion. Until recently, Sally had had the best of life with George. She did not have to work, even though they had no children. She could go out for lunch with her friends, and support the Women's Institute, without too much commitment. She was there for the fun.

Sally was not one of those girls that went to bed with every male or female. She thought she still possessed some dignity, like Mrs Thatcher. The madness of the sixties and seventies had whooshed by her. They had too many worries about money and, although she had an inkling that George was a womaniser, he was a man, after all, a strong man, and if he saw women on the side, she knew that he only did it in Hungary. He could be forgiven for being sentimental; the Communists robbed him of his childhood and his family.

Her own father had loved George and this was the best possible testimony for the character of a man without a pedigree. George's joviality and jokes, his amazing strength in making money, and his talent for survival had impressed the old doctor. Sally had not been her father's favourite, but the minute she brought George into their house her position changed: she was respected. Perhaps George represented everything that her father could never achieve. He was Jewish, never a fighter; a highly intelligent man that would shy away from any conflict, even with his own wife. Sally turned out to be completely different. She could fight. She grew up into a Yorkshire bitch, like her mother used to be: refined, but ready to fight back, if necessary. George knew that and respected her, too.

This was why she could not understand his carelessness by not mentioning that his niece was coming to visit. She arrived at half past nine, introduced herself, sat down on the sofa, and fell asleep. She smelled like a druggy and her long hair, although in plaits, looked unwashed. Obviously, she was exhausted. Sally observed her face, which reminded her of George's mother. She had seen pictures of the old lady when she was young, holding baby George on her arm: the same rounded chin and arch of the nose lay in front of her. She was beautiful in a quirky way and God, so young. Velvety skin, untouchable, pretty. For a moment, Sally felt a twinge of sadness. Her own daughter could have turned out to be like this; well, no use to give in to melancholy, you take from life what you are given and make the best of it. Then an episode of Only Fools and Horses came on, and she watched it nodding off from time to time, with a half-smile on her face.

When the eleven o'clock local news popped up again, Sally was shocked to see the burning police cars in the middle of her city. Princess Street was blocked and the BBC warned people from going downtown. It was more amazing that this girl had arrived here safely. How could she have avoided all that madness coming from

Piccadilly? How lucky she must be, having got on a bus and arrived in Openshaw. Mind, they lived at the opposite end of Manchester, but still, she must have an angel, she thought.

George arrived at 11.30 p.m., full of beans and with a slight waft of whiskey and smoke. She liked his smell, even if tinted with alcohol. It made her want to feel his hands around her waist. George was embarrassed. He didn't close early, although he heard about the riots. The men wanted to linger on, talking about the illness of the government; the bloody rich sucking their blood; the dole that was not enough for any family; the blacks that cannot stay put; the lazy bastards always wanting havoc; the Irish committing suicide and Maggie not acknowledging their political status, which is ridiculous, there they have hundreds of thousands of supporters. The woman had guts, visiting Belfast at the end of May, but she should not go back now; wherever she goes there are riots.

Sally stopped him, pointing at the sleeping girl, 'why didn't you tell me that she was coming?'

'I didn't know about it myself. I just got a phone call from a customs officer at the pub at lunchtime. I'm sorry that I didn't warn you. You know that my head is always so full.'

'Wake her up, she smells awfully.'

George gently touched Sofie's leg. 'Sofie, wake up my darling.'

The girl shook and shuddered, looking at them in surprise, as if she did not know where she was. Then she forced a smile on her scared face. 'Uncle!'

They hugged and Sally went to the kitchen. Sally did not feel the need to go through introductions again. While making tea she heard them talking. They mixed Hungarian words with English. Sally was grateful to George, who seemingly turned back to English as often as possible, for she knew that George did this out of respect for her.

'Let's go West, ha? I hope nothing too terrible happened to you on the border.'

The girl had a terribly childish Hungarian accent, pronouncing every r and t with a trill like a Scotsman, yet, turning up the ends of sentences like the French.

'I thought they would never let me free, but it was much worse in

France; I almost got raped.'

Sally, now honestly curious and worried for the safety of this innocent girl, arrived with the tea and butted in, 'Oh, dear, how could you put yourself into such danger? Aren't there enough trains on the continent?'

'I was saving up the money for here.'

Sally just nodded. Frugality was one of the qualities she possessed, too. Very laudable in such a young person. 'Have a cup of tea, you'll feel better,' she said, while George grinned at his niece, becoming George the jovial, ready with a joke.

'Rule number one: a cup of tea solves all your problems.'

After tea Sally told Sofie to go and have a shower. She showed the girl how it all worked and gave her a dressing gown to wrap up when she finished. Then she moved back to the kitchen and prepared some leftovers from dinner – a good opportunity for George to open a bottle of wine from Hungary, a bull's blood. He poured her a glass of wine and looked into her eyes deeply, as if on a first date. 'I can give her work,' George said, pensively.

Sally pressed her lips together. 'So, this is not jut a visit?'

'No, she came here without a visa. I promised sponsorship. She is to stay in England.'

Sally was contemplating what and how to say it, when Sofie appeared with wet hair and smelling like a baby.

'What are your plans for the future, Sofie?' asked George, expecting a sound reply from a girl, shocked and traumatised, who had just walked in through the door.

Sally was surprised when she gave a salient answer.

'I want to study modern European history. Here they'll at least teach me the truth.'

'The truth is, luv, that you're a little late. From this year, for foreigners, it costs a fortune to study here,' Sally butted in again, not capable of letting go of the point.

Sofie looked at her uncle questioningly.

'Yes, sweet, Sally is right. Hundreds of pounds a term.'

'The best thing for you would be to marry an Englishman. You would get the citizenship at once,' Sally added, quite sure that she would hit a spot, assuming that Sofie would be just as rebellious as her uncle.

'I wouldn't want to marry just for that.'

Of course, who would? Sally thought to herself. *I did not marry your uncle for that, either.* Nevertheless, she preferred to tease her further. 'Who knows, you might even meet somebody you like.'

By now Sally could sense that *clever little Sofie* would always be ready with her answer.

'I'd rather work and save the money for my studies.'

George was there to her rescue. 'I can give you a job in the pub, no problem. I should be your sponsor, anyway, I'm expected to do so.'

Sally just frowned, imagining the drunken blue collars courting the poor little girl and grabbing after her bum. *So be it*, she thought. 'It's time that I showed you the guest room.'

'Can I go to the loo first? I think I must have got a bug.' With that Sofie ran to the toilet and they could hear her retching. George looked at Sally with concern.

'She needs a couple of days rest, I guess,' Sally replied to his look. 'She must be exhausted.'

George nodded and lay his arm around Sally's waist. His hand slid down on her hip.

'Do you like her?' he asked, pushing his face into her neck.

He smelled of smoke and wine and Sally could feel a hot flush rising in her body, but she just shrugged. She would not let him get away with this surprise so easily.

Chapter 26

Sofie woke up groggy. Her eyes wandered around the tiny room. *Where am I?* She was amazed that, opposite the bed, on the light blue wallpaper, was an amateurish copy of Van Gogh's *Vincent's Bedroom at Arles*. The colours were not the same, but the person who'd painted the copy had managed to bring in the light, nevertheless, expressing the joy of expectation. *Vincent was let down and chose the door like I did; but for me, the door meant freedom* – leaving all the constraints of a life behind; Samu was part of it: she'd had to leave him, too.

She recalled that Samu had asked her to call him when she arrived in Manchester. Meli's phone number was etched onto her memory, she had called Samu there so many times, but she resisted the urge to call him. *He doesn't deserve it.* For her, it was all over. It was better to start a new life with a clean sheet, without Samu and his abusive father, his loyal friends and all that baggage.

She went to the bathroom. She was amazed by the luxury she had not noticed the night before because of exhaustion: the tiles, toilet, sink, and bathtub were all in the same shade of green. An octagonal shaped mirror hung over the sink. A porcelain coronation mug with the face of the Queen, suspended in the metal holder, contained several toothbrushes and toothpaste. The green sink impressed her with its colour, although, technically, it was a great disappointment. Two taps instead of one, with a C and H each. One for cold and one for hot, at least ten centimetres apart. How was she to wash her face now? There was no plug either. The tap on the left gave out extremely hot water, while the one on the right was ice cold. *God, what kind of world have I entered?* she thought, washing her face with cold water. When staggering out of the bathroom she could smell burning flesh. It took her a few minutes to realise that it must be breakfast.

In the kitchen, Sally was busying around, full of energy. Her ashen hair seemed very thick and in big waves. She wore a yellow, short-sleeved shirt and a blue apron over her knee-long, pastel green skirt, almost the same shade as the bathroom. *It must be her favourite colour,* thought Sofie. Her mother only wore an apron on rare occasions when she was baking. Sally's was light blue and pristine. It must have been freshly ironed. Sally seemed joyous. She put the bacon and eggs on the table and beans in tomato sauce. It looked like a huge meal for breakfast, but Sofie obediently sat down at the table.

'Sally, I don't eat meat, you can have the bacon,' she said.

'Oh, no problem. You should have told me that you are a vegetarian. Or are you a vegan?'

'What is a vegan?'

'No animal products at all, which means no eggs either.'

'No, I eat eggs and I drink milk, thanks. Only the blood is what I detest.'

'Fine. Enjoy,' Sally said, picking up the bacon on her fork and placing it back in the pan.

They ate in silence and Sofie could feel the energy returning into her body. She was pleased that her vegetarianism did not cause an uproar here in her uncle's house, while in Hungary it made her into an outcast.

'I saw a painting in the bedroom. Did you make it?' she asked Sally still half-dreaming, but Sally took a few moments to realise what she meant.

'Ah, that? Yes, it was just a silly thing I bought at Waitrose. Painting by numbers.'

'My favourite Van Gogh. It's so simple and cheerful,' added Sofie with a big smile.

'I'm glad you like it, even though it's a terrible copy.'

'Where is Uncle?'

'He's gone to work. It's twelve-thirty. I let you sleep; we could see it on you last night that you really needed it.'

'Thanks,' she mumbled through her toast. 'The beans in tomato sauce are really nice,' she said.

'We call that baked beans.'

Sofie just nodded, chewing on. 'I'm glad I have met you at last, Aunt Sally. How come you never visited Hungary?'

'No, no. I never wanted to go. I've heard so many terrible stories from George about Budapest. Instead of me going, we invited your grandmother to come to us.'

'What kind of stories?'

'The standard of living, first of all. Poverty, lack of good workmanship.'

'Bathroom taps work better in Hungary.'

'Really? How?'

'They mix the water.'

'That is not a question of quality. It is a question of tradition.'

'You mean the hot and cold suffering in the morning is due to tradition?'

'Yes. English products are so good that they last for hundreds of years – even if they are obsolete.'

'That doesn't make any sense.'

'Nor do Hungarian taps make sense if they leak all the time.'

'You're right, but you don't need to come to Hungary to find that out. I would say that there is more to Hungary than leaking taps.'

'Well, I'm not interested. I don't want to see how people suffer there.'

'You might be right about that. It's just strange that you never wanted to see where Uncle grew up.'

'He spent most of his life here; he is a respected individual. That's enough for me.'

The telephone's shrill ringing interrupted their conversation. It was Uncle, reminding Sofie to phone home after four, which was five pm in Hungary. She said she would. Then she asked Sally whether she wanted to go for a walk, but she refused. In fact, she gave her a bicycle. Sofie was surprised as she did not imagine Sally to be a rider, but the bike turned out to be about a hundred years old, and Sally admitted that it had belonged to her father, who had cared a lot about physical exercise to keep healthy.

'I can see, the good English workmanship,' Sofie said smiling.

So, she got on the black bike, feeling a bit strange and went on her journey. The streets were very quiet, considering that this was a red-brick estate. No children or women in the streets. The sky was grey and the clouds hung low in the sky. She took pleasure in the lush green of bushes and hedges in the front yards then came to some free grounds and biked through a park. She turned left at the end of a street, entered a more industrial estate. When she ventured forward, she bumped into a police cordon. Real bobbies forming a chain.

'You can't go any further, luv,' said the policeman. This was the first time Sofie had ever met a nice policeman. The bobby even smiled at her. She looked over to the other side of the street, where a group of well-dressed men were standing around and talking to each other. They seemed to have blocked most of the street.

'What's happening here?' she asked.

'That's Laurence Scott's. Industrial dispute.'

At the gate there seemed to be a commotion. Another group of men blocked the entrance.

'The road is closed, young lady,' said another bobby and Sofie realised she had to go home. The bobby was talking to his colleagues, 'the Bailiffs have arrived. We're going in.'

Sofie sensed the familiar fear in her stomach, but this was different. She could not understand the violence or the fight between these groups of people: workers fighting for their jobs, police protecting property, as if she was transported back in time, reliving the history lessons about the Great October Revolution, the cruiser Aurora at Saint Petersburg. These workers had no guns, yet they were militant, and the bobbies seemed worried about them. Yet, she herself was only a bystander. Although she could sense the upheaval in the air, she was allowed just to watch, uninvolved. She could walk away, and she would be safe further down the street.

She got on the rusty bike again and rolled on, not really knowing where she was going. After a while she got onto a busier road and arrived at a black painted wall and old-fashioned bar doors. Over it in shining white letters the sign said Revolution Pub. She entered with a huge grin on her face. In the dark belly of the pub, behind a curtain of smoke, she saw her uncle at the bar, reading a newspaper. Another man was sitting in the corner and the radio boomed pop songs. 'All you need is love' embraced her and she was transported into her dreams, only this was real.

'Are you a Beatles fan, Uncle?'

'Yeah, aren't we all?' he replied with a wink.

'My Dad isn't, and Demis Roussos was my mum's favourite. In fact, I don't know whether they ever listened to the records that they bought for me.'

'But they did buy them, don't forget.'

'Yes, and all those expensive records fetched good money on the black market. I had to sell everything before I left to be able to buy foreign money.'

'Don't worry. You'll earn enough in no time and you can buy yourself your favourite records.'

Sofie beamed a big smile at her uncle. 'Thanks, I love your positive spirit.'

'Thank you for coming in to join me for lunch, you just have to go and get it.'

He gave Sofie some money and she had to go and get fish and chips from next door. In the chippy Sofie stuttered, embarrassed by her broken English, but the woman over the counter smiled at her welcomingly. She could only understand 'luv' from all she said with her Manchester accent, but it all worked out with pointing and smiling. The fish and chips were wrapped into brown paper bags and then into a newspaper. Sofie looked at Johnny Rotten and a half-naked girl on the front page of *The Sun*, worried that she'd missed some vital news. The package was still hot enough to make her want to run back to the pub as fast as she could. When she turned out of the chip shop the remnants of a sudden shower were steaming on the hot tarmac. On her arrival, the pub took her in, already like home.

Her uncle had decorated the walls with photographs and framed newspaper cut-outs from English newspapers that reported on the Hungarian Revolution in 1956. Sofie was just as proud of him as he was himself. Uncle tapped beer with the lunch, and she did not resist it. She was only worried about how she would bike home later.

Sweeping around with her eyes, looking at the silhouettes of Russian tanks in the streets of Budapest, she sighed. 'I'm just so glad that I could leave. They were after my brain.'

'Well, you did it and I am proud of you,' her uncle's acknowledgement made her feel so welcome.

'I hope you didn't misunderstand Sally. Life is not easy for us now. The unemployment is high, the government has raised the taxes on beer and cigarettes again. All the interest has gone up and on top of that I've just had to increase my manager's wages.'

Sofie became serious. 'I didn't realise that it would be so hard for you.'

'No, of course, you didn't. People in Hungary think that life is a bowl of cherries here.'

'I don't want to be a burden for you.'

Her uncle rushed to reassure her, 'you won't be. I need a hand in the pub. You could live with us and save for the university.'

'What would Sally say to that?'

'I'm sure she will agree. You could be our daughter in the place of the one we've never had.'

'Thank you, Uncle. When shall I start?'

'Give yourself a couple of days to recover. How about starting next Monday?'

'Sounds fine. I already love this place.'

Uncle laughed. Sofie liked the semi-darkness of the place, the dark walls, and the music. They kept on drinking and later Uncle introduced her to a bald man with a flat nose: Robert, the manager. He wore jeans and a denim jacket over a black shirt. It turned out that he used to be an amateur boxer.

'He was the best candidate for the post of a manager, believe me,' said Uncle, laughing.

Then Sofie remembered that she had to phone home. Uncle led her into the back room, and with the music, in the background, she managed to talk to her mother, who was in tears. The alcohol fuelled her courage to face this heavy task, much harder than any of the adventures of the last week. Her mother had always been on her side, and she did not deserve to be lied to.

'I'm so sorry, Mum. I did not want to get you involved, that's why I kept quiet. Please forgive me. How are Dad and Nan?'

'Your Nan is positive, your Dad is worried.' Then the line became distorted, and they agreed to talk again, in a week's time.

'I love you, Mum,' she still managed to say. The cracks in the line made her feel free of guilt, as if they were an excuse enough to lie. She knew that, from now on, all their calls would be monitored.

Chapter 27

She did it! Samu could not believe it. *How could she just go on her own?* He was angry, but he admired her courage at the same time. Now he was even more stuck in the cage of his own making. He did not know how to avoid the professor. It would have been a lie to say that he did not like the sex with the old man, but he did not want to repeat it either. It made him feel too submissive and too good at the same time and he was worried that sooner or later the professor would take away his masculinity, making him into a sissy. *Is that possible?* Could the professor eat away at his hardness? He could not tell but did not want to risk it. On the other hand, he wanted to remain friends with the great man. The attention made him feel important and powerful. At least now Sofie was not there to witness and sense his struggle. And it turned out that she had been right.

Samu travelled home to his hometown, Kaposvar, on a half-hearted mission to find out why he did not get his new passport for the Eastern bloc. Nearing military service, he was not sure that he would get one, but he owed this to Sofie, so he did have to try. He had handed in his application, which was accepted, but now he had to go into the town hall and visit the council offices to enquire about it.

The man at the counter found the application at the bottom of a drawer. When Samu said his name and hinted that his father was a captain of the army and he would be very disappointed if he did not win a swimming competition to be held in three weeks in Czechoslovakia, the man apologised.

'I'm so sorry, it must have been put into the wrong pile the last time you applied. I will rush it through for you, of course. It should be with you in a week.'

His mother was too happy to see him. She made wonderful food.

At the dinner table his father declared, 'I had to inform my intelligence agent about your friend. She was reading a dangerous dissident paper. Let her know that she should get rid of it before she is caught.'

Samu carried on eating, but now with an enormous stone in his stomach. 'Thanks, Dad, thanks for the warning. I will let her know.'

'Tell us about your new job,' butted in his mother, saving him from the unpleasant conversation, 'do you have a chance to learn while you are there?'

'Oh, yes. You can imagine that the country's most successful painters work there. I always listen when my boss is teaching. He is a great teacher, Mum.'

'Did you have success with your Matura?' his father was keen to know.

'I did Hungarian, Maths, and Biology. That's enough. Basically, they could consider me for entry next autumn.'

'After your service. You know, son, in your place I would be volunteering. Volunteers get a better treatment and if you get a place at university you only have to do one year.'

'I know, I will try to get a place, Dad.'

After dinner, when his father left the table and moved into his study, Samu helped his mother to tidy up the kitchen. She pushed a five hundred *forint* note into his jeans back pocket. Samu hugged her and wanted to kiss her ear under where she liked it, but when he pulled her close, the woman wailed and frowned. Samu pulled up her long shirtsleeve and discovered the bruises on her arm. He kissed her there, instead.

'I'm so sorry, Mum. I thought he only hit me.'

With tears in her eyes she turned away. 'Don't be sorry, he is a good man. It was all my fault. I provoked him.'

'How?'

'I threatened him with leaving again. Then he held me too tight. I was silly to dig up the past. It wasn't fair.'

Samu sighed and hugged her again, more gently. 'I wish I could help you.'

'There is nothing that you could do for me. If you want him to respect you go to the military, be a good soldier, and he will be proud of you. But don't do it for me. My life is on his side, no matter what.'

'You could leave him when Brigitta is old enough.'

'Perhaps. But I might not want.'

'Do you love him?'

His mother turned away and from the movements of her shoulders, Samu guessed that she was crying. He did not feel that he could touch her again.

He went to bed. He had a funny dream about Sofie wearing medieval armour, making rusty, cluttering noises when she moved toward a red brick wall overgrown with tiny pink roses. She cut the rose bush in a heroic way, a Monty Python way, feverishly, but not too effectively. Her sword became overly powerful, like a bulldozer, knocking down the red brick wall. Behind it, to Samu's surprise, he noticed even in his dream there was a bed. When she stepped closer Samu could see with her eyes the face partly covered with brunette curls. She leaned forward and kissed the rose-coloured lips, unveiling his face.

Samu woke up with a jerk. Now he could see it crystal clear that Sofie had abandoned him, she could not wait for him another week. But then, embarrassed by his own selfishness and the recognition that Sofie had always been right about his father, he burst out in an angry cry.

In the morning, he moved on. He did not feel that he could stay there to wait for the passport if it ever came. He went back to work in Budapest, although he did not want to. The looks of the students and the professor made him feel suffocated.

In a break between modelling sessions, as Samu stretched out his creaky limbs, trying to regain the suppleness of his body, the professor approached him.

'I'm having a party on Saturday, do you want to come?'

'What kind of party?' Samu could not hide his suspicion.

'Just a few friends to celebrate my birthday. Are you coming?'

Samu visualised his two-storey apartment in Buda Castle, the bay windows overlooking the River Danube and the Buda Hills. He longed to be there again, just to see the streetlights coming up in the dusk.

'What would you like for your birthday?'

'Oh, don't worry about it. Anything would do, even just a kiss.'

As it was Tuesday, Samu had the big chunk of the week in front of him. He first worried about what to get for the professor, then he worried about what could happen to him again; who would be there that might know him or of him. Whether there would be any other gay men that might want to have sex with him, or indeed, if it would be an orgy of homosexuals? He was not sure whether he wanted to be there or not, was he too curious or too frightened? Was he a chicken, as Zoli had accused him so many times? What did Zoli, or Sofie, for that matter, know about growing up in the shadow of a violent brutal father? *What did they know about having to listen to random noises, on the alert, waiting for this monster to appear, not sure what would happen; what he would find wrong that would give him the impetus to lash out, to take off his leather belt and set off again?* How could you not be a coward when you lived in fear? Everything he had done so far was an attempt to get over that fear, to forget it. He needed to do more and more cantankerous, bloody-minded, dangerous things to break the law that his father represented.

He was willing to forge a passport if necessary. He had watched Zoli carefully cutting away the top surface of the photograph in his old passport and replacing it with his own. Samu could do the same with somebody else's that he could get or even buy one off someone of his age. He had to escape and the professor could help, if necessary.

The party in his house in Buda Castle was much quieter than Samu had expected. There were five men and three women, one of them the professor's daughter. She brought her boyfriend, Kari, a university student, who had long straight hair and thick glasses. It turned out that Juli, his youngest daughter, was still underage and studying at a boarding school for her Matura. The name of the grammar school rang a bell: the best of the best. She had long brown hair, very much like Sofie's, and she talked sweetly and extremely kindly to Samu, who was introduced to everyone as a very talented model at the Academy. The other two women turned out to be the professor's housekeeper, who served the food, and the professor's ex-wife, Anna. She looked knowingly at Samu, not having bought the introduction. The woman could see through him. She must have known, all too well, that Samu was a potential, if not already established, lover. In her innocence, Juli did not notice this and by all signs, she did not know anything about her father's inclinations. She suffered under her parents' divorce, but she seemed to have grown up with it.

The other two men presented the biggest part of the puzzle for Samu. A tall man with black hair and an incredibly fair-skinned face surrounded by a black beard was introduced as Stefan, the professor's lawyer. He had his friend with him, who was nearing fifty, robust and shorthaired. Deeply impressed with the company he found himself in, Samu recognised one of the most successful actors of the country. He wore jewellery on both wrists and many rings on his fat fingers. He became the centre of attention, of course, but tried to play it down, paying compliments to the host.

The dinner that he had been so worried about turned out to be extremely pleasant, as if Samu was floating on a cushion of whipped cream. Every one of them was terribly nice to him in their own, pointed way, only Juli and Kari were indifferent. They were innocent and his own age. The actor was forgiven for his ambiguous behaviour; everyone took his open homosexuality for acting as if it was meant to entertain them. Samu guessed that Stefan was surely his partner, but he did not give it away, just as the professor would not give away anything in front of his family. A strange sense of safety made Samu feel free. He gave the professor a bottle of wine as a present; he seemed to be happy with it. Juli, Kari, and the professor's ex wanted to leave early, as they lived at the other end of the city. Samu used the opportunity to go with them, getting a lift to the city centre. The professor squeezed his hand when he said goodbye, but he pretended not to notice. Relieved, he got away.

He got off at 7th November Square and went to a disco. He danced like a dervish in a trance, imagining that Sofie was watching him. When he went to the bar he noticed a pretty blonde. While Samu ordered and paid for his drink, he lazily watched the girl, who now was dancing for him. He must have looked too bored, for the girl stopped abruptly and walked up to him.

'Hi, I'm Rita. I watched you dancing. It was fantastic. All your muscles were moving.'

'That's how it should be, or not? Anyway, I was dancing for my girlfriend.'

Rita turned and had a good look around in the now nearly deserted disco. There were no other girls except for her. 'Oh, I didn't know you had one. Where is she?'

'She is in England.'

Rita giggled, 'can she see you?'

Samu nodded seriously.

'She is magic.'

'Then I better don't upset her,' she said with a smile and slid away like an eel.

Samu went to the toilet. In front of the mirror, he combed and fastened his hair into a ponytail. Touching his own curls he remembered Sofie's pubic hair, how black and silky it was.

Chapter 28

Sofie was numb. First, she had been just focussed on the journey, but when she arrived in Manchester she suddenly fell asleep, switched off and now she was sleeping all the time, just watching the dream. Like a fish, just moving and breathing, looking. Nobody could have touched her, only the painting reached her soul, deep inside her chest with its vibrant green. *Where am I?* She asked herself every morning opening her eyes and looking around in this tiny room, where there was a bed, a window, a bedside table and a cupboard and a painting on the wall. Sometimes she was inside it. On this side of the painting, the bed was very old, Victorian, perhaps. The cupboard, too, was dark mahogany. It was hard to open its doors and they made a screaming noise as if she was violating their dignity. The cupboard was mad. Yet, the painting, Vincent's bedroom was beaming light and she preferred to think that it was the extension of this room, the crowded Victorian room reached out for freedom, the freedom of art.

In the following days, she learned to ride a bike again. She even got used to riding on the wrong side of the street. She got lost many times but loved the monotony of the estate; the houses all looked the same to her, yet the people were very different. From her safe place, she watched the calamities at the factory, like an interested bystander would be watching a scene of an accident. The bailiffs were flown into the factory in helicopters to talk to the workers that refused to leave. The bobbies cordoned off the building so that no one could come in or go out.

Sofie developed a deep bond with Uncle George, deeper than with her own father. Sofie regarded her father as a weak man, who always chose the safe way. Uncle George was a daredevil. She spent her days working in the pub and listening to George's stories about the Revolution and her father's part in it. Every night Uncle George would drink and give her some too, and talk, telling his wonderful stories. She learnt a lot. Not only about the right handling of taps and taking money, but real stories of history. She began to understand that her mother was a communist, for sheer want of belief. When her grandfather came back from the Siberian camps, where he had spent five years as a war prisoner, he was already a communist.

'The Russians converted my father; this is the truth. Your mother wanted to be with him after the divorce of our parents and she blindly followed anything he said.'

'I know. She told me the story, too. She was her father's daughter.'

'I always took my mother's side and I wanted to stay with her. I rebelled against everything that my father brought with him from Russia. It was inevitable that I went out onto the streets and fought when the time was ripe. If they had not divorced each other, it might have happened otherwise. Your father was my friend, and he was in love with my sister. Nevertheless, he fought with me. When it was a question of leaving, however, he chose to stay with my sister. I respect him for that.'

'It's a miracle that he has never been persecuted.'

'Oh, you don't know that. He was an intellectual and never shot anyone. I gave him permission to push everything into my shoes if they questioned him after I left.'

Sofie became accustomed to the traffic on the left side of the road, and she was happy to bike. When she started to earn money, she also got used to phoning home from red telephone boxes.

'Samu asked for your address. He will probably write to you.'

'Tell him, I'm happy and life is wonderful in England.'

When she finished the sentence, the pennies cascaded in the phone like a waterfall. She did not have any more change, so she turned to go. Just as she stepped out onto the pavement it started to pour. It did not look very promising, but she tucked her head down into her collar, trying to race home on the bike as fast as possible. Cutting the corner was a bad idea. She only thought about this when she faced a screeching bright yellow car and crashed onto its bonnet. A sharp pain shot through her. The driver, who seemed very dark in the depths of his sports car in his brown suede leather jacket, quickly got out of the car and rushed to help her.

Sofie looked at the young man, totally lost. 'I'm so sorry.' And she meant it.

'I'm sorry,' the guy said with perfectly rolled vowels.

It was the first time she ever heard this accent spoken outside the television box. He sounded like Mrs Thatcher. He had dark brown, unkempt hair and dark green eyes. He grabbed her arms and helped her to stand up. He took off his blue paisley patterned scarf, which seemed like a handkerchief to Sofie, and tied it on her shin, but it immediately got blood-soaked. A pang in her stomach, seeing her own blood told her, that *something awful is going to happen.*

'I think, I should take you to a doctor.'

'I can't leave the bike, it belonged to my aunt's father.'

'No problem. I'll put it in the boot.' He did so, and although half of the bike did not fit in, Sofie managed to sit in, too, and the guy, who introduced himself as Justin Browning, took her to a doctor's surgery, where she got an injection, two clips, and a bandage. She did not have any more money, neither health insurance. The guy called Browning agreed to pay the bill.

Browning drove her home and even half-carried her up the steps. It turned out that Sally knew him well.

'Hello Mrs Lantos.'

'Hello, Justin. This is my husband's niece, Sofie. I'm sorry that you must meet her this way.'

'It was an accident. I'm awfully sorry.'

'But Justin, what have you done to her?' Sally's voice was teasing.

Sofie did not understand why. Did Sally want some compensation?

'It was entirely my fault. For a moment I forgot that you drive on the left side,' she said quickly, to defend the guy.

'I took her to Dr Livingstone. It's all settled.'

'Thank you, Justin,' Sally said. 'Join us for a cuppa?'

'This was the least I could do, but no, thanks. I should be at the agency by now.'

'Well, have a good day. Come and see us soon.'

Sofie gladly saw him go, she did not know why. His kindness was exaggerated.

'Smile, Sofie, smile,' whispered Sally between her teeth, while waving after him. Sofie smiled, relieved that he had gone. Sally was overjoyed.

'Gosh he fancies you! And I thought he was gay!'

Chapter 29

Sally adored the fact that Browning knocked down her niece. There they had a match made in heaven. She knew well that Browning came from an affluent family. No wonder he drove that old Ferrari. She decided that she would invite some friends, including Browning, to celebrate her niece's arrival from Hungary. She made turkey, even though it was summer; it always went down well. She tried to get Sofie involved in the cooking, but, of course, she was a vegetarian. So she baked some Camembert in the oven for her, too.

'Shall I set the table?' asked Sofie, while Sally was setting the timer for the cheese.

'Do you know how to?'

'We do use knives and forks in Hungary, you know.'

'I'd better show you: first the starter, then the soup, the main course comes the closest to the plate. The dessertspoon comes on top. Look, the dessertspoon is slim, the rounder one is for the soup. All right?'

'All right. I see. Where is the Queen going to sit?'

'This is not a joke, Sofie. These are fine English manners. Very important, if you want to get ahead in life.' She folded a napkin. 'So, and you make a lovely crown.'

'It's very impressive.'

'Well, I hope you'll be, too. I invited all our closest friends. You'll see.'

'What do you want me to be, Sally, a puppet?'

'Don't be silly! You should ask yourself what I want for you. I want the best for you.'

George arrived home late, as usual. He seemed a bit drunk, too.

'George, finally! They'll arrive in an hour!'

'I'll go and have a rest.' He staggered up the stairs, but Sally knew he would recover soon.

'Put your silk jacket on, darling.'

She did her utmost to turn the evening into a success. Her guests loved the food, even Sofie liked her baked French cheese. The Sandwiches were their friends, from a long time ago. Jackie used to go to grammar school with Sally and they got married nearly at the same time. Both had thought that they might remain spinsters, but luck smiled at them at work, for they met their husbands in the factory. George was a supplier of catering then, while Jackie's husband, Tom, was a foreman. George used to walk in there with his bills and always forgot to leave again; standing around, asking Sally idiotic questions about the bill, till one day he popped the question and asked her to go out with him. That question changed her world for good and now she was Mrs Lantos. They got married soon after, but she never looked back. She was happy.

'I did not guess for a long time that George came from Hungary,' Tom said. 'Yes, he has a funny name, but we didn't care about these things in those days.'

'Yes, he has a very colourful past. When I first met him, nearly twenty years ago, he had just arrived from Alaska.'

'Did you have the gold rush?' Tom asked one of his silly questions.

'We could say, if oil is the gold of modern times. I worked on a rig. It was an amazing experience. It gave me the seed money for my business.'

'Yes, George told me that three of his colleagues died in a storm,' Sally said.

'You must be a master of survival, George,' Jackie said, and smiled.

'I was lucky. I used to be very lucky. When I came back to England I went every night to the Casino and won. I won more than I was able to spend and in half a year I opened the pub.'

Browning seemed impressed, 'remarkable.'

Sally smiled at him. 'You could write about him, couldn't you?'

'I suppose, I could. Sofie's escape would have a stronger effect, though. It's fresh and truly amazing.'

'Yes it's truly amazing. She risked her life,' said Tom, eyeing up Sofie.

Sofie stood in their midsts like a traumatised monkey. She clearly struggled to understand them.

'Isn't she brave for a woman?' asked George.

Sofie still did not say a word, but clearly, she was embarrassed. Sally thought she did not deserve all this attention, after all. She served them the soup, adding, 'and desperate. A lady would have chosen a less demanding path. Using her wits, I suppose.'

'Do you mean a lift in a carriage at midnight?' asked George and they all laughed.

Sofie still did not react, but Sally watched her playing a pantomime. She pretended not to know which spoon was for the soup and took the dessertspoon for the soup. She started stirring her soup with it, so that everybody could see her mistake. George grinned at her, encouraging; Sally could not believe her eyes.

At last, Tom looked at Sofie and asked her, 'is it so terrible in Hungary?'

'Not if you compare it with Africa or China. Everything is relative. For me, personally, it was suffocating, and I couldn't go to the university I wanted to, unless I bought into the system. I hoped to be able to study in England. Now I need a lot of money to buy my entry. Isn't it grotesque?'

'Yes, I can see the paradox,' said Tom. 'To find your way in life takes a lot of compromising.'

'Compromise does not suit me,' said Sofie and everyone smiled knowingly.

'We all said so when we were young,' blurted out George.

Justin Browning came to Sofie's rescue, 'well, I cannot promise anything, but you might find that your situation changes if you give me an interview.'

'Do you think I would be offered a place just for telling my story?'

'Probably not, but if people get interested in you, you might get a scholarship.'

'Well, it's something to think about. It's only that I am very shy.'

'You won't get anywhere by being shy,' said Sally, but Jackie distracted her.

'What a nice mushroom soup, Sally. You're a wizard.'

'Have some white bread with it, Jackie.'

When she went to bed, Sally was still pleased with herself. She granted George lovemaking; a passionate one: on top. Afterward, they fell asleep in each other's arms like babies. Sally dreamt her recurring dream about being a mother, but now with Sofie as a young girl. They walked down Manchester Piccadilly holding hands and for some inexplicable reason, as it is in dreams, her father's surgery was there, too. They walked in and Sally proudly showed him the child and her father took her into his arms. He said 'thank you' to Sally, as he always did in these dreams.

Chapter 30

Sofie had a few stitches in her shin. Sally convinced her that she should walk to work until the wound healed completely. Passing the factory, progressing at a slow speed, she could observe everything better. The men were much less happy than the last time she stopped there. The police had built a strong cordon around the building. When the bailiffs finished, there were some more talks at the door and the police got instructions to move in. The workers left the building reluctantly, but they stayed in the street, waiting for something, swearing and dejected. There was a lot of commotion and the BBC arrived with its van.

Sofie discovered Browning in the crowd of journalists. He was standing taking notes on a small pad in his hand, probably in shorthand, for he was keeping pace with the talker. Sofie sped up her steps not to be noticed. *A journalist. What I wanted to be*, she thought with some admiration. *He is writing the truth.*

She was working behind the bar and could not help but notice how many more men came in that day. The general mood of the people required alcohol, clearly. Her heart beat a bit faster when she saw Browning coming in.

He smiled at her with his big childish smile. 'Nice to see you. Is your knee all right?'

'Yes. What would you have?'

'A lager, please. It's hot outside.'

As it was already muggy and smoggy outside, Sofie took this as a metaphoric description of the political situation in the factory. She smiled, knowingly. To confuse her even more, Justin took off his jacket to reveal a short-sleeved checkered shirt and his white arms covered in a bush of fine reddish curly hair. He had freckles all over his arm. Sofie shuddered, but the sun broke through the clouds outside and the hairs sparkled like the red shoes in *The Wizard of Oz*. It seemed truly magical.

'That's fifty-three pence,' Sofie said.

Browning put the money on the counter and gazed at her. 'So, you grew up in Budapest. It's a beautiful city.'

'Yes. A bit like Paris.'

'I visited for five days last year, but I know little more than that.'

'What was your impression?'

'The border was strange, and perhaps more soldiers than anywhere else, but we had a great time. Don't you miss it?'

'Yes, I do. Very much.'

'Would you tell me how you came here and why?'

'Why do you want to know that?'

'I'm always after good stories.'

'Excuse me, I'll talk to you in a minute.'

Sofie had to serve another customer at the other end of the bar. She could feel Browning's eyes on her all the time. She shouted at him over the music, trying to roll the vowels and bite off the 'r's, with little success.

'I left Hungary because I was harassed by the police. Perhaps, I was really under surveillance.'

'Perhaps?'

'It could just as well have been paranoia. I can't explain this. It's a feeling. A tightness. But I also belonged to a circle that were on the verge. The unacceptable. A friend of mine wrote a pamphlet criticising the system. I brought a translation with me. I smuggled it out.'

'That must have been daring.'

Sofie laughed. 'Do you think? Sometimes I think that I was just seeking adventure against my father's will. I'm headstrong, you know. Anyway, that pamphlet is more important than my story.'

'Can I read it?'

'Of course. I translated it as well as I could. I will be more than happy to lend it to you.'

They kept chatting and Sofie had a drink, too, which gave her the courage to be cheeky with Justin and ask him, 'why do you talk like the television?'

Justin laughed, embarrassed. 'What do you mean?'

'You talk like the BBC.'

'Ah, that's called received pronunciation or RP. I went to a public school, that's how.'

'Aren't all schools public?' she asked.

'No. You have to pay for public schools.'

Sofie did not have much time to marvel about yet another contradiction and total contrariness to what she thought to be normal, like driving on the left side of the road and taps that did not mix the water, or men wearing skirts, to that matter. She just nodded, for she could see that she had hit a sensitive spot with Justin, who looked even more embarrassed than generally.

'I'm not too proud of it. My parents thought that a public school would provide the best education and anyway, my father is a diplomat, and I could not have stayed in one school for long.'

'Why are you not proud?' She could not let it go. If Justin opened the can, she wanted to see and even taste the worms.

'Although public school education opened some doors for me and I used the advantage it provided, I don't think it's fair that only people with money can give the best education to their children. There are many talented children in the working classes who never get any chances, just because they have no money.'

'Yes, I agree with you on that. But you should not have used the advantage if you think so. Like I did not join the Communist Youth Party just because it would have meant to get one more point towards my university admission.'

'Well, you must be more enlightened than me, but to defend myself, I must say that I was only eleven when they put me into that school. I used the advantage it had given me for my first job, anyway, which was with the *Financial Times*. I left them very soon, for figures and stock market news didn't really interest me. I got my second job at the *Manchester Evening News*. They write about real issues.'

'Well, your accent is lovely.'

She noticed Uncle George at her side, who butted in, 'it will rub off on you, never mind. I lost my Hungarian accent, didn't I?'

Sofie and Justin looked at each other and grinned and nodded.

'Yes, only when you are drunk it comes back and that is nearly all the time,' Sofie said and hugged her uncle knowing that she had gone too far.

He pushed her to the side. 'Cheeky, be careful!'

They all laughed.

The next time she saw Browning he admitted that Victor's piece of writing was original and had many new ideas that he had not heard about, but it was based on Victor's prophetic vision and discussions with Jesus, which made it less credible. Anyone in their right mind would question his sanity, or the pamphlet could simply be downgraded as a religious piece of writing, something like Jehovah's Witnesses would produce. Sofie argued with him, but generally found that Browning was a leftie. He thought that the system in Hungary was fairer. It provided more opportunities for everyone and people could work, while here in Britain the workers had to fight for their jobs.

'I love living here in Manchester. The workers have a voice here. Did you know that the Labour Party was founded up here?'

'No, sorry. Do they want to change the system?'

Browning laughed. 'No. Capitalism works. But they want better living conditions for all and perhaps a better distribution of wealth. The workers make it all happen.'

'My country was always oppressed. First the Kuns, then the Otomans, the Habsburgs, the German, the Russians – it has never been free, even then, for just a very short time. The people have never been their own masters. They tried to become free many times. There had been at least four revolutions, or freedom fights throughout Hungarian history, but they lost and every system was forced on them. This is like an illness. You can't even imagine how it feels.'

'That's true, I can't. We're very different, but we can learn from each other. So where is this prophet friend of yours now?'

'He is in London. He doesn't even know that I'm here and that I brought his pamphlet.'

'Well, I could help you to find him, perhaps. I would be interested to meet him.'

'Really? Wow. Would you write about him in your paper?'

'The readers of the *Manchester Evening News* are more interested in stories of real people than political theories. They would love to read your story, I'm sure.'

'Well, I have to think about that.'

Justin offered to give Sofie a lift home. Robert promised to close the pub and she left with Justin. Stepping onto the pavement, she looked up at the banner hanging over the door – and smiled at "Revolution". Her uncle had humour. Browning caught her eye.

'What are you smiling at?'

'The only revolution in this country,' she said, pointing at the sign.

She was tipsy and light-headed and in the next moment Browning was pushing her against the wall, nearly squashing the air out of her lungs and they were kissing. It was a passionate kiss; something she had never expected from him. She kissed him back, melting into his body, the waves of excitement shaking her throughout. When Browning pulled back, seemingly fully aware of his own power over her, he behaved very sober, gentlemanly, as they say, as if the whole thing had been a put-on or a show.

He smiled very kindly and asked her, 'I don't suppose we could cultivate this encounter in a more suitable atmosphere?'

Sofie, gasping for air, was even more shocked by his tone of voice than by the presumptuous attack. 'Is this the kind of language that you use in your paper for real people?'

'OK. Point taken. Would you like to come to my place?'

'Sorry. I don't want to be rude but I'm not feeling very well, and I don't know you at all.' She lost her balance and Justin hugged her closer. He did not want to let her go, so she panicked and tore herself out of his hug.

'Let me give you a lift home.'

'No. I'd rather walk.'

Browning got into his car, looking dejected and hurt.

Sofie walked home, shivering, for it started to rain. When she got home, after the short walk, her head was still spinning. Why did she feel so abandoned? Did she catch Justin's existential loneliness by kissing him? English people were so friendly, yet she was an alien. It said so in the stamp they put into her passport. She tiptoed into the living room and dialled Hungary.

'Hi Mum, sorry for phoning so late.' She enjoyed every word she uttered in Hungarian. Her tongue slid around in her mouth like a kiss. She shuddered again. 'I've been working. Have you heard any news from Samu?'

'No, he has not phoned since I gave him your message that you are happy and free. Are you all right?'

'Yes, I'm fine. I just miss you and him, too. It's so much harder here than I thought.'

'Sofie, you must write. These little talks are too short, and I need to know everything about you. Or get your uncle to lend you a tape recorder and talk to me on that. That'd be nice.'

'OK, Mum, I will.' She could hear Sally going to the toilet upstairs. 'Give my love to Dad. Goodnight, Mum,' she whispered and put down the receiver as quietly as possible.

She had agreed not to use the family phone for international calls since she had started to earn her own money, and she had kept to her promise until tonight. Worried that Sally would notice, she did not dare move. She just rolled up on the sofa, deciding to wait until her uncle arrived. He arrived soon, fumbling with his keys in the door, and woke her from a half-sleep.

He whispered, 'what's wrong, Sofie? You seemed so happy tonight. Did anything happen with Browning?'

'Nothing happened. I just got too drunk. But I miss everyone at home, Samu, too.'

Uncle sat down at her side and pulled her over to sit on his knees, something her father had not done to her since she was perhaps seven. Another surge of emotions let the tears well up.

'Look, darling. I'm sorry if I disappointed you, but I had to learn that you couldn't be a rebel all the time. The Revolution is over.'

'And you call it your second home.' They grinned at each other.

'Yes, but that's only sentiment. I'm doing the best I can for you, believe me.'

'I don't know what's happening to me. I drink all the time now and I almost gave in to making love with somebody that I only met a few days ago.'

'You mean Browning? I'll talk to the bloody jerk, if you want me to. Did he go too far?'

'No, don't. It's my fault. I led him on too much. Anyway, I think I like him.'

'Then, what's wrong?'

'I'm confused. I mean, the sex.'

'Call me old-fashioned, but it is better to go slow if it's supposed to be a relationship. Your father would tell you that, too.'

'Are you joking? My father would have killed me if he had seen me kissing in the street.' From the expression on Uncle's face, she could see that he was now confused.

'What? I'll kill that guy.'

Sofie pushed her hand on her mouth and tried to suppress laughter. Uncle laughed too.

'Let's not wake the mistress. We better go to bed, it's late.'

Just in that moment they heard Sally coming out of the bedroom and going to the toilet for the second time. She banged the door noisily. They sneaked into the kitchen and had a glass of water. Uncle made a ceremony of drinking water, too, clinking his glass against Sofie's.

'To your health. Stick to this next time you meet Justin.'

'I will,' she promised solemnly, giving him a big smile. 'I love you, Uncle.'

Sofie scurried into her bedroom and switched on the light on the wooden bedside table. The painting on the wall, opposite her bed shone back at her with its whole south of France daylight. She smiled at the naive copy and slid under the duvet. She could not sleep, however. The walls in this house were not thick enough and she could hear Uncle staggering into their bedroom next door. Sally must have been in bed already, waiting for him. Her voice slapped her sharply like a cold facecloth, as if she was talking through the wall, directly at her.

'She's been on the phone to Hungary. For half an hour. Didn't we agree that she will make such long-distance calls from the street and with her own money?'

'She's upset, she's missing her family.'

'George, I think this is too much of a favour for a poor relative. She lives here free, isn't that enough?'

'I will talk to her, darling, but be a bit more understanding. She is only eighteen.'

After a pause, she heard some muffled shuffling. Her uncle sounded smiley and mischievous.

'Sally Lantos, you did promise to obey.' Her voice turned soft and womanly, 'no, George, you are drunk.'

'Show me your breasts, at least,' said uncle, begging, and Sofie blushed. She pulled the duvet over her head, ready to cover her ears, if necessary. Sally's voice was deeper now, 'no, it's too cold.'

'Your left breast,' he carried on in a childish voice. Sally giggled and he sniggered. Then, regular breathing turned into snoring. Sally searched for something in her drawer, then she switched off the light. And that was that.

Chapter 31

The next morning, Sally slept in, for she had her earplugs in her ears. In the kitchen, when she arrived downstairs, George was already making breakfast. Passing the green Wedgwood ashtray next to their cream-coloured telephone, she glimpsed two pound coins. *George must have paid up for his niece's mistake.* She pretended not to have seen it. Keeping busy always helped to get over a frosty morning. George whistled some old passionate Hungarian tune; Sofie was eating her breakfast at the table, clearly hung-over, and Sally turned on the radio to hear the news about the Royal Wedding, but they only repeated the same announcement as last night. George and Sofie emanated the stale smell of the pub – it must have been hiding in that big hair of the girl – and it reminded her why she never liked working in The Revolution. She hated drunkenness; the only person she could forgive it in was George. She disliked the blue collars that frequented the pub, too, for she knew them too well. She had been a secretary at Lawrence and Scott's for twenty years, until they made her redundant. The constant strikes and industrial action wore on her nerves. She had to play the buffer between the management and the workers. She often had to suffer the anger and the abuse that was directed at the workers from the management; when she produced their payrolls to them the workers' remarks annoyed her. She could not understand why they couldn't accept that they were cogs in the wheels of machinery. The skilled workers were at least better. They had more dignity, and this was, according to Sally, the most important quality any human being could have.

They ate their breakfast in silence at her father's oak table. Their new little family, heavily sunk in thoughts. Soon enough, the telephone rang, and Sally answered it.

'Justin, good morning.' Sally chatted to him like a schoolgirl, knowing too well that he did not want to talk to her, but to Sofie, sitting at the breakfast table, still half asleep, and signing with her hands vehemently that she did not want to talk to him. Eventually, Sally gave in to Justin. Sofie squeezed the phone onto her ear, full of tension. Sally could not hear what Justin was saying, but it did not look good.

'It's OK, it could have been my fault. Let's just forget it,' Sofie said, turning her back on Sally.

'Is there anything else?'

Sally moved into the laundry and let them get on with each other. It seemed like a good match: Justin and Sofie. She had a feeling that Justin would do anything for this lucky little duck from Hungary. When she heard that they had finished, she moved back into the kitchen, patiently waiting to be filled in with the news.

'He wants to write an article about me.'

'An interview?'

'Something of a kind. But who would want to know anything about me?'

'Oh girl, you would be surprised. People like adventures.'

'That's what he said, too, that he was very interested in my adventures. Indeed, he would rather write about my journey than the Royal Wedding.'

'Oh, he is flattering you, isn't he? I told you he fancies you.'

Sofie laughed. 'No, I'm just an excuse for his socialist sympathies.'

'Even so. I would never swap your story for the one of Lady Diana, but still, I can read both, can't I?'

George hit the nail on the head, 'it could even fetch you a studentship at university, remember that.'

'Well, I agreed, and he will write it. I am going to meet him in the city.'

'Well, the city is clear now, but still, you have to be careful. Don't get into talks with any punks. Just listen to me and you'll have a ball, luv. Let me give you something to wear.'

She took Sofie into her bedroom and laid out a few outfits she got in the sale last year from Harvey Nichols. 'What do you think of this orange?'

'Very nice.'

'No, perhaps not. It wouldn't suit your tanned face. You need something darker.'

She found a dark blue suit, but it was too formal. The gal was not going to a business negotiation; she had to look sexy and innocent at the same time. 'You must look, pretty, Sofie. It's your first date with him.'

'It's not a date, just a discussion. He fancies me anyway, even too much. It's annoying.'

'Annoying? Are you a virgin?'

'No, I'm not. I had a boyfriend in Hungary. But only one. Justin threw himself at me last night. I got scared.'

Poor little girl. She wanted to hug her, but too much tension wedged between them, and the fact that she had broken the rules. 'What a nuisance. But he is a friend. You don't have to worry. I'm sure he will make up for his mistake.'

Sofie turned away towards the window. 'We'll see. He can have one last chance.'

Sally found another dress that she adored. 'Isn't it fantastic? I fell in love with it when I first saw it on Twiggy. You are not so thin, of course, but never mind. That is exaggerated, anyway. She looks ill, don't you think?'

She could see on Sofie's face that she hated that dress as well. Could she ever please her?

'You should wear it, Sally. It's really you.'

'What's your problem? I heard that you phoned home last night. I should be cross, not you.'

'I am really sorry, I was drunk and desperate. It won't happen again, and I put some money there, anyway.'

'You did? Well, let's forget it then. This is the day of forgiving for everyone, I can see. I think I have a dress that you'll like after all, but it's up in the attic, I'll fetch it in a minute.'

Chapter 32

Sofie arrived in a red and white polka-dot dress, seemingly, to the only café in Manchester. Sally, who lent it to her, thought that she had to look nice if she was going on a date. Even though it was horribly old-fashioned, Sofie liked the dress, remembering her mother's photos from the sixties. The outfit was leftover from the late fifties; one of the relics Sally could not get rid of, for sentimental reasons, just like the bicycle; but she remained silent about the origins of this attachment. It was her secret; Sofie suspected that it had something to do with meeting Uncle for the first time. It was an honour to wear this meaningful dress with its vast and mysterious history, even though it limited her movements and squeezed around her waist. The seam kept gliding up; it did not even cover her knees. Still not a miniskirt, but something much more frivolous than Sofie was used to. After a long verbal battle, which Sofie assumed that she had won, Sally sneakily managed to spray a waft of Chanel No. 5 on her when she was leaving. Sally swore that it would bring Sofie good luck, for it used to be the favourite perfume of Marilyn Monroe. Now she was worried that the wasps might find her and had a vision of a 'crazy' red-skirted mushroom with white dots moving ahead on thick stomps, smelling like Marilyn Monroe.

The dress did have an effect, for Justin jumped up to stand when he saw her and pulled out the chair so that she could sit down. To go with the dress, she had tied her hair in a knot on the top of her head, just as her mother used to wear hers in those old pictures. The bird's nest made her look a good bit taller, but at least some air could circulate around her neck. It was unusually hot that July day; the sunshine seeping through the grey clouds creating something like a greenhouse over Manchester.

'Hello. Will this table be all right for you?'

'Fine. How are you?' Sofie had become accustomed to asking this polite question, not expecting an answer, just to prove the superficiality of English manners.

'I was feeling guilty after you ran away. I hope I can make up for the unfortunate start.'

'Let's not talk about that. What shall I tell your readers?'

'About your journey, and why you decided to leave Hungary.'

'OK, I was always interested in history, but I found out that we were not told the facts of the past, that we were lied to by our own government ...'

Browning switched on his Dictaphone and listened. He did not have to write, so his eyes rested on her face. Even though Sofie felt exposed and almost naked to start with, she enjoyed opening up to him. The intensity of his attention reminded her of Janos and the nights they had spent talking. It was good to know that someone was really interested in the story that she had not yet put into words. Articulating it empowered her; she started to feel that she was a human being with a rich history, not just an intruder or an alien, after all.

Thoroughly impressed, Justin thanked her and went back to his office to type up the article. She decided to walk home from the city centre, or as far as she could in her tight and sticky sandals. Unencumbered, having rid herself, she walked light-foot, she was almost hovering like a butterfly. The city was preparing for the Royal Wedding; people were hanging the Union Jack on every lamp post. Although there were no plans that the royal couple would come to Manchester, people were excited, getting ready to watch it on TV, and for later that night, street parties were in preparation: a huge celebration for the people. Something she got to know on May Days when she was a child, but different. This was not just an excuse to drink and make jokes about anything to cheer them up, but it seemed to create a feeling of community: belonging. They were looking forward to an excellent show that proved to them that they were still a great nation, the richest nation; in it together. Sofie observed from a distance, being an outsider, too. For a fleeting moment, she felt sorry that she could not share the excitement with anyone. She missed Nan, who would be all over herself, but Sally did not seem to enjoy it in the same way. She was ready to criticise every little flaw if there was one in the young bride. Sofie was better left on her own, observing the national hype from a distance, even though it brought a smile to her face. She walked and walked till her feet began to hurt.

Embedded in the bright sandstone, on the edge of her perception, she glimpsed some dubious dark places that looked like dancing clubs. A group of young men were sitting on the kerb, enjoying the sunshine, hugging pints of beer. They all had very short hair and army boots, army trousers. One of them hung up his bomber jacket on a railing, scratching his tattooed arm in the sunshine. Sofie suddenly felt terribly out of place and vulnerable in her red dress, balancing a bird's nest on her head. She guessed that they were skinheads but was not sure whether to trust or fear them. She first perspired then shivered, speeding up her steps. When she was passing a betting office, she heard her name called.

'Sofie.'

She turned to the voice and saw her uncle sitting on a highchair. He waved her to come in, while his eyes were glued to a television screen high up on the wall. Relieved of her tension, she entered, eager to find out what he was watching. The horses neared the jump. Uncle jumped.

Sofie got excited. 'Did you win?'

'No. I just thought it was my horse.'

'Uncle, you've told me that you have debts.'

'I'll win and you will be able to go to university.'

'Don't do it for me, please, it will ruin you. I will manage, really.'

George gazed at the betting clerk's hands, paying off a winner. 'I'll only go up to fifty pounds, then I'll stop.'

'That's a fortune. Nearly three weeks' wages. Save it for me, please, come with me.' When she stepped closer, she could smell the alcohol on his breath. Sofie managed to pull him away. 'Let's go.'

'You look pretty. Where did you get this dress from?'

'Sally lent it to me. I thought you knew this dress. She is very attached to it.'

'Nothing to do with me,' he said sadly. 'She has her wedding dress, too. That has something to do with me,' Uncle said, forcing laughter. 'She was twenty-six when we married.'

They went to the pub and sat down in the snug. Her uncle was in a dreamy mood, apart from being drunk, and Sofie welcomed his chattiness.

'You're so beautiful.'

'Sally is beautiful, too, in her own way.'

'Sally is the fair-haired queen of the north, but you are the dark princess of the south.'

'Thanks. You're a charmer, Uncle.'

'Yes, because I am feeling so rich since you're living with us. I'm no longer the poor beggar from Hungary. I'm proud of my women. You know, we'd been trying for a child for so long, but Sally lost them all, one after the other. Then we stopped trying. It hurt too much to carry on.'

Uncle's eyes were brimming with tears.

'I'm so sorry,' said Sofie.

'I could never follow why she could not carry a child and after a while I started to feel rejected and doomed, as if the Hungarian blood was not allowed to mingle with the English.'

'So, what did you do?'

'I fought for her even more. This is how we are, stupid men. I became a publican, a patron. I gave the English guys what they wanted, and I got admiration in return. It was a good idea to call the pub *The Revolution* just to remind them that the owner was a fighter and ready to fight if necessary. The tough men ate from my hands and that was it. Sally could be proud of me, too. I'm just sorry that business has not been so good for the past couple of years. She has to stand in for me when I go to Hungary to see your gran. It's like a bitter pill for her, but she understands. Your grandmother cannot travel any more. Sally understands that. She is a good woman, even if a little stiff.'

Unsure what to reply, Sofie could not lie that she really liked Sally, even though her natural curiosity made her want to find out more about her. 'How did you two meet?'

'When I came back from working on the rigs, I was a bit lost on the mainland. I had too much money and frequented the clubs. I'm a gambler, deep down, now you know.'

Sofie just nodded sadly.

'In those years, however, I won. Anyway, have you ever looked at

Sally's hips?'

'Not really. Why?'

'They were always terribly lively, like a ballroom dancer's, almost indecent. Well, I fell in love with those. I met her in a ballroom, and she danced. Luckily, your gran in her wisdom had sent me to dance school when I was a young boy. It was an essential part of a good upbringing in those days. I knew all the steps of the tango and the foxtrot, and they came in so handy; I had enough skills to lead Sally around the ballroom floor on Saturday nights.'

'It couldn't be just her hips, Uncle. I can't believe it.'

'No, you're right. Even though she was nearly a spinster's age, she was hard to get. She kept me guessing for a long time. When, after six months of casual meetings, nights at the pictures, and long kissing sessions in alleyways, she finally introduced me to her parents, I fell in love with them, too. They were ordinary, decent people. Her father was a doctor with the NHS, her mother a fine lady. She had two sisters, but she seemed to be towering above them, even though she was the middle child. Like a holy statue, mature. Sally was the only one of the three that worked full-time. She was a secretary at Lawrence Scott's.'

'The one that is closing?'

'Yeah, the reason for all these upheavals. I don't know what I will do when the factory closes. For it will, you can be sure. No workers can stop the owners. It will take away all my good customers and I might go bankrupt, too. Have you seen all those houses that are empty in the area? All of them will be demolished soon.'

Later, after some coffee and food he asked Sofie not to mention to Sally their little secret. Sofie promised not to say anything.

Chapter 33

Browning phoned Sofie the next day and let her know that the article was well on its way, and it would be published in a couple of weeks, after the Royal Wedding. He had to go to London at the weekend and, if she wanted to, she could accompany him.

They left very early in the morning. With an all-knowing smile, Uncle George had given her two days off. She tried to hide her excitement from Browning, but she knew he was aware of it. He watched her ever so intently all the time, even when he was driving his yellow flashy car. They stopped twice on the way to London to get fuel and to have a break.

'I must go and see my aunt in Kensington for a short time. You're very welcome to meet her. Afterwards, we can go and see Victor,' Justin announced, searching her eyes over his tea.

Sofie did not dare to suggest that she could do without seeing his aunt and spend some time on her own in the streets, but she was too grateful to Justin for taking her. She just said, 'that's great. Then we both will have a place to sleep.'

Justin sighed. 'You don't have to worry about me. I know my place.'

They arrived in London in the early afternoon and drove straight to his aunt's flat in Kensington. The old lady opened the door and ushered them in. Sofie was introduced as Justin's Hungarian friend. The old lady had to be addressed as Mrs Brunswick. She offered them tea with triangle-shaped cucumber sandwiches. Sofie knew not to say anything until spoken to and the old lady got used to her quiet presence. The walls were covered with tapestries and huge oil paintings. On the commode, there were beautiful objects: small Oriental-looking statuettes. Sofie enjoyed the private art show. The china was finer than she had ever seen in her life, blue and gold-rimmed, with a beautifully painted pansy at the bottom. Sofie worried that she might break them just by touching them. The old lady had cut off all the crust from the white bread, each little sandwich was a creation. When she complimented them, the lady said, 'Goldie is good at making sandwiches. I'll tell her your comment later.'

She interrogated her nephew about life in Manchester and was very pleased about Justin making progress with his journalism.

'You could get a job at *The Guardian*, darling, and move in here with me. You know I'd love having you near me.'

'I don't respect *The Guardian*, to be honest. They are just the mouthpiece of the government. Did you read their article about the Irish Hunger strikers? It's appalling.'

To Sofie's surprise the old lady clapped her crinkly little palms together. Her eyes were sparkling with delight. 'That's my boy! A rebel forever.'

Justin laughed, but looking at Sofie's surprised face he added, 'Aunty Mary was one of the first women studying at Oxford. This was the only reason I went there, to see the place she had conquered.'

'Well, it was hard for us girls there, but we won. Even without smoking,' she added winking at Sofie.

'And what did you study if I may enquire,' asked Sofie shyly.

'Well, I did Art History and Business Studies, of course, to be useful in the firm, but I have retired. Nowadays I like to think of myself as an impresario.' She turned to Justin, 'do you remember that quirky little pianist I discovered? She had a concert at the Royal Academy last week.' Justin blushed. 'You know the one you fancied,' Mrs Brunswick added. 'She is a little devil that girl. She had a fling with the cellist as well.'

'Oh, yes, I remember,' Justin said, looking over to Sofie sheepishly, who pretended not to be there, smiling like one of the artworks, like a Thai Buddha.

Mrs Brunswick turned to Justin. 'I like your friend. Sofie is a good name, I shan't forget.'

'She is a Hungarian princess. Her father came from a noble family.'

'Really? Tell me about it.'

Sofie was embarrassed.

'They used to control the milling industry in the south of the country but lost everything in the twenties.'

'Just when I got into university it happened to some of my friends' families, too, and they had to quit. I thought I did it to impress my father, but, he had other plans for me. They kept giving balls in my name to sell me off to some magnet. In the end, I married Brunswick. But not because of his wealth. I met him at university.'

'I would really like to go to university,' Sofie said half aloud.

'What keeps you? Go for it! Girls have to fight for what they want. I can tell you that.'

'Yes, I will. Thanks for the advice.' Sofie was sure that this lady had no idea about how she had to fight for what she wanted. Perhaps, the lady did not know about the raised university fees for foreigners, newly introduced by Mrs Thatcher, but she did not want to seem too clever or to start talking about her own journey through the green borders. After some more chit-chat about family matters that she did not want to listen to, they were ready to leave.

Outside in the street, when they got into the car, Sofie glimpsed an off-license with the name BRUNSWICK over it. Until then she had not noticed but now realised that she had seen so many of these before. Justin caught her eyes and nodded.

'Yeah, that's her. She owns the whole chain and some breweries.'

Justin tried to play it down as much as possible, but Sofie could see that he was somewhat embarrassed. All of a sudden, Sofie understood the man. Poor Justin, he could never be sure whether girls loved him for himself or for his potential inheritance.

On the way to Bayswater Road they crossed Hyde Park and passed Buckingham Palace. The black fence with the golden tips and the seal with the lion and the unicorn impressed her enormously. The Queen wasn't at home. She must have been on holiday at Windsor, away from the crowds that were already gathering for her son's wedding. When she asked Justin whether he knew where she was, he just shrugged. He was not interested at all.

Arriving at Bayswater it took them some time to find the flat in the basement of the tall Victorian building painted brilliant white. When Victor opened the door Sofie could hardly recognise him. He had cut off his beard and sheared his hair, now tied in a ponytail. He had dark brown rings under his eyes and he was even thinner than in Hungary. He forced a smile and looked searchingly at Justin as if he was a plainclothes policeman.

Sofie introduced him. 'Justin is a journalist. He is very interested in your work.'

'What work?' Victor said with an embarrassed snigger.

'*The Criticism of the Dialectic Materialism*,' replied Justin.

'Oh that, come and sit down. I make some tea.'

While Victor made the tea, Sofie had a good look around the room. It smelled of mould and it was sparsely furnished. Sofie admired the fireplace with the glowing embers, noting that the heat it emanated was necessary. Even though it was the end of July, it was chilly in the room. A double bed and a desk were lined up under the window that had bars outside for protection. It looked like a prison cell to Sofie, but she forced herself to look at it in a positive way. Victor was free, after all.

They had cups of tea again and chatted. It turned out that Margaret had flown to Venezuela with the Red Cross and she had let him have the place while he was looking for work. He said that the only work he had found so far was dishwashing. He had to cut off his beard, for it was hanging into the dishwater, and they made him wear a hat for safety reasons that's why he had shortened his hair. He worked at nights and got his dinners in the restaurant, too. Victor had the television on all the time they talked, looking at it anxiously from time to time.

'I'm waiting for the news. There was something about riots. I have to board up the window if they come. That is my instructions.'

'Surely, they won't come here,' Justin said.

'You never know. The British are racists. No wonder these guys have had enough.'

The news came on. Another policeman was killed by the IRA in Northern Ireland.

'They fear the IRA might retaliate and come over here, you know. I'm not surprised. This is a very hard, cold-hearted society. It's ruled merely by money. I don't know whether the ordinary people here have any honest feelings for each other.'

'Isn't this your world as well?' asked Sofie not knowing what to say.

'That's just it. I've changed and I'm scared by it. I've become much more materialistic and egoistic, too. I'm worried about my shelter and my food.'

'Shall we pay for the tea?' Sofie meant this as a joke, but Victor remained serious. 'Of course not. But maybe next time you come I'll ask you for it.'

'Victor, it doesn't matter what you believe. I love you.' Victor smiled at her, unbelieving. 'I brought your manuscript, Victor. You can get it published here, look, it's here.' She took out the manuscript from her satchel.

'Thanks, but if you go to any church, you will see they are full of this kind of writings. Jesus came to me in Hungary to save my sanity, that's all.' With these words he stepped to the fire and threw the manuscript onto it. Sofie screamed.

'Don't!'

She tried to pull the burning sheets out but did not want to cause a fire. Finally, she just squatted down in front of the fireplace and stared at the flames eating away the manuscript. She sensed the weight of Justin's hand on her back. Victor had moved back in front of the television, engrossed with the news. For Sofie, he became just as cold as his environment.

They slept on the floor of the damp room in their sleeping bags. Early in the morning they left, but instead of going towards Manchester, Browning wanted to take her to the sea. Sofie refused, saying that she had to work the next day and she would rather go home. They did not talk much on the way, although Justin was trying to console her saying that the manuscript was not very good, after all.

'Are you talking about my translation?' she hissed at him to shut him up.

Sofie had caught Victor's depression. She thought that Victor, this beautiful man full of light, refused to be part of any society. From the bottom of one society, he entered through the asshole of another, and in her eyes, he had committed suicide by destroying the manuscript. He was like those Irish guys, starving themselves for some basic rights; by leaving Hungary Victor lost his purpose. Instead of freedom he found paranoia and isolation.

She thanked Justin for taking her.

'I'm sorry that it did not work out as you had imagined,' he said.

'I don't know what to say. I'm just sad and I must think it all through,' she replied, 'see you some time and thank you very much for taking me.'

That night Sofie went to bed with a huge void in her heart. She missed her mother, her Nan, even her father. But most of all she missed Samu.

Chapter 34

After ten days his passport arrived in a light green envelope. It was a Wednesday, July 29th; a day that Samu would never forget. His mother sent it on to Meli's address with a letter in her pristine handwriting.

Dear Samu,

When you were here last Monday, I could not talk to you, but there is so much to say. I feel so guilty that I did not manage to protect you from your father. He meant good, but he is a hard man. I owe you the truth about why I left him so many years ago, before Brigitta was born. He had an affair, but not as usual. I found him in our bed with a man one afternoon. I came home from work too soon. A colleague, I believe from the Army. They were only kissing and fumbling with each other, but I knew from the look in their eyes that it was a foreplay they were used to. I walked out on him. You were only a year old, and I took you with me. We lived apart for a year, but you would not remember. I found it very hard on my own with a child and he did his utmost to beg me back, especially because of you. He said you needed a father. I agreed and moved back with him, but under the condition that he would never have sex with a man again. He promised and as far as I know he has been faithful to me ever since. I did not know that he was beating you for a long time, until that awful night when I discovered that your back was bleeding and it needed stitches. We lied in the hospital. We said that you fell, and you agreed to lie. Nobody questioned the Captain of the Army. Your father used his power everywhere. That was my fault, too, but also the first time that I recognised that he let out his anger about me, on you. This might explain why I never really tried to stop you from going to a boarding school or leaving us for good. I did not want to be the cause of your suffering. This is why I am sending you this passport, without him knowing, and wish you a safe journey. Don't stay here because of me. If you have to go, just follow your path. I love you. Good luck and take care.

Mum

P.S.: You know what to do with this letter.

Samu read the letter once again, as if wanting to memorise it. His tears were flowing, but he was on his own, he let them show. Then he took out his Zippo lighter and burnt the letter over the sink. His mother's words hurt him in many ways, but they set him free, too. He would go – he had his passport for Yugoslavia. He would follow Sofie and find her.

Chapter 35

On the day of the Royal Wedding, on her way to work, she lost the bicycle while she stood in a phone box, talking to Nan, boasting about how wonderful her life had turned out. She was telling her how happy she was and how her uncle George was helping her to get on, and they would all be watching the wedding on TV at the pub soon, together with the whole nation, while some ruthless thief pushed away her bike. Sofie suspected that Sally would never forgive her for this carelessness. She arrived at work late and cried. Uncle promised her to help with Sally and to explain it all to her, but she could not trust him anymore. Since she had found out about his gambling habit, Sofie saw her uncle in a different light. He was an addict and addicts could cheat and lie to get the object of their addiction.

The next morning, perhaps still dazed by national pride and the pomp of a wedding dress, diadem, glass carriage, and all, Sally was more considerate than Sofie had expected. In fact, she tried to play it down, hiding her real feelings, but Sofie could see that her eyes became wet.

'Yes, it belonged to my father, but what can we do. Unfortunately, the world is full of dishonest people these days.' She looked at Sofie with burning eyes. She understood the hint.

When the article was published, at last, Sofie was shocked by its language and the lies that it was speckled with. Sally showed her the *Manchester Evening News*. After a week of cold-shoulder treatment, she was surprisingly animated and kind to her.

'Look, Sofie, you're a star.'

The headline said: 'Innocent Hungarian Teenager Escapes Communist Dictators'. Sofie could not believe her eyes. 'Oh my God, this is ridiculous.'

'I think, it's fantastic! I wouldn't be surprised if the *Manchester Mirror* didn't phone. You'll be a celebrity soon.'

Sofie read the article. Justin painted her in the best light, while making the Hungarian government seem like a bunch of killers.

'Can anyone believe this? It sounds like a film script; full of special effects.'

'Sure, Justin is a good writer. It could make a good film. Why not? Do you know how much money you can get for a true story these days?'

'No, but this is not true. I'm not innocent and they are not communists. They are not even dictators.'

'Sofie, don't complicate it. Get real! Words are just words and money counts. I think Browning is good news for you.'

At the pub, Uncle threw a party for her, inviting each one for a drink. Browning brought Sally in his car. They walked in victoriously, or at least, Sally seemed to be on top of the world, enjoying her niece's fame. Justin came to the bar. Sofie tried to avoid him and his inquisitive eyes as if she was put on a pedestal against her will.

'Did you like my article?'

'You made me sound like a victim. Like some casualty of the Cold War. I'd rather be an adventuress.'

'Perhaps, that was my feeling after having met Victor. He is indeed a casualty of the Cold War. But you're not. I'm sorry if you didn't like the tone of my writing, but you must win people's sympathy if you want them to help you. I can assure you that, for me, you're the strongest eighteen-year-old I've ever known.'

'Thanks.'

Mr Chapman, an old drunk, butted into their conversation, 'how was life in Bucharest, luv?'

'You mean in Romania? It was dangerous. Dracula came to visit me every night.' Sofie could see Browning laughing and she winked at him. At the same time, she had a terrible déjà vu, remembering Samu and the time he had told her that Zoli, his blood brother, had sucked his blood. Sofie's head spun and she had to run to the toilet. She was washing her face when Sally entered.

'What's this ugly face? Aren't you happy? You've achieved it all and only within a month of coming here.'

Sofie could not hide her disgust with herself and Sally. 'I bought into this system.'

Sally just laughed. 'Was it better in Hungary, then?'

'No, I don't mean that.'

'Don't bite into the hand that feeds you, I tell you. This is the best democracy in Europe. Take it or leave it.'

Sofie lost her mood for celebrating. Browning reminded her that he still owed her a trip to the sea. She asked her uncle for the rest of the day off, only too happy to go.

They arrived in Blackpool around seven in the evening. Although it was the height of summer, it felt like an early spring afternoon in Hungary. She was still grasping the fact that the sun set only at nine in August in this country, yet the air had a tinge of coolness. They climbed the fake Eiffel Tower and then on the beach they had fish and chips from newspaper. The walk in the sand was chilly, but also silly and romantic; they chased each other and got soaked up to their bottoms. Grateful for the sensation of sand between her toes and the now familiar smell of the sea filling her lungs, Sofie only worried that Justin would fall in love with her.

'I hope you don't think I just want to play with your emotions.'

Browning put his arm around her shoulder. 'Emotions? What are they? Have you never heard of the slogan: No emotions, please, we are British?'

Sofie laughed. 'I think that slogan should say: No sex, please, we are British.'

'That's it. But talking about "emotions" is just as dirty as exposing intimacies, like sex.'

'I hope you're joking. In Hungary we do nothing else but talk about emotions, all the time. But can anybody separate sex and emotions?'

'Some people can. For instance, prostitutes.'

Browning took a lock of her hair and kissed it with irony. Sofie pulled it back with force but smiling.

'I can see that you have feelings and I want to be honest with you, Justin. I cannot give you what you want and there is a danger that I will hurt you in the end.'

'Why would you hurt me?'

'Because I am an adventuress.'

'Wow, then I might have to take some risks as well. How long has it taken you to grow your hair so long?'

'Since I can remember. It was always long.'

'It's ravishing.'

He buried his nose into her hair and Sofie enjoyed her own power over him, like a magnet, pulling him close. He was being drawn into her aura and she did not want to resist it.

They drove back to his place when it got dark. They spent the journey in silence, listening to New Order. The lights floated by on her retina, creating an impressionist nightscape of the world.

Justin's flat was a cross between a linen mill and a town house.

'How did you get to live in this place?'

'I moved in.'

She giggled. 'I can see. And?'

'I didn't ask for permission. We call it "squatting".'

This confession put Browning into a new light in her eyes. He was a rebel, after all, as his Aunt Mary had said. Sofie was terribly impressed by his courage and the place that seemed to reflect his personality. Most of the rooms had whitewashed walls. There were just a few pieces of furniture, but so much space that she could dance around. It was so vast, free, and different from the tiny little room under the red star where she grew up in Budapest, but even from her present bedroom at Uncle's and Sally's house in Openshaw. He had a life-size poster of Patti Smith on one of the walls in his living room and a huge old blue velvet sofa in the middle of the room. Sofie threw herself onto it.

'Wow! So much space!'

'It will be demolished, soon,' he said.

'Hopefully not with us inside,' she meant it as a joke, but Browning repeated it with an Eeyore-like voice, 'hopefully not with us inside.' He hugged her and they kissed. Sofie enjoyed it this time more and she did not want to stop. Then he disentangled himself and put some music on. 'I think, you'll like this.'

Sofie was engulfed in the sweet melody and the most depressing lyrics ever by Joy Division. Love could tear people apart. It was true, so true. He started to undress her slowly and she did the same to him. One for one, as if they were equals. When they were naked, they reclined on the huge blue velvet sofa, and he caressed her chin and face with the middle of his palm and carried on her back, all over. The walls of the room emanated cool, while his hands were soft and hot, but they stuck to her skin with magnetism. There was so much care in his slow motions. He was attentive, always watching her, and they looked into each other's eyes all along. She kissed her breasts and tummy and massaged her thigh with his half-erect penis. He entered her slowly, watching her reactions, as if they had all the time in the world. She did not think it was possible to be so intimate with someone without exchanging words. In her world it had to be talking, a lot of talking, and then physical touch. With Justin touch seemed to replace words and skin to skin had more to say than any of his words as if they had been developing a new secret language of their own.

But of course, she might have just imagined it all. Justin offered himself, but nearly embarrassed about it, she did not think that she could love him back. She was too frightened of hurting the lonely little boy in him that she could feel was always there in reaching distance.

She insisted on going home and not sleeping at his place, so Justin gave her a lift. Silence crept between them, for she was not sure that she had done the right thing. When they arrived he did not force a kiss. She gave him a peck on the cheek.

Justin only said, 'don't worry, I'll be OK.' As if he had read her thoughts.

'Thanks. I mean, thanks for taking me to Blackpool and all,' she mumbled and jumped out of the car and hurried into the house.

Sally was still up, sitting in front of the television, watching the news and Mrs Thatcher.

Wearily Sofie sat down on the settee. 'Hi Sally. How come you're still watching TV?'

'Another hunger striker died today in Northern Ireland. I was watching the news to see whether Mrs Thatcher would say anything about it.'

'Did she?'

'Not a word. You know, one of the women in the club is from Northern Ireland. I just thought I needed to be prepared. We have a meeting tomorrow.'

'I thought you never talked about politics, only charity and stuff.'

'This is not politics. This is personal. You can see that Moira is affected by all that madness in her home country, even though she does not say a word.'

'Why do you want Mrs Thatcher to say something? Can't you show compassion without her approval?'

'Of course, I can. But it would be easier if she had said something. She is our prime minister, after all, and she is the one that would not give in to the Hunger Strikers' requests.'

'I don't understand, to be honest, but I don't approve of violence.'

'Then you came to the wrong place. There has been more violence in this country this year than in yours in the last twenty years. But anyway, how was your trip to the sea?'

'Good. Blackpool is fun.'

'Only good? Not fantastic, or wonderful?'

'No, it's becoming rather boring. Perhaps it's just the Hungarian temperament. We don't show so much enthusiasm.'

'Well, I would say you are right. Is he hooked?'

'What do you mean?'

'You know if he does not propose you will have to give him a hint. Most men need a little hint, otherwise they'll never know. They need directions, you know?'

Sofie could not cope with this madness anymore. 'Goodnight, Sally.'

'Is this your reply? Instead of "thanks, Sally, thanks for the advice?"'

'I'm too tired to discuss this, Sally. Goodnight.'

'Then go to sleep.'

'I'm going, even without your permission.'

Sally turned away towards the television. From the side she looked so much like Mrs Thatcher that Sofie got the shivers.

She went to bed, but she was confused. *What have I done?* It had been a mistake to make love to Justin. *The day he knocked me down*

with his car it was all decided. I was bleeding and I had a premonition.
She promised herself that she would finish this, whatever it was, the next day. She fell into a deep sleep, praying that she could resolve this, but woke again after some time, for next door she could hear Sally's angry voice mixed with Uncle George's.

Sally nagged, 'I can't bear it! She is so impudent with me! She knows everything better!'

'I can't put her on the street, she is my niece for God's sake. Be more tolerant, please. I'm responsible for her.'

'You always defend her, what about me?'

'I'll talk to her, will that do?'

Sofie pulled the duvet over her head and turned towards the opposite wall.

Chapter 36

Uncle George did not talk to her the next day, or any other day. He knew about the thinness of the walls in his house, and he must have been too embarrassed about his wife's behaviour. He kept disappearing in the afternoons from the pub. Sofie guessed that he went away to gamble. Every time he came back, she could read on his face whether he won or not, and most days the answer was no. Yet, she did not talk to him about his little secret, either. The relationship with Browning was on hold; he seemed very distant and Sofie was free to think about whether she'd made a mistake. The work started to annoy her, for the people in the pub got drunk very soon in the evenings and she could feel their anger and depression about the factory. Luckily, Robert, the manager, was always there to help when they needed to send someone home, even if Uncle George was not.

After the success of the article Browning told her that he got a new assignment to write about refugees in Merseyside, so that he had to go away for a whole week. Funnily, Sofie started to worry about him, but then just put it down to boredom. After a week, however, when she had not heard from him, she started to feel sorry for herself for having slept with a man that had no emotions at all. He never called her, therefore he was cold-hearted, for sure, and she had made herself ridiculous when she was worried about his feelings for her. *What an idiot!*

Her self-chastising and boredom abruptly ceased one morning when the front doorbell rang, and she went down to open the door. She could hardly recognise Samu, who looked exhausted, but happy. He grinned and they hugged and Sofie realised that she had been missing him all along. Uncle was surprised to see him, but Sally seemed to like him from the first moment when he bent down and kissed her hand. It was ridiculous, but it had worked with Nan in the past, too. *Women were hopeless idiots*, Sofie thought, but at least now everything had changed, and Sally was more malleable.

Samu brought a breath of fresh air with him, and they wanted to know his stories. He had crossed the Yugoslavian border in the boot of a car rented by a Canadian. It was hard to believe that anyone would risk so much, but Samu added that the man was originally Hungarian; he had left in the early seventies, and he was a friend of his friend from the Academy, the professor.

'How come the professor helped you? I thought he was a commie, after all,' Sofie asked him.

'When I got enlisted in the army, I was desperate and I asked him for help. He fully understood that I could not stay in Hungary and this friend of his was visiting. We agreed that we would meet in Zagreb, so I took the train there. He smuggled me through two borders, took me to Calais. I sneaked onto a boat and travelled by night, but before we reached Dover, I jumped off and swam to the shore without being noticed. I slept in a cave; would you believe it. The next day I started to hitch-hike all the way up to here.'

'He must have been a very good friend to risk so much,' Uncle George remarked.

'To be honest, I think the professor paid for this. But I'm not sure. It all went very smoothly and the Canadian was very nice to me.'

'Did he ask you to join the CIA?' Uncle asked.

Everybody laughed.

'I'm serious. This guy sounds like a people smuggler. They are employed by the CIA.'

'No, nothing alike,' Samu replied with a tired smile.

'I was approached after '56 to become one of them, but I did not want to risk my trips to my mother with stuff like that,' Uncle said.

Samu seemed confused and Sofie came to his rescue. 'You're so lucky, Samu. I'm so glad you didn't drown,' Sofie said with admiration.

Sofie took Samu with her to work and he fell asleep in a dark corner in the pub. She worked all day, checking the corner, not believing her eyes. Looking at his fine frame and long brown hair partly covering his face Sofie fell in love with him again. It was amazing that he followed her without any arrangement. Sofie was happy. She asked Robert to close the pub on her behalf and they escaped to the city to the Rafters Club. Sofie proudly introduced the music of Depeche Mode to Samu. These guys were very well dressed, Sofie thought they could even find Sally's approval. There were no punks in the club. The fashion seemed to subside. Skinheads speckled the scene here and there, but she was not afraid on Samu's side. They danced and raved together as they used to in Budapest.

They were like puppies in bed that night, playing, till they made love and she melted into the sounds of his body, the hairless muscular chest, the touch of his skin. She could hear Uncle and Sally making love in the next room, too, and Samu smiled at her, with his wise, knowing smile. Life seemed to be right again, just right.

Just as with herself, when she had first arrived, the next day they had a family sit-down at the breakfast table. Uncle and Sally were very happy, they kept touching each other fleetingly, as if they had fallen in love again, as well. Uncle wanted to know their plans. They had decided that they wanted to go to London, to find work and to explore the city.

'Are you sure you want to give up what you have here, Sofie? It might be better if Samu went ahead, found work and a place to live and then you could follow him.'

Sally butted in, 'I'm sure they want to be together, let them go, George.'

Uncle George seemed annoyed but put up his hands, giving up. 'Do whatever you want, but your mother will be worried about you.'

They decided to leave the following week. Sofie had saved enough money so that they could take the train and there was enough to rent a room somewhere near Victor's place in Bayswater. She still had the two hundred pounds she got from Nan. She was very rich, after all. She had enough to fall back on if she got into trouble, which she was sure would not happen. They were warned that work would be very scarce everywhere, but they decided to go to Margaret's father, the minister, who surely would be able to help them to find jobs.

Uncle organised a farewell party in the pub on the last Saturday. Sally invited her friends from the Women's club and the Sandwiches turned up as well. Uncle George played all his favourite Beatles' songs, John Lennon, and the Wings. Sally danced like a queen of the ballroom, she really enjoyed herself. Blondie was singing 'The Tide is High' and Sofie was singing along to Samu, dancing in her jumpy crazy manner, when she glimpsed the silent, sophisticated, dark shadow of Browning behind the drunken faces. It was only a second and he was gone.

The last days in Manchester were emotional. How much she had grown to love her uncle! She tried to do her best to show her respect and love for him, but he started to push her away, perhaps unable to show his emotions. Sofie did not understand and the last night, when they were in the process of closing the pub together, she asked him, 'Uncle, are you cross with me for going to London?'

Uncle George stopped putting up the chairs on the tables and looked straight into her eyes.

'Your parents will be very disappointed in me for letting you go. I promised that I would look after you. Now, I suppose it will be Samu's job to do that.'

'We will stick together, don't worry.'

'London is a different place, Sofie. Don't go anywhere near Brixton or Notting Hill. Avoid staying out long at night. Take care of yourself.'

'I will.'

'I must say that I don't trust that Samu can do it. You have to look after yourself.'

'Uncle, Samu is strong and intelligent. Don't worry about us. We will be good,' she said with a naughty smile, but Uncle did not like her joke. He remained serious, so she added, 'anyway, it was time for me to go. Sally will be happy to be rid of me.'

'Now this is unfair. We did everything in our might to make you feel comfortable; don't be ungrateful.'

'Yes, I am very grateful. I love you.' She hugged him and they left it there.

She could not really tell her uncle that she was looking forward to realising her dream and Vincent's dream of the artist community. Surely, Samu was an artist. He could paint and play the flute; and herself, she loved history and languages – one day she would be studying at the university. She could become something one day, who knows, the future was bright, full of promise. In the morning, before leaving, she put down the house key on the kitchen table and dutifully thanked Sally for her hospitality.

The Door

Chapter 37

When they arrived in London Victoria, they chose to ride buses to do some sightseeing. London smelled different than Manchester, perhaps less sooty, but much more suffocating. The asphalt radiated heat and the smell of exhaust burnt her nose. Passing Big Ben, Sofie shouted over the noise to Samu.

'Do you remember the snow globe on my Nan's table? I showed it to you when we visited her once.'

'Oh, yes. You pushed it into my face.'

'I used to play with it during every Sunday visit. Shook it and watched the snow slowly covering Big Ben and the Houses of Parliament. And now I am here.'

They had to get off the bus and wait for the chimes to realise Sofie's childhood dream before going on foot, walking through the streets towards Hyde Park. He enjoyed watching some punks. Samu had never seen any man with a turquoise Iroquois crest, in heavy boots, army uniform, and heavily chained up with piercings and all the paraphernalia. They seemed to be parading in Hyde Park as if to make a statement of their anger, their existence. At Speaker's Corner a bald man with a goatee was arguing against Capitalism. He had a yellow sign in front of him saying that he was a representative of the British Socialist Party. Samu looked at Sofie, who seemed just as shocked and nearly paralysed as himself. When Sofie caught his eyes, she started to laugh uncontrollably. He could not stop himself giggling either. Finally, he took her hand, and they ran away and collapsed on the grass. The lawn was soft like a thick carpet under his feet. Sofie took off her sandals.

'In Hungary we were never allowed to step on the grass,' Sofie said.

'Yeah. This is the free West,' laughed Samu. 'They even ask you to walk on the grass.'

It was getting dark when they arrived at Bayswater. The windows of all the downstairs flats were boarded up. Some broken bottles lay on the ground in front of the entrance door, so the boards made sense to Samu. They had to sit on the steps and wait until well after midnight, for Victor was working in the restaurant, but Sofie could not tell him which restaurant.

Victor did not show too much joy at seeing them; he seemed too tired after work. Although Sofie had warned him, Samu was shocked when he had to face his old friend's changed demeanour. The shorter hair and the lack of his long beard revealed how thin he was. He looked like some starving homeless person. Yet, when they went into the flat, he perked up, made a fire and tea, and they sat up until the early hours talking about their experiences, means and manners of escape, and Victor's thoughts about the West.

'I had a blue passport for the West and came on the Orient Express from Budapest straight into Victoria Station,' Victor said.

'What? Like a tourist? How come?' Sofie asked him amazed.

'I had to get a visa for all the countries I crossed, which was more difficult, for I had to show that I had Western money. Luckily, I had that stashed away as well.'

'Unbelievable,' Sofie uttered.

'You see, I had applied for a passport three years ago, when I had a job as a teacher in a primary school. My girlfriend was still alive. We had planned to go away together to Paris, for a fortnight, like lovers do. I had planned to propose to her on the Eiffel Tower. I had the money, the passport, everything, but when she was knocked down in the street, I had a breakdown.'

'I cannot imagine it. I thought you were always a hobo and never had a proper job.' Samu was amused by Sofie's naivety.

'Well, here you are. I wanted to take my own life after that, but Jesus appeared and instructed me to live the life of the prophet, the leader.'

Samu was more interested in his life as a man, and dared ask the question: 'And have you served as a soldier, as well?'

'Well, I did, like everybody else. I had to do a year before studying to become a teacher, but they dismissed me for health reasons.'

'What happened?' Samu asked, curiously.

'I lost my gun. When they put me into prison for that, I ate chalk. They thought I had epilepsy. So I'm not fit for military service.'

'That never occurred to me but seems like a good way out.'

'I don't recommend it to anyone. It's too dangerous to play with your mental capacities.'

Victor happily agreed that they could stay there for a while, till they found a place to live. He advised them about places to avoid, such as Soho, and places where they would not have to pay money but could enjoy themselves. For instance, the British Museum had no entrance fees.

The next day they went to the British Museum and explored the Egyptian department and found great relief sitting amongst huge sculptures and sarcophagi, admiring ancient artefacts and the mummies.

'Looking at history always puts your present into perspective,' Sofie said with her wise, put on voice, annoying Samu for a moment.

For him it was all beauty, for her it had to be ethics or philosophy. She could never just be in the moment. Samu was not allowed to enjoy himself too long, for there and then they decided to pay a visit to Margaret's father, the minister.

He lived in Ealing, which was very far out of the city centre. They stopped in front of number nineteen Ealing Broadway. It was a two-storey corner house with much smaller windows than the houses in the inner city. It was hard to imagine that a minister would be living there. The doorplate read: Rev. Steel.

'Now I understand,' said Sofie, 'he is a minister of religion.'

Samu just whispered, 'I see, a minister for all occasions. Maybe he can give me a job?'

'Playing the organ, for instance,' Sofie replied, half-seriously.

It did not seem to occur to her that Samu perhaps had never played the organ. As far as she was concerned, Samu was superman. He rang the doorbell. A middle-aged woman opened the door.

'Can I help you?'

'I hope so, we're looking for Margaret Steel.'

'I'm sorry, she's not here.'

'We met her in Budapest, and she told us to visit her if we ever made it to London,' added Sofie. She was smiling.

'I'm sure she would be pleased to see you, but she is in Bolivia. She has a very important mission with the Red Cross.'

From inside they could hear an old man's shaky voice, 'Winifred, why don't you ask those young foreigners in?'

So, they entered the building. It smelt very clean and of bleach as if the floors had just been washed. Opposite the entrance, a huge crucifix hung over the door, and they could see a small picture of Margaret as a young woman, wearing a cap and gown, clutching a scroll. They went into the living room where Reverend Steel was reading under a lamp in front of a tall glass-fronted cupboard full of books. He stood up and greeted them and asked his wife to make some tea and bring some biscuits.

'It's very difficult for us to imagine what life is like in Eastern Europe. Margaret told us some pretty gruesome stories about censorship and oppression, of course,' said Reverend Steel.

'Well, I have only been in England for a short time, but people seem to be better off here and more relaxed.'

'What I can see is people are desperate. We have very hard times. The unemployment is higher than ever,' said the reverend, 'religion is a comfort, of course, but that's all I can help with. Margaret loved Budapest. How long are you going to stay in England? You must go and see Buckingham Palace and St. Paul's Cathedral.'

'Actually, we're staying here for good,' said Sofie. 'We had to leave Hungary illegally and we will not be able to return for a long time.'

The atmosphere in the room changed. Samu could see that they were not the welcome visitors anymore, but the alien intruders.

'How terrible!' said Mrs Steel. 'How can you bear that? Not to see your home country and your parents?'

'I didn't feel safe in Hungary and the police were always asking for our papers, at every corner,' said Sofie, but Reverend Steel shook his head disapprovingly.

'That can happen in London, too. Especially at night.'

'Really? We've never been stopped in England,' said Samu, but immediately his stomach churned.

'Yes, everybody who looks dangerous, I mean, like a terrorist or a rioter, will be checked out at night. You need to be careful on the streets. Stay indoors at night if you can.'

Samu started to plead, 'two weeks ago I got my papers to go to the army. But it's against my faith to murder on command, so I left Hungary.'

'I can sympathise with your dilemma, young man. It's very sad that in many countries men of your age still have no choice in this.'

'Would you know anyone that could help me? I need work.'

'Well, young man, I can make some enquiries. Leave it with me for a while.'

Mrs Steel took a piece of paper and wrote down an address. 'This is the address of the club of Hungarian Immigrants in Notting Hill. They might be able to help. We get an incredibly large number of immigrants in this country and they all have their own clubs.'

Samu and Sofie thanked them and left. They took the tube and a red double-decker bus to Notting Hill. Two Rasta men were playing music on the bus. Samu enjoyed the music and the mood immensely. When they drove into Notting Hill, the black men stopped playing. Everybody was just watching the outside scenery. Sofie squeezed Samu's hand fearfully when they passed some shopkeepers boarding up their windows in a hurry, even though it was in the middle of the afternoon. One of the houses was completely burnt out and on the wall graffiti said, 'Nigger-Free Zone'. They were so shocked by what they saw that they missed their stop. When he noticed, Samu pulled Sofie onto her feet and they jumped off the bus at a red light.

In the Hungarian Club an old lady immediately offered them some more biscuits and some more coffee. When they accepted it she also produced a small plate that had a piece of brown wrapping paper on it. On the paper someone had drawn '*Köszönöm*' with a shaky red pen. There were a few pennies already sitting on the plate. Samu threw a few more in. There were two older men and a young woman with a child sitting around. They all spoke Hungarian, although the young woman expressed her embarrassment, for she had a very strong English accent. One of the men, Mr Horvath, Samu's namesake, started to talk to him, but first they had to clarify that they were not related.

'Before the Revolution, people that criticised the system were taken away in black cars so that they would never be seen again. Nothing is as bad there now. People can travel, even.'

'Only old people can travel. Young people have to join the army.'

'Why don't you change it? We took the guns and fought.'

'And you lost,' said Samu, seeing that he had no chance with this man.

'Yes. We paid the price for your freedom.'

'I wouldn't call that freedom. The censorship, the Russians in the country. They forgot to go home after Kadar brought them in. What do you think about that?'

'It's just a show of power. Unfortunately, there are bigger forces playing this game.'

'Could you help me to find some work? I need to feed another mouth, too,' Samu said, nodding with his head towards Sofie who stood further away, talking to the young mother.

'Work? Let's see. Have you got a driving licence?'

'No, but I can drive.'

'I can only take people with a licence. I have a haulage company. I learnt driving in the Hungarian army, by the way. It gave me my profession.'

Samu could not carry on with this conversation. He took another sip of coffee and moved on, to another veteran of the 1956 Revolution, but he was losing hope that he would achieve anything with any of these men.

Sofie arrived back from the young mother she had been talking to. She was exuberant, having been cooing to the baby.

'I promised that girl that I would look after her baby sometimes. She is very nice. And you? Have you got anything?'

'No. What an old bugger. Just like my father, let's just go.'

For Samu it seemed that they left the building like beaten dogs.

Although they intended to look for suitable accommodation, when they passed some boarding houses where it said 'Vacancies' on the windows they also discovered under the signs the host's reminder: "No blacks, No Irish, No dogs". Disheartened, all Samu had energy left for was to go to Victor's before he left the house for work in the evening. He just wanted to fall asleep and hopefully awaken from this nightmare.

Chapter 38

They had been searching for an abode for two weeks. Every morning they went together to look for accommodation, but some people did not even open the door for them. Sofie noticed that old ladies in old houses were frightened when they saw Samu, so she took over. Nonetheless, they did not get very far. Only the museums offered shelter, where they found some harmony.

They got the first good result in the second week, when they passed a university in Westminster. Sofie wandered in to check the smells and to see the inside of the building. The space was enormous, just like at home, but she sensed much more movement. Students were coming and going. The place seemed much more alive than the university in Budapest. Samu walked up to the doorman's cubicle and read a sign that said that they were looking for cleaners. Sofie asked the doorman how to get the job.

'Come back this afternoon at two. You can join the group then.'

'Can my boyfriend come, too?' asked Sofie.

'Doubt it. They're all women,' he said, and grinned while measuring up Samu out of the corner of his eye.

Sofie got herself a job that afternoon, at the best place she could think of, working at the university. She was paid a pound per hour, which seemed like a fortune when she converted it to *forints*. Samu promised to carry on looking for accommodation on his own, but he seemed to become depressed by his own lack of success.

One Friday they went back to the Hungarian Club in Notting Hill, where they first met Emily and her baby. The minute she saw Sofie, she decided right away that she would go out that night. She left her one-bedroom studio flat and her baby to Sofie and Samu.

The gorgeous baby fell asleep soon after Emily had left. Samu and Sofie had a bath together and made love standing against the bathroom door, for Sofie did not want to mess up Emily's bed. Sofie fed the baby at eleven again, slightly worried about Emily. Luckily, the baby seemed happy enough. They sat down in front of the television and watched *Only Fools and Horses*. The humour seemed alien to both, but they managed to laugh a couple of times. They fell asleep on the sofa, to be woken by Emily stumbling in at around three in the morning. She checked on the baby and scattered into her bed. Sofie went back to sleep.

In the morning, Sofie fed the baby, letting Emily sleep. She woke up hours later terribly hung-over, but she said that she had met a man the night before, and she thanked them.

In the streets of Notting Hill Sofie was reminded of Uncle's warning to avoid the place. It seemed so ridiculously prejudiced. On nearly every corner they bumped into a Rasta man who had long dreadlocks and a cassette recorder under his arm that boomed the music of Bob Marley. To Sofie and Samu it seemed like paradise. They passed a house with high stairs and broad double winged doors. A metal sign, slightly tilted to the side, hung in the window with red letters that announced, 'Vacancies'.

Samu ran up the steps and rang the doorbell. A young black girl wearing a white dress opened the front door and ushered them into the front room of the house, where the vacancy sign was hanging in the window with its back to them. A short, jumpy black man, with bloodshot black, intense-looking eyes and greying dreadlocks falling onto his shoulders, came to the door.

'Thank-ya Shirley, dear,' his voice sounded croaky, but he introduced himself with a huge ivory smile, 'Can me help you?'

'We're looking for a room to rent,' said Sofie nodding towards the sign.

'Yeah, 'ave an upstairs, come.'

He led them up the stairs to the first floor and opened a door to a room that had a double bed, a fireplace, and two large windows to the street. There was a dressing table with a mirror and a chair in front of it and even a small table with a reading light. It all looked perfect.

'This cost you ten pound a week and you share a bathroom with Mr Ahmed an' 'is family. You do no' take food in room an' no pets. You can use kitchen downstairs, man. I show you.'

They had to follow Mr Whingley to the kitchen at the back of the house, under the stairs. On the way down Samu squeezed Sofie's hand to mean that he liked the place.

'Do you like it?'

'Yeah. Don't you?'

Sofie nodded reluctantly, she always took time to make up her mind.

The walls of the kitchen were painted dark red, the semi-darkness embraced them like a womb. The sudden warmth together with a strange odour lingering in the air made Sofie's stomach contract. High up on the walls were shelves full of dolls, each with long hair and beady eyes. Samu admired the dolls.

'Amazing.'

'Where a' you from?' Mr Whingley enquired.

'Hungary.'

Mr Whingley hit his knees with delight. 'Puskas, soccer, Hungary!' Mr Whingley jumped into the air and kicked an imaginary ball and made the noise of a cannon.

Neither Sofie nor Samu liked football but grinned like crazy to show their national pride.

'Do you want the room, kiddos?' Mr Whingley asked but he seemed to be talking to Sofie's long brown hair.

Samu looked as if he was already living there, his limbs relaxed and hung down much looser on both sides of his body. He seemed tired, but also comfortable. He sat down on a chair grinning encouragingly at Sofie, nodding his agreement. 'Amazing, man,' he said, pointing at the exhibition of dolls. 'Fine work, man.'

'OK,' Sofie said. She took out ten pounds from the wooden box that she kept all her notes in and gave it to Mr Whingley. 'For the first week.'

'OK, Saturday be rent day, then.'

'All right.'

Mr Whingley gently touched Sofie's hair, but she shrieked away.

'Me never see so beautiful hair. It's worth good money.' He pointed at his dolls. 'All good hair. Real.'

'Are you a doll maker?' asked Sofie.

'I make wigs. Dolls me hobby.'

Mr Whingley took down a box from a shelf and opened it. There, in a soft bed made of silk paper lay an array of miniature dolls. He took one out and put it into Sofie's hand, but she dropped it.

'Sorry,' she said.

Mr Whingley gently picked it up from the floor and ferried it on his ivory-coloured palm to the table. 'Effigies,' he said, proudly. 'I make 'em.'

'Are they used for Woodoo?' asked Sofie worried, but Mr Whingley just laughed.

'No way. They're wish dolls. You tell 'em wha' ya wa' an' they carry it out while you sleepin'. Some used in t'eatre just like wigs me make.'

'How very strange.'

Mr Whingley shrugged and swirled a slight wave with his dreadlocks.

'Anyway. You move in. Don't forget: Saturday – rent day.'

On the way up to their new home they met Mrs Ahmed. She wore a black burka and she seemed to be fat underneath. She turned her eyes away when they passed her.

'Hello,' said Samu.

Mrs Ahmed nodded.

On second sight, the room seemed bigger than before.

'I always dreamt of having a fireplace. I think it's a wonderful tradition,' said Sofie throwing herself on the bed. Samu dropped himself down next to her. The bed responded with a squeak.

'And you always get what you wish for, even without effigies.'

'Don't talk about them. They're creepy.'

'Well, he's a bit creepy himself. But I like his creepiness. Did you smell the weed?'

'I thought it was food, the smell, I mean.'

'No, it was real weed. Bob Marley, remember?' said Samu turning onto his stomach.

'I wonder what Mrs Ahmed would say to that?'

'She probably cannot smell it through those layers.'

'You're funny,' she said snuggling under his face on her back. They kissed. Sofie looked around once more. There was a bed, a table, and chair in front of the window.

'We have a home,' whispered Sofie to Samu's smiling eyes.

Chapter 39

In a week Mr Whingley had already figured out that Sofie worked, but Samu did not. Samu spent most of the days in the house, playing his recorder, drawing whatever was in front of him, but mainly the vista from the window, and trying to score some 'herb' as they called it. Mr Whingley was fun to be with and he was generous with the weed. He claimed to have met Bob Marley in London a few years before, which was a life-changing event in his life. After that he converted to the Rasta religion. He was trying to be helpful, suggesting that Samu went to the police to register and get himself a work permit. He told him he might even get some benefits as a refugee.

Although somewhat apprehensive, they followed Mr Whingley's advice and went to the police.

Passing Kensington Market they entered and descended the stairs into a maze of cubicles selling smelly stuff, as Sofie called it, incense, palm reading, and clothes. Even the street entrance smelled of sweet and dubious Nag Champa. In front of the tattoo parlour there was a tall mannequin wearing shiny skinny leggings and a black top. It had strong muscles and shoulders and very short spiky hair. Yet, it was female. A silver chain hung down from the shoulders and the mannequin had many rings in its ears. Samu admired it.

'Fashion is usually crap, but this looks wonderful. I wish I could get it for you. It really turns me on.'

'I don't know,' said Sofie, and Samu could see her pupils shrinking with fear.

'But I do. Your father wouldn't approve,' he prompted her.

'I suppose you would like me to get a tattoo on my left shoulder, as well?'

'Would you have one on your bum? Just for me?' he boomed and kissed her laughter away.

At the police station they had to sit down with two officers. It was a small and stuffy room without any natural light. The whole place looked in dire need of refurbishment with its dark walls and glass-walled cubicles. The walls were covered with metal shelves packed with files in paper boxes. Mr White had a nameplate on his table; the other man did not. He never said a word – he made notes of everything spoken in the room.

'Mr Horvath, Miss Benedek, I hope you don't mind my colleague sitting here.'

'No, I don't mind,' said Samu, trying to stop his shaking knees.

'Mr Horvath, when did you enter the United Kingdom?'

'A month ago.'

'Did you have a visa?'

'No. As you can see my passport it has no visas. It is for the Eastern bloc.'

'Where did you enter?'

'I jumped off the ferry near Dover.'

'Hm, so you are an illegal immigrant. Why didn't you come to the police sooner?'

'I went to visit my girlfriend, Miss Benedek, in Manchester and I did not know that I had to register with the police, to be honest. I was only told a couple of days ago that I could get refugee status.'

'Who told you that?'

'Our landlord,' butted in Sofie.

'Mr Horvath, regarding your right to political asylum, it is very unlikely that it will be granted, as you have no proof of your political activities against the Hungarian regime at all.'

'Isn't it sufficient that we left Hungary illegally, through the green borders?' asked Sofie shocked.

'I'm afraid not. But if you have been persecuted for any political reasons you can claim asylum in Britain.'

'We were constantly molested by the police,' said Samu.

'The police would "molest" you here too, if you behaved suspiciously. The police's task is to keep order in the public.'

'And I did not want to become a soldier of the Hungarian army. I refused military service for I did not want to serve the Russians.' Samu hoped that this would make his point, but Mr White's face remained the same: blank and emotionless.

'Refusal is passive resistance. It is not political activity as such.

There is no precedent that you could get asylum with that argument.'

Samu remained silent. He was getting very annoyed by the scribbling of Mr So and So colleague.

Sofie looked at Mr White questioningly. 'If he cannot get an asylum, then how can he get a work permit, Mr White?'

'Mr Horvath needs to find an employer that will become his sponsor. He has a month to do so. After a month he has to come back and if he has not done so, he will have to leave the country. For this month he has to prove that he has enough income to support himself while he is looking for a sponsor. Can you show that you have two hundred pounds to come by, Mr Horvath?'

Samu's eyes widened. Mr White and Miss Benedek were discussing his fate over his head, and of course, he had no money in his pockets. He just watched silently as Sofie quickly pulled out her wooden box from her satchel and laid out two hundred pounds from the money she had from her grandmother on Mr White's table.

'Yes, we have enough money to come by.'

'OK, noted. Well, if he has an employer that will be willing to vouch for him, he will get a work permit for that particular job. On the other hand, Miss Benedek, you can get indefinite leave for the United Kingdom, for your uncle has already vouched for you. You can get it stamped into your passport outside at window 19, after paying the administration fee of ten pounds.'

'Thank you.'

Then Mr White turned to Samu again. 'Mr Horvath, is Samuel Horvath a common name in Hungary?'

Samu could feel the blood leaving his face. 'The Horvath is a common name, I've just met a man in the Hungarian Club who was my namesake but not my relation. Why are you asking?'

'And what about Samuel, Mr Horvath. Is that common?'

'No, Samuel is less common,' Samu mumbled, trying to hide his trembling hands.

'Mr Horvath, would you say that Samuel Horvath is a rare name in this combination?'

'Could be.'

'Thank you, Mr Horvath, that's all. This interview is finished, and I look forward to seeing you again in a month's time. Ah, your sponsor should be a British Citizen, by the way.'

Mr White shook Sofie's hand with compassion while he ushered them out.

Chapter 40

Samu left the building to get a smoke while Sofie was getting her stamp. The streets were busy, life was moving at a fast speed, while everything seemed to have stopped inside his brain. Samu was wondering where Zoli could have ended up with his passport. It was clear to him that he was the only Samuel Horvath in the UK. If they met someone else with the same name, it must have been Zoli.

They went to Kensington Gardens. Sofie seemed happy, lying on the lawn, enjoying the sunshine, but Samu started to be very unnerved. He imitated Mr White's smooth manners.

'Miss Benedek, Mr Horvath, I love you, but you must leave this country in a month's time, will you?'

'He was doing his job. He could have been much worse. I think he was nice, much nicer than the police in Hungary.'

'Bullshit. He wants us to talk to the intelligence, but I won't sell my soul to the devil.'

'What? He didn't say a word about the intelligence.'

'Who do you think was that Mr Anonymous? Jesus Christ in disguise? He became totally agitated when he heard that my father is an army officer. Just think how much I could tell them. I grew up almost as part of the army.'

'He didn't say a word.'

'He lifted his eyebrow.'

'He lifted his eyebrow? Are you serious?'

'OK, you didn't notice. Your papers are all right, why should you care? But I won't be granted asylum if it's up to him, I tell you.'

'Then you will have to find a sponsor. They cannot send you back to Hungary, that's for sure.'

'Don't be so naive. I don't believe a word they tell us. Look how they treat their own people.'

'I think you're paranoid.'

Samu shrugged his shoulders and looked around. A man in a grey cardigan sat down on a bench near them. He folded out a newspaper and started to read, but, he was listening to them. Samu was sure of that.

'Silence means agreement,' said Sofie. She started to pretend that she was blind, or not seeing him, tapping the air around her. 'Samu, where are you?'

'You're so silly,' he said, 'let's go home.'

When he pulled up Sofie onto her feet he could have sworn that the man in the cardigan was looking at them for a moment. He rolled up his paper when they left, ready to go, too.

Samu saw the dog first, but he did not notice it. He was too preoccupied with watching his own back.

'Everything will be all right, I have faith in you,' said Sofie, 'and I still have the money my Nan gave me.'

Samu looked back again and noticed that the dog was following them. Sofie stopped and turned back. When Samu turned he could see the man in the cardigan passing them.

'My god, a stray dog!' Sofie screamed. 'How do you do? This is my friend Horvath Samu.'

Samu tried to pull her away. She was extremely childish. 'Isn't he charming? Let's take him home with us.'

'Do you remember Mr Whingley: "no pets"? And anyway, we have enough trouble making ends meet as it is without another mouth to feed.'

'It doesn't matter, he needs us. We'll find a way. Let's call him Twist Oliver.'

Samu grinned, they were in England, after all. One or two more orphans, who cared?

'I don't mind. All right. Come, Oliver. I'll show you your wonderful new home.'

They smuggled the dog in under his jacket and it was good enough to be quiet. The house on the other hand was very noisy. Mr Whingley's workshop door was open, and they could glimpse some very young black girls busily assembling large white ostrich feathers. Caribbean music boomed from a tape recorder, and they could hear Mr Whingley's delightful laughter.

They sneaked up into the room and fed the dog. Sofie seemed just as happy to look after the dog as she had been to look after

Emily's baby. *Girls are strange creatures*, Samu thought. Luckily, by now they knew Mr Whingley's habits. They reassured each other that he would either be stoned or working in his studio, listening to reggae music, so he would have little chance to hear when the dog made any noise. Anyway, their next-door neighbours, the Ahmeds, had the nocturnal habit of screaming the walls down. They also listened to the Muezzin on their radio every four hours, busily praying, no doubt. They had no time to care about little dogs making little noises.

Sofie and Samu had to smuggle the dog out twice a day for toilet matters, and they did this in turn. Usually, Sofie did it in the morning and Samu did it at night when she was at work. Sofie got a basket for Twist Oliver to sleep in and to be taken out in, which was originally a picnic basket with a lid. Nobody ever cared what they did with it outside or inside. So, everything worked out fine, just as Sofie had foretold.

The exciting preparations of Mr Whingley and his granddaughters carried on all week and turned out to be for the Notting Hill Carnival. Samu got to take part as a drummer, sitting on top of a parade lorry and he learnt the rhythm very quickly. He was proud of himself, for even the drummers acknowledged that he had a talent. He became part of a community, where every man had an open heart. Although he was at first apprehensive for having a different skin colour, the Rasta men took him in without comments. He played the drums well, this was sufficient. It was not certain whether the procession would go ahead, but they prepared for it, anyway. Mr Whingley said that the police might stop it all, if they found that it was too dangerous for the people. They did not want any riots.

'They have no respect for us, you know?'

Samu knew it too well. The police were not respected and had no respect in return in Hungary either. But they were wrong. Mr Whingley was convinced that through His Imperial Majesty, the Rastafari messiah's intervention, a true miracle occurred. A good relations officer was appointed by the police to safeguard the carnival, and in the end, the Notting Hill Carnival became a symbol of good relations between the communities. It was peaceful and for a long weekend the streets were whirling with crowds of dancing people, black, coloured, and white. They had a wonderful time, even though they later heard that someone was murdered.

Chapter 41

Samu had only a few weeks left to get a sponsor. His first journey took him back to the Steels, in the hope that Reverend Steel would help him. When he arrived at the house, Mrs Steel opened the door. She apologised for her husband's absence.

'Oh, the Hungarian gentleman. I'm sorry, my husband is away, but he left a note for you.' She produced an envelope.

Samu opened it and found a twenty-pound note; a purple sheet of paper depicting Romeo and Juliet. *How tragic*, he thought.

'My husband said he was very sorry, but this is all he could do.'

Samu's suspicion of not being liked by the Steels was confirmed. He thanked the woman and left, not even considering asking for any more help. He went on to Kensington and Notting Hill, looking for church institutions, but none of them had work or sponsorship. He even went back to the Hungarian Club, picking the old lady's brain about possible sponsors, but she was just as unhelpful. Meanwhile, he had the distinct feeling of being followed. Once he saw a man in a beige Mackintosh at a bus stop. Samu stopped and waited for the bus as well but did not get on it in the end. The man took the bus and left. He looked through him, through the bus window, yet Samu could feel that he was looking at him.

Getting home that night he took out the dog, then went back and he was in bed by the time Sofie came home, just at eight. She put on some slow jazz on her tape recorder and undressed slowly, knowing too well that Samu was gazing at her through the blind shutters of his eyelids. She glided under the duvet slowly and started to caress him all over, but Samu did not feel like having sex at all. He did not respond; he turned to his side.

The Ahmeds started to quarrel next door; Mrs Ahmed screaming in Arabian. Samu glimpsed a mouse in the corner searching for food. He jumped out of bed and caught it with his bare hand. Sofie laughed. Samu could not hide his anger with her; he held the mouse by the tail and flung it towards her. She squealed. The dog woke up in the basket and whimpered. Samu dropped the mouse and jumped to Twist Oliver to press his hand on its mouth. From there he could see the mouse scurrying back into the crack in the wall. He could feel his tears running down his face and his lips opening and uttering uncontrolled laughter.

When he saw Sofie's scared face he said, 'I hate this life.'

They fell asleep hugging each other.

Samu woke up early in the morning, for Twist Oliver was scratching the door. Sofie was sound asleep, so he hid the dog under his coat to take it out. He silently opened the door not to wake Sofie, neither to make any noise to reveal Twist Oliver's existence, but when he got to the bottom of the stairs Mr Whingley's studio door opened and the old man pushed his greying curly head into the gap. He was grinning. Samu gave up. He let Twist Oliver run to Mr Whingley, jumping up on his leg. Of course, he charmed the old man, too. However, Mr Whingley decided that they had to pay a fiver more now weekly because of the dog. Samu gave in without resistance. They broke the rules, it was just as right. The only problem was that he had no money and he was fed up depending on Sofie.

He went to Queen's Park to watch the runners. Twist Oliver was sniffling around, pissing happily on each tree. Samu wished he could change places with him for a moment. Being a dog without worries was more appealing than his present circumstances. All of a sudden one of the runners, a young guy in tight shorts, sat down beside Samu, panting.

'Have you had enough?' asked Samu, looking into his eyes under the sweaty eyebrows.

'Oh, yeah. Hi. I'm Jack.' He reached out his hand and Samu shook it with pleasure.

'I'm Sam.'

It all happened very quickly. He touched the other's arm and he didn't pull it back. They ran together into a tunnel and started to kiss. It was different with a young man. It all made sense. Jack told him to be there in the afternoon and he said OK. He ran back to the house full of energy, more alive than ever. Something good was going to happen.

Chapter 42

When Samu got home that Friday morning, Sofie was already getting ready. She had a shower in the shared bathroom, trying to wash away the depression caused by Samu's awful mood the night before. She was even more surprised when he got back from the walk with Twist Oliver and came in through the door beaming with joy.

'What happened?'

'It's out in the open. Whingley-man doesn't mind, as long as we pay fifteen pounds a week.'

'Five pounds more? For such a little dog? How can he be so greedy?'

'I'm sorry, Sofie, but sooner or later it would have come out, anyway.'

'It's all right. Don't worry. I earn twenty-five in the week. We can always use my Nan's money as a last resort.'

'You should never touch that.'

'Hey, I've got a feeling that you'll be lucky today. You'll find a job, too.'

'I hope you're right. But let me have a sleep first. I'm exhausted.'

Sofie forgot to tell Samu that there had been a phone call from Margaret. She just left a note. *Hey, could you meet me after work? Margaret wants us to go and visit her and Victor.*

After work Samu was not there waiting for her. She waited for fifteen minutes but decided to go on her own, as she had arranged to meet Margaret at the tube station. Twist Oliver might have eaten the letter – he liked eating everything.

Margaret was very agitated when they met.

'I don't know what happened to Victor. He has been behaving strange lately. So much so that I decided to stay at my parents. This morning I had a call from his workplace looking for him. They said that he hasn't been to work for two days and they threatened to kick him out.'

When they arrived at the flat they could hear some noise from inside. When Victor opened the door the chain stopped it. He just peeped out suspiciously through the gap at Sofie, seemingly not recognising her.

'I have no information, go away,' he said.

'Victor, it's me, it's Sofie. Margaret is with me, too, please let us in.'

'What for?' asked Victor.

'I've come to see you, Victor, please let us in.'

'Nothing anti-socialistic is happening here.'

'Victor, I've come to see you, I'm not interested in politics.'

He took off the chain, hesitantly. Sofie pushed the door open. It was terribly smelly and cold in the room. Victor was naked. He ran into the far end of the flat. His body was full of drawings, in red and black ink or biro, obviously done by himself: red stars, hammer and sickles, swastikas. Sofie and Margaret followed him slowly. He curled up in the corner, muttering to himself.

'I know mankind is imperfect. Even if he is the most developed of the animal kingdom. Is he? What about the spiders and the ants?'

'Who are you talking to, Victor?' asked Sofie laying a blanket over his shoulders. Victor stood up to attention.

'Comrade Stalin is going to help us; he is our hero.'

'Can you see him?' asked Sofie, but Margaret had better ideas.

'Victor, Stalin is dead, Lenin too. They cannot see you.'

'Comrade Stalin cuts a red star into my skin, hooray.'

'I can't believe this,' whispered Margaret, 'he must have taken LSD.' Sofie just vehemently shook her head. Victor never took drugs.

'Victor, please listen to me, tell Comrade Stalin to go away. Tell him that you are in the West now and he doesn't have power over you anymore.

'Mr Lenin and Mr Stalin are helping me.'

'Don't believe what they are telling you. They only want to get you into a mental asylum, to take your freedom.'

Then as if by magic, Victor changed completely. He became calm and sober and looked at Sofie with recognition. He was himself. 'You're really crazy with this mania for freedom,' he said. He knocked his forehead. 'It only exists here, not in the West.'

Sofie and Margaret laughed, relieved. 'Really? And it drives you mad.'

They persuaded Victor to put on some clothes. Sofie was so upset she nearly cried, but she managed to stop herself. They helped Victor into bed and hoped that he would sleep until it was time to go to work. Sofie promised to stay there to wake him up in time and to send him to work and to spend the night there to be there when he came back, to make sure that he was still all right. Margaret gave him an ultimatum. She declared that he had to pull himself together and find a place to live. She could be helpful in finding a room, but this was as far as her help reached.

Sofie walked with Victor to his workplace and on her way back she phoned Mr Whingley and left a message for Samu, so that he was not worried about her. Victor stumbled home after work, thoroughly exhausted, and he was happy for the company. He was sound and healthy when she left him on Sunday morning, as if the madness of the last couple of days had not happened. He admitted that he experimented with mescaline and the breakdown was the after-effect. His trip had been mind-blowing, however, he found out that his totem was a Siberian wolf, a pack leader and very wise, but when he went on the run with the animal in the snow, somehow, he got lost in Siberia and his trip turned into horror. Indeed, he met Stalin's ghost who was trying to possess him. He thanked Sofie for helping him to come back to reality and he swore that he would never take mescaline again.

Sofie went home on the bus on Sunday morning. London basked in sunshine and the light was playing a magical show on the dew-covered lawns of the parks. The bus glided like a boat, like a cradle, rocking her into relaxation. Her limbs were mellow and there was love all around her. Passing Queen's Park she saw Twist Oliver and Samu, running towards a tunnel, so she got off sooner and decided to walk home through the park. She wanted to tell Samu about last night's anguish and her subsequent success with helping Victor out.

First she saw Twist Oliver snuffling in front of the entrance of the tunnel. When she got to eye level, she looked in and saw Samu kneeling in front a man, performing fellatio. She turned as if stung and started to run – she ran home as fast as she could.

She pretended to be asleep when Samu arrived back later that afternoon with the dog. She observed him through half-shut eyes, his every move. He was humming to himself. Sofie had never seen him so happy. Her heart shrunk into a prune, dry and inconsolable. She was not a big woman. If she had been, she would have been able to keep him. Samu confused her even more by kissing her awake. He kissed her feet, her arm, her hair. He was kissing her with the same mouth that was holding a penis just a couple of hours before and his lips were sweet. When she could not pretend sleep anymore, she sat up abruptly.

'I had to stay with Victor last night. He was in a very bad state.'

'Yes, I was wondering where you were. I was worried about you.'

'I think, Victor will soon have to move out from Margaret's place. She is fed up with him.'

She did not say anything about the mescaline, or the madness, or even about her success in getting Victor back into reality. Samu did not have much to say, either. Perhaps, he felt rejected.

'Well, I'm sure you will want to know. I still have not found a job yet, but I'm looking.'

'Do you think I care?'

'I thought you did.'

'Well, sorry, I should be.' She turned towards the wall to hide her tears. 'I think, I'm coming down with something.'

She stayed in bed until twelve the next day, when she had to get ready and go to work.

Chapter 43

After work Sofie did not feel like going home. Instead, she went to a pub near her workplace in Soho with one of her workmates, a Polish girl called Katka. They had a couple of beers and later she went home. Still Samu was not there. So she took out Twist Oliver and bought a couple of more beers in the off-licence – a Brunswick. She was gently reminded of Browning, but her mood dropped a million storeys thinking about her adventure with him. Well, Samu was doing the same to her, only with a boy. She thought it was what she deserved, a hilarious twist of fate. *Instant karma's gonna get you.* Of course, this was an open relationship and Samu was free to do what he wanted. This is what they had agreed to a long time ago, in Hungary, sometime around John Lennon's death, now she remembered. She could not recall why exactly she had agreed to it, but now all of it seemed to be wrong. She was monogamous, after all. She was hurt and thought that Samu only turned homosexual because she was not a big or strong enough woman to save him.

She wandered around Holland Park, then sat down on a bench, drinking her beer. From her spot she could see a huge poster of a werewolf over the entrance of the Odeon cinema. A long queue of curious people had formed: the film was a sensation. Normally, she would be too scared to want to watch a horror, but in her misery, she wished a werewolf came and tore her guts out. A young Latino guy sat down next to her. He had dark skin and gorgeous almond-shaped eyes. His hair was longish and framed his face gently.

'Hi. I'm Pablo.'

'Sofie.'

'Are you OK?'

'Thanks for asking. You Latinos are so beautiful people.' She could feel her tongue messing up the accent, like Uncle George used to when he was drunk.

'Have you got a boyfriend?'

'I think so.'

'What will he think when he knows you're here with me?'

'He doesn't care. We're very open, you know?'

'Then you better come home with me, I'll look after you.'

'No.'

Pablo looked at her worried, like a father. She was lingering on that for a few moments. She could let go and fall into the arms of this angel. Then she heard a voice that was very familiar.

'Sofie, I've been looking for you.'

Samu leaned closer to her face, and she recognised his high forehead, the pronounced knobs on each side where the horns grow out of the devil's head. Samu shook her and reached under her arms to lift her up. Her soft legs obeyed and she was standing, waving like a reed on a frozen lake. She could see Pablo still on the bench and announced to him, 'this is him, Samu.'

'Thanks for looking after her, man,' said Samu to Pablo.

They moved on together, stumbling and struggling against the wind or some other vicious substance, the streetlights floating around her, while Samu's voice echoed in her ear.

'There was a bomb alarm in the tube. I thought you were caught in it. Come, let's go home.'

'Samu, this is very nice,' she slurred.

When they got home, Samu undressed her like a child.

'Samu, do you love me?'

'I love you.'

She heard him say before she fell into a dark mist of complete oblivion.

In the morning Sofie was still in bed when Samu left with his usual, 'See you later, alligator', which she reciprocated with a 'good luck Donald Duck', forming a plan of great proportions in her hung-over head. She jumped out of bed and opened her wooden treasure box, but after some consideration decided not to touch the money. She had a shower with ice-cold water and dressed. Her hair was still wet when she painstakingly cut it with her manicure scissors. She revered, loved, caressed, and kissed goodbye to every little bunch she cut. Her childhood, her mother, her grandmother, her father, the kindergarten, the primary school, the Balaton, the grammar school, all her friends, Janos, Gabi, Budapest, Hungary. She addressed, considered, and said thanks for each lock. When she finished, she went down to Mr Whingley's studio. She knocked on the door.

'Come. Ah, what nice surprise!' he said.

Sofie laid the hair out on his bench like a samurai sword between them.

'How much?' she asked.

'You don't pay rent for a month,' he replied.

Sofie panicked. 'I want money.'

'Then me can give ya half of it. Thirty pounds.'

Sofie shrugged her shoulders and got ready to leave, but she knew that Mr Whingley would not miss noticing her trembling fingers.

'OK, OK, forty poun' an' two weeks no rent. Here.' He took the money from a drawer.

'Give your word,' Sofie said suspiciously.

Mr Whingley put his hand on his chest and grinned like a child. 'Cross me heart a' hope ta die.'

Sofie turned her back on him and sneaked out of the room like a shadow. She went to the kitchen and got some oil to rub it into her hair and spike it up. Incomprehensibly light-headed and weightless, she hovered into the street. The money burnt between her fingers. On her way to work she bought a black outfit in Kensington Market: tight miniskirt and tight top with a silver chain dangling down from the shoulder. She bought Doc Martin boots, high up to her knees, black too, and make-up. Her Polish and Philippine work colleagues laughed when they saw her. Everybody wanted to touch her short hair, running their fingers through it, but she denied them the pleasure, too worried that they might spoil the spikes.

She put on the new gear after work, intending to surprise Samu. On her way back through town she started to notice the change in the way, people perceived her. They seemed to be attentive when she got near them as if the clothes had given her some status: status of the strong, of the outsider. She could not slouch sitting on a chair anymore, she was too worried about exposing her crotch. She remembered that the last time she wore a short skirt was in primary school when she flashed her knickers at the boys. *Dear God, I ever did that?* She smiled to herself. Now she rediscovered the pixie of her childhood in herself again. People smiled at her. Her hair worked as an antenna, exploring the environment like a snail's eyes, searching, tasting the air. The air in between the antennae seemed to energise her, and wake her up. The short skirt allowed her legs to move more freely. She walked with long steps, wading through the dirt of London.

In the house at Notting Hill, when she was rushing up the stairs to the room, she passed Mrs Ahmed and her little daughter but she did not seem to recognise her for a moment, so Sofie stopped to explain to her, 'I changed over to wearing black, too. It does really make a difference.'

Mrs Ahmed did not say a word; however, she pulled her daughter closer.

When entering the room, Samu laughed. Clearly, he liked what he saw. He was amazed.

'Jei, you are exquisite!' he boomed at her, running his fingers up her legs.

They went to Soho, drank beer in a few pubs, and visited a few sex shops. There were machines where, for some money, you could peep in and see porn films. Neither Sofie nor Samu liked the films very much and after a while Samu said, 'it's too boring, they do the same thing in every one of them.'

They went back to the pub and drank tequila. Samu loved it and it made them smile and grin and kiss, but after a while, Samu started to peer at a man in the corner, who seemed vaguely familiar to Sofie. He was middle-aged and wore a grey blazer. He drank beer and read the newspaper. Samu raised his glass to the man, but he just looked through him. The man did not seem to notice him at all. Samu turned back to Sofie and held her short hair between his fingers.

'It's very, very sexy. I know you did this for me. Thank you.'

Although jealous and frightened, Sofie summoned up the courage and asked him who the man was behind her.

Samu shrugged his shoulders. 'He's been following us all along.'

They drank more and left the pub, and the man did not come after them, so Sofie just forgot about him. They passed Il Paradiso, a transvestite bar. Samu admired the men in feathers, wearing headdresses like Mr Whingley's granddaughters at the Carnival; he traced his fingers along the outline of their strong shaved legs and painted faces and discovered a note in the window that said, 'Vacancies'. He wanted to go in to enquire about the job straight away, but Sofie pulled him back.

'You're too drunk. Do it tomorrow.'

Arriving home, they chased each other up the stairs to their room, followed by a just as joyous Twist Oliver. They fell on the bed as if exhausted, and then Samu started to kiss her. Deeper and deeper, rolling on the bed. When they fell on the floor they laughed. Mrs Ahmed turned up the volume on the record player and they laughed even more. Arabian male choir filled the air. Sofie had a flash of memory. Afghan soldiers she had seen in a documentary, standing in a circle, swinging Kalashnikovs and singing to their lovers, or whoever was beyond the clouds of comprehension; but the yearning, undulating music seemed to turn Samu on. Humming into her ear, he rolled her onto her tummy. Sofie, not being able to see his face anymore, got scared.

'Be gentle,' she asked.

He entered her gently, but within a minute he became very excited and wild. Instead of enjoyment, Sofie was in pain, but where did it come from?

'Stop!' She pleaded. Sofie swallowed a scream of pain; she did not want Mrs Ahmed to hear after all and Samu only stopped when the dog started to bark at him. He collapsed then on top of her back.

Sofie lay stiff, and at last, he whispered sorry and started to kiss her back and neck, but she was immovable, like marble. She only turned her head towards him, when she felt his hot tears dropping into the creek of her neck.

'Please get off, you're suffocating me,' she said and then she saw that he was properly crying, booing like a small child. He was shaking with sobbing, the snot and tears smeared on his face. Sofie lay down on her back and took him into her arms. The thought of having to comfort him, when she ached inside out, seemed absurd, yet she did it. They fell asleep arm in arm, even though her sensible self wanted to run away.

The next morning, Samu left early to go back to Soho, trying to get that job, whatever it was, while Sofie stayed in bed a bit longer. She was slumbering, her body trying to get used to yesterday's rejection, the aftermath of pain, wondering why it all had happened as it happened. Why could she not accept him, for sure, it was all her fault? Why couldn't she just have given in to him, surrendering? Where was the love of giving?

Twist Oliver started to get agitated, and she could hear some noise from behind the door, so she quickly put some clothes on and opened it. Zoli was standing there like a ghost. She stepped aside and let him come in. He sat down at the end of the bed. He seemed exhausted.

'Hi Sofie, is Samu home?'

'No. As you can see. Can I get you some tea or a glass of milk?'

'Yeah, milk would be good.'

Sofie went down to the kitchen for a cup for herself, too. By the time she got back, Zoli was asleep, sitting up. She knocked him on the chest and he fell back, stiff, like a corpse.

Chapter 44

Outside the office of Il Paradiso Samu was waiting for his interview. One wall of the office was made of glass, so he could observe the boss sitting behind his desk, his long legs carelessly thrown under the table. The walls, just like the corridors, were decorated with the photographs of the transvestite divas wearing feather outfits. The boss looked at Samu from time to time, but he averted his eyes, being too nervous. There were two girls sitting next to him. The one on his left was a Polish girl who spoke very bad English, wringing her hands nervously. The other girl was a punk, something like Sofie had become. Her legs thrown apart, her mouth chewing gum. She had a ring in her nose and three more in a row on her ear lobe.

She asked Samu, 'Do you know what the job is?'

'No idea, but I'd take anything.'

The girl grinned at him. There was something not right about her teeth. Samu, when he allowed the wave of confusion to subside, got the picture that she was a dyke. He snuggled closer to her and looked into her eyes.

'Your rings are fabulous. Is there anymore?'

The girl looked back annoyed.

'No chance, man, fuck off.'

Samu enjoyed the abuse. Sofie would never talk to him like that, although he would have deserved it, like last night. What the hell had come into him to go at her like that? Like an animal. His ears were burning when he thought about it. *Poor Sofie, she deserved so much better.*

The dyke was called in first but came out very quickly. When she left, she just looked at Samu and said: 'All yours. He's a prick.' So Samu went in apprehensively.

The boss's name was Trevor Tender. He was thin and tall and there was nothing gay about him. He folded his arms and legs in a lanky way and asked what Samu could do.

'I'm an artist and I can play the flute.' Samu had brought his plastic recorder with him and he took it out. He was brilliant at improvising, he knew. He gave the guy a quick performance.

'How delightful – a talent,' said Trevor, lazily clapping his hands together. 'Hm, the flute.' His voice went up two octaves and now he trilled in a falsetto. 'Well, all our music is recorded, unfortunately. We don't need musicians, but we need a dishwasher. What would you say to that?'

'OK, no problem. Any job will do. Would you be able to give me a note for the police that you employ me? I can only work if it is official.'

'Of course, everything is official here. We love uniforms,' he said again turning up the end of the sentence with a slight giggle. 'You can start tonight, and I will sort out the paperwork tomorrow. How's that?'

'OK, call me Sam.'

'Great, Sam, see you tonight.'

On leaving the room Samu managed to give an encouraging smile to the Polish girl, even though he suspected that he had just grabbed the job from under her nose.

Samu was victorious. Although by now he knew that he could have a lucrative career as a rent boy, he did not want to go down that route. Jack gave him twenty quid each time without even asking how much and he even brought Samu another customer for the blow jobs, but he wanted to stop. It could grow into a deadly addiction; illegal work, no matter how well paid, would not help him to secure his stay in the United Kingdom.

That same night he started working in the club, while listening to the music that shook the walls of the kitchen. The divas had deep voices, some of them quite beautiful. Trevor kept checking on him from time to time, forgetting his hand on his bottom. Samu just waved him off with the sponge and they laughed like friends.

While Sofie was happy for him and she seemed to be proud of him, Zoli, who had been staying with them for days, of course, was totally dismissive of his new workplace. He called the divas fags and other awful names so well-known from their childhood in Hungary. Samu was not happy to see his old friend this time. He had a dangerous air about him, a lot more aggression than Samu remembered and he actually confessed, behind Sofie's back, that he was a dealer. Although Samu admired his old friend's courage, he knew that he would never do anything so illegal. He thought it was shameful to profit from people's addictions and he did not want to have contact with the dark side of society. He knew from films and hearsay that dealers had a short lifespan. Sooner or later, they would be killed.

They were sitting in the dark corner of an all-day chippy one day, having breakfast. The place seemed deserted, having no customers to speak of, except for an old woman, wearing a long grey coat and billy hat, her head tilted to the side, gazing out of the window, as if she was in another world. While they were relaxed and playful, Zoli seemed nervous. Samu kept wondering whether Zoli had become a user, but he had never seen him taking anything. So he shushed his worries. Nonetheless, Zoli's behaviour started to remind him of Al Pacino, playing Scarface. His dark eyes were darting from side to side, his head sunk between his shoulders, and he had become jumpy. Sofie, being the goody-goody, was in a celebratory mood, trying to entice Zoli's admiration.

'This is fantastic. You have a job, sponsor, and even money.'

'The Home Office can fuck off now,' said Samu.

'And you're a real cunt now, as well,' butted in Zoli.

'Who cares? Is your job better, perhaps?'

Zoli understood the hint, but, of course, he could not go into too much detail in front of Sofie.

'I'm a business traveller between here and Amsterdam.'

Samu laughed. 'What about my passport? Did you burn it after you escaped, as you had promised?'

'Which passport?' asked Sofie and Samu remembered – he had never told her why he had to stay behind and Sofie had to leave Hungary on her own.

'The first one.'

Sofie visibly checked the gravity of this revelation. She became very agitated and turned to Zoli.

'Did you burn it or are you still using Samu's identity for your little trips? Answer now.'

'Of course, I did, as we agreed.'

'Show me your papers then,' Sofie demanded, putting out her hand like a beggar.

'Show me your papers,' Zoli mocked her. 'Are you the police, or what?'

'If you're such an honest friend, you can.'

'Sofie, shut up. This is not your friendship,' interfered Samu, but he was just as shocked as Sofie when he saw Zoli taking a gun out of his pocket.

He put it on the table and looked at Sofie, who understood the hint. Zoli seemed to enjoy his power, so he took some time before he spoke again.

'It's for sale.'

Samu became interested. 'Wow! Is it loaded?'

Zoli grinned and nodded.

Samu could not resist touching the gun. He started to pose with it like James Bond, humming the music. He asked Sofie, 'it looks masculine in my hand, doesn't it?'

Sofie seemed disgusted and frightened. 'Put it back, it's awful.' But he did not listen.

'How much?' he asked Zoli.

'For you it's two hundred.'

Sofie interfered again, demanding, 'put it away.'

Samu leaned over to her and touched her short hair with the gun's barrel, drawing an ice cold line behind her ear. 'I like your hair, baby,' he said with a deep voice, but she shook her head in tears. She stood up and ran out of the café.

Chapter 45

Outside in the street, Sofie, on the verge of a nervous breakdown, was walking up and down, waiting for Samu. She could not understand this relationship between Samu and Zoli, just couldn't. Idiotic Samu would follow Zoli blindly, like a slave. She was a pacifist, she hated guns. Only weak boys needed guns to feel powerful. Or even each other. There was absolutely no individuality in these guys. They were just ticks, leaches, mini *Smurfs*, who could only feel strong in a pack. She stood opposite the café, in the bus stop, watching the door. Zoli left first. He came out and looked around. Pulling his head down into his collar, he disappeared in the crowd.

When Samu's bright face appeared in the door, Sofie walked over to him.

'Stop being so angry. He is my oldest friend,' he said.

'He is using you and you don't even want to see it.'

'In Hungary, we had a lot of fun together. But I have distanced myself from him, I must admit. Not as if it mattered to you.'

'What kind of fun?'

'Boys' games. Games that I can never play with you. Because you never challenge me.'

'Are you suggesting that I should make a man out of you?'

She could see the range of emotions on Samu's face and knew that she hit him below the belt. She was about to apologise, but he was faster. He became scarlet and jumped close to her, grabbing her by both arms. He squeezed her wrists and sneered into her face, 'Ha-ha. That's not funny and not even fair. And you know that.'

His hold weakened and Sofie freed herself. She could see that she had touched a very deep wound in him and she tried to make it better. 'Sorry, Samu. Believe it or not, I love you.'

All the way home they did not talk to each other. It was OK, for the noise of the tube and the rocking sensation made them even more tired. They sat side by side, their shoulders touching, but Sofie was light years away from Samu. His body was just another rock, carelessly thrown into space, lame and listless.

Twist Oliver greeted them barking and wagging his tale happily when they got home. By now he was Mr Whingley's favourite tenant. He was getting fat being fed so much food in the downstairs kitchen, and he had the freedom to run around in the backyard that was full of mysterious statues and ornamental chairs that Mr Whingley kept for his 'meetings'. From the smell that often crept in through their bedroom window Sofie always knew when he was sitting there, even on his own. He had a huge water pipe in the yard as well; there were no secrets about that. The black men, whom Mr Whingley called 'elders', not only discussed matters of race and riots but also played reggae music.

Such a meeting was taking place in the backyard when they arrived, so they just scurried up into their room, trying to be invisible. Samu collapsed on the bed. Sofie went to have a shower in the communal bathroom, trying to wash away the madness of this day. When she returned, Samu was already tucked up, half asleep. She lay down at his side, wondering whether this would be the last time she shared a bed with him. She was wordless. She put off the light and watched the flashing streetlights reflected on the ceiling, listening to the mix of incomprehensible murmur and music reaching her ears from the back yard.

Samu began to talk.

'You know, before I left, I found out something awful about my father. My mother confessed it in a letter to me that my father had a male lover once. In truth, he is a latent homosexual. He suppresses his desires for the sake of fitting into society, or just because he wants to have a family, I'm not sure. I thought about it a lot and finally understood that he wanted to make a man out of me, for he was frightened that I would become a gay man.'

Sofie was speechless. She did not know what to say. She could only whisper, 'Are you? Are you a gay man?'

But Samu did not answer. He turned on his side and he might have been sleeping, she could not decide. She snuggled closer to him and hugged him from behind. This was quite the opposite of the times in Hungary when they were camping together in the wild, undisturbed by the outside world, far away from society. Then,

Samu had snuggled up to her from the back and they'd fallen asleep without making love. This time she just hugged him from behind and tried to protect him – of what, she wasn't sure.

Chapter 46

When Sofie finished work the next day she was pleasantly surprised to see Samu, who was waiting for her outside the university. They strolled along Tottenham Court Road arm in arm and it all made sense to her; they were still a couple. Passing some shops on the way down the road, Sofie remembered their discussion after seeing Zoli.

'OK, here is your challenge. Steal something from the next shop we pass.'

Samu looked at her in surprise. The scare in his eyes gave her a fleeting feeling of satisfaction. *So be it, he asked for it.* He slowed down his walk. Sofie enjoyed his hesitation but would not let go of him. In the corner of her eye, she saw that he was nervously eyeing up the next shop in the street, which was a greengrocer. The fruits displayed were meant to attract customers, but they were either of inferior quality or fake. Perhaps too many were stolen here, near to the university. Samu fixed his eyes on a bunch of green bananas in the last basket, almost hanging down to be picked. When they got closer, he grabbed it and they ran.

The next moment they were surrounded by police. A man wearing a grey blazer walked up to them. Sofie recognised the man from the pub in Soho. A police van appeared out of nowhere and they were pushed into it. It all happened in a second and it was all so shocking, Sofie nearly forgot to breathe.

When they arrived at the police station, Sofie was told to sit down on a bench, for she did not do anything, except for running. Samu was taken in for interrogation. A very tall and very wide shouldered police officer was waiting with her, standing on her side. She saw handcuffs and a billy club hanging from his belt in the corners of her eye. Sofie was a mouse at the feet of an elephant, but in truth it was the law that towered over her. She was small and guilty. *Mea culpa.*

'It was all my fault, please, can I make a statement?' She asked the policeman repeatedly.

'Miss Benedek, please stop bothering me. Your friend is making a statement right now.'

After an hour or so, Samu was released.

'Come, Sofie, we can go.'

'They don't want to talk to me at all?'

'No, they are after Zoli. Come on, let's go.'

Samu was already late for work, but he was quite sure his boss would understand. They went their separate ways.

Chapter 47

It was ridiculous that the challenge Sofie set him had turned into this huge disaster. When Samu was questioned by the police he found out that they had been watching him since the first interview, for his name was known to them.

'I didn't know I was so important,' he said.

'We have received information that in certain circles there is talks about Sam the dealer, a Hungarian, who made a name for himself with making a quick career: a rise from nothing to becoming a middleman.'

'But that's not me,' Samu kept saying.

They were sitting in this glass cabinet, with thickly painted grey walls and doors. DC Richardson, a man with baggy eyes and nails chewed to the root, seemed more nervous than he was. 'Well, we don't believe you. As you said to Mr White in your immigration interview,' he said, pointing to a brown paper file in front of him, 'Horvath is a common name in Hungary, but Samu is not. This cannot be a coincidence.'

He turned the file over and pushed two photos in front of Samu, showing Zoli. In one of the pictures he was in Amsterdam, entering a club, in others he was in the streets of London, talking to some suit-wearing heavy guy.

'This is the guy. Do you know him?'

Samu hesitated for a moment. 'No, I don't know who this is, but it's clearly not me. You have the wrong man,' he said finally.

The DC left the room. Samu was alone with another policeman, waiting – seemingly for hours.

When DC Richardson returned, he declared, 'Mr Horvath, your girlfriend, who is being questioned next door, has already confessed that she knows this man.'

Samu's eyes were stinging. He just shook his head in disbelief. Did Sofie really hate Zoli so much? What had he done to her?

'Mr Horvath, it would be better for both of you – you and Miss Benedek – if you admitted it too.'

'Why?'

'If you decide to help us to catch this man, who is obviously using your identity, you can stay in the UK. If not, you and Miss Benedek will be extradited. She is your accomplice, after all.'

Samu thought, poor Sofie had probably given in when they threatened that they would throw her out of the country. Of course, he did not want to spoil Sofie's future. Zoli was not her blood brother, after all. He had to save her, this he owed her. It was a logical conclusion that he had to admit that he knew Zoli. He could not let them hurt little Sofie.

He told them everything; stupidly, he even confessed that he had given Zoli his passport in Hungary, although it was not really their business.

DC Richardson did his best in helping him to feel even more miserable. 'This is the worst you could have done, Samu.'

He began to believe it. When he found out from Sofie that she had not even been interviewed, he understood that he had fallen for the oldest interrogating trick in the world.

The next time he met Zoli, he suggested that they worked together. Zoli was reluctant, as if he guessed that something was amiss.

'OK, but I only want to use your address. A parcel or a letter will arrive in your name,' he said and grinned and Samu could see in his eyes how much he enjoyed his cruel joke; like in the old times, having no compulsion in using his identity, 'and you will have to give it to me. That's all I want. You will be paid, of course.'

Samu called his mentor, DC Richardson. He had been told to report to them when Zoli was due to come to collect the parcel. The police would pick Zoli up there and then, with the evidence in his hands, and that would be it. He would get his identity back and Zoli would be their problem from then on.

Only, the parcel did not arrive. When Zoli came for it, there was nothing to pass on.

'They sent it exactly a week ago. It should have arrived.' Zoli became agitated. 'Somebody must have nicked it.'

All letters for the tenants were kept on a low table in the hall of the building until they were collected. When Samu tentatively asked Mr Whingley whether a parcel had arrived and whether someone could have mistakenly taken it, all Mr Whingley could say was that they had a 'meeting' and someone had picked it up because of the shiny stamps.

'Do you mean a child?'

'Or man,' Mr Whingley said in his usual dreamy manner. 'Our community we not allow the monkey business … we don' allow our kids do synthetic. Herb is holy plant. Everything else make you ill.'

'How could you know what was in it?'

'If you get a thick letter or parcel from th' Babylon Amsterdam, man, an' you never been there, it's clear what it contains.'

'Mr Whingley, you're playing with my life here.'

'God's ways are th' mysterious ways. It'd be often th' seeming worst disaster turn into a blessing.'

When Samu explained to Zoli that his parcel had been taken by 'divine intervention', he became agitated and very angry.

'Are you serious? They'll kill me.'

So it was Samu's job to find the money for the replacement consignment. As a measure of caution, he also rented a PO Box at the local post office. He did not imagine that DC Richardson would pay up and the number of people that could have helped him to get the money were very limited. He was resigned to being a gigolo, but the maximum number of clients he could manage a day was less than ten and the idea of being watched by the police while doing it did not make him any more confident. He started to feel like a love machine and this made him even more desperate. He developed a septic throat and the glands in his neck swelled up. He began to think that he would have to take drugs to survive this business. *But what kind of drugs could help?* He did not know. Weed would have made him indifferent, so that was not very good for the activities he had to perform, but that was all he could get. He was very tired by the time he arrived at work in the evenings and Tender noticed that something was wrong with him.

Tender waved him to come into his office.

'What's wrong, Sam? Are you ill?'

Samu had heard of some mysterious illness that had been brought over from the States. It took many members of the gay community off their feet in the neighbourhood. Tender must have alluded to that, therefore he just shook his head.

'I'm not too well these days, for I have problems.'

'Do you want a few days off?'

'No, actually, I got into some trouble and I need money.'

Without asking any more questions, Tender opened the drawer of his desk and handed out a hundred pounds.

'This is an advance for a month. Or if you wish, it can be a loan. Whatever you want.'

'Thank you, so much,' Samu mumbled.

It was such a relief to know that he had a friend and he was wondering why it had never occurred to him to ask for his help. He had been too worried about any strings attached, but this was so easy and Tender never made any fuss about money.

Chapter 48

Sofie took out Twist Oliver for a walk; her only companion during the weekends, when Samu had to work. When she left with the happy dog dancing at her feet, she saw a shiny dark blue Jaguar waiting in front of Mr Whingley's house. Sofie recognised her uncle's car. He rolled the window down and called out.

'Sofie?'

Her uncle looked fantastic, with the winsome shine in his eyes that he only seemed to have when he was on the way to or just back from Hungary. They went to a pub, of course, to have a beer. Not every pub allowed dogs in, but Sofie knew one a few blocks away, near Portobello Road.

They sat down in a quiet corner. Uncle was visibly shocked by her appearance, and Sofie enjoyed the show. No doubt, he had expected to see Saint Sofia. *Well, no more.* She was used to her punk hair and the Doc Martins by now, but it was interesting to see the effect on her uncle, the middle-aged womaniser.

'I'm on my way home back from Hungary. Everybody was asking about you.'

'How is Nan?'

'She's ageing, rapidly. But she said she trusts that you'll do well, and you'll achieve your goals.'

Slightly embarrassed, Sofie was trying to remember her goals. Too much had happened recently and she had to admit to herself that she had lost touch with her own life and she was too involved in Samu's. Tiredness overtook her.

Uncle George broke the silence. 'What happened to your hair?'

'I sold it.'

'Are you starving?'

'No, I needed money for sex.'

Uncle swallowed and trying to hide the shocked expression taking over his face, put on the mask of authority. 'Sofie, your parents are very worried about you. They want me to help you.'

'I don't need help. I've got a job now. I work at the university.'

'Let me guess. You're cleaning after the students.'

'At least I'm closer to my aim there.'

'Browning was asking about you. He talked to someone at Manchester Uni about you.'

'Ah, really? He just wants to get into my knickers.'

'What sort of talk is that? You're going downhill, Sofie. Everybody thought that Samu wasn't good news for you.'

'I love him.'

'You're his slave.'

Sofie could feel the tears of anger burning her eyes and turned away. Uncle George put his hand on her arm and went on, 'come with me back to Manchester. We'll make you better; you can have your job at the pub. Everybody likes you there.' Sofie shook her head but could not stop the tears. Uncle uttered a big sigh and threw back his whiskey.

'OK, let's go. I'll take you home.'

Uncle George wanted to give her a lift home and, although it was only two corners away, she agreed, for she was aware of the heaviness in her limbs. When she sank into the soft seat she was thrown back to Hungary to when she first sat in a Cadillac on their way back from Kaposvar to Budapest, sensing for the first time that she might have got lost in the vicious web of her relationship with Samu.

They were rolling down a sloping street alongside Holland Park Gardens, when she noticed that they were going in the wrong direction. 'I think, we're going the wrong way,' she said to Uncle George, but he did not listen. The radio was playing 'Slave to Freedom', a wild hard rock song. It sounded as if the guitar was being torn into pieces. 'Hear?' He turned up the volume, grinning, but Sofie did not think it was funny. She shouted at him, 'stop the car. I want to get out. I'll jump out if you don't. I don't care if I die.' As a reply, Uncle switched on the central lock in the car. She couldn't open the door. Sofie screamed and kept bashing the window, and Twist Oliver started to bark ferociously. At the traffic lights, Uncle could not bear the worried looks of people and drivers around them any longer. He released the central lock. Sofie and Twist Oliver jumped out of the car and ran. *No man, no bloody man in this bloody world has respect for my freedom.*

She was nearly asleep when Samu arrived home and sneaked into the bed beside her. She was happy that he did not initiate sex. She knew that they had gone beyond that.

In the middle of the night, she was woken up by his shouting. 'No, don't please.'

And she was wondering who might want to rape him in his dreams. Then she was reminded of the fact that she had been raped by her boyfriend, by the man she loved. It was inconceivable, but true. The gentle, placid Samu she had known had turned into a monster. He needed help, but who was able to help him?

The next morning they took the dog for a walk together. When they entered Queen's Park, Samu grabbed her hand. It was as if he was leading Sofie into his kingdom, but, of course, he did not know that Sofie had seen him here before with a man. They sat down on a bench, far away from the tunnel, yet Sofie was so painfully aware of its dark presence, as if it was pulling her and Samu together into its depth. She kept seeing Samu there in the same pose, kneeling in front of a man, while Samu started to talk about his boss, imitating his manners and voice.

'Sam, my dear, would you come into my office?' He waved his hand in a loose motion, as if trying to shoo away a fly, adding that he had first thought that Trevor could not control his limbs simply because they were so far away from the centre of his body.

'But since then, I've found out that this is what they call "camp". It's the way homosexuals show themselves.' Samu was sounding so light and happy when he said this. He was never camp and could not be, he was a boy that she fell in love with. Unexpectedly, there was harmony between them. Sofie spontaneously leaned closer, wanting to kiss him on the lips, but he jumped away abruptly as if he'd been stung. With a deep gash into her heart, Sofie was turned inside out. Samu seemed to become conscious of what he had just done and tried to hug her. 'I'm sorry,' he said, but something snapped in her.

She shrugged him off and walked away without a word. She walked around the garden slowly, like a queen. She took in every bit of it, knowing that she would never return here again.

When she got home there was a message from Margaret. She called her back and Margaret simply told her that Victor had moved out and had not left a forwarding address. She was worried, but she could not help him anymore. She asked Sofie to get in touch if she heard from him.

She climbed the stairs to their room and lay down on the bed. Samu was already gone to work, but he'd left his coat hanging on the door. It was a warm day. She was just staring at the coat, imagining his body in it, the strong muscles, the beautiful chest, all that she could not touch or feel anymore. Then she saw the bump. There was a strange elevation in the height of the chest, as if his heart had been left in there. She stepped closer to feel it, but instead of rounded edges, a weight; when she slid her hand in, she touched cold metal. It was a gun!

First, she threw it on the bed with a sudden disgusted reflex. Then the thought of betrayal conquered her mind, and she ran to check her wooden box to see whether there was any money missing. The box was empty. Nan's money was gone. Exhausted she lay down beside the gun.

Chapter 49

The streets in Soho were riddled with prostitute boys. The shutters on the tube station were down and Samu saw that he had missed the last tube. He had to wait for the late-night bus to get as close to Notting Hill as possible. On his way to the bus stop, he could hear some boys shouting. At first he thought they were coming after him, but no, the guy was shouting 'Help!' When he got closer to the noise the guy was not shouting at all anymore, but he ran. Samu could see his curly hair, guessing that he was black. He became a flash of dark light, turning into a shadow, extinguished in the distance. Now alone in the dark street, Samu was petrified. He started to walk faster but could hear some laughter and some words floating towards him like shots of slag, talking about some 'nigger fag' in the belly of a corner, and someone lit a match. In the glow a group of four men were lighting up, one after the other. They noticed him.

'There's another,' someone said, 'Do you want a fag, queer?'

They laughed, but Samu did not have the nerves to stop or to say anything, anymore, he started to run towards the lights, where he had seen the black guy disappearing a minute before.

It was nearly three o'clock when he got home. He stumbled into the room. When he switched on the light on the bedside table he was facing the cold barrel of a gun. He nearly freaked out.

'I thought you hated guns,' he said to Sofie.

'And I thought you were a pacifist,' she said.

He snuggled closer to her, trying to give her a kiss to shut her up, but Sofie pulled away, hard as stone. She pointed the gun at his chest from close, so that it hurt. He thought she wanted to punish him for hurting her feelings earlier that day. 'Sofie, I said sorry.'

Sofie would not budge. 'I have the power now, for I have the gun. I tell you what you'll do, you'll put on make-up.'

Samu laughed nervously. It was too late for silly games. 'Are you serious?'

Her face was cold and desperate. There was no way that he could have argued. So, he sat down at the dressing table and started to paint his face. Lipstick, eyeshadow, foundation. He was trying to make a show of it in the hope that he would make her laugh, but her demeanour did not change. When he was finished, Sofie examined his face. She sat down on his lap and made him look at himself and herself in the mirror, head by head. She looked like a girl that wanted to look like a boy, and he looked like a boy wanting to transmute into a girl. They broke out into hysterical laughter.

'You took my grandmother's money for this?' she asked, waving the gun in front of his face.

'It's mean, I know, but I needed it. I was only going to borrow it, anyway. I was going to put it back as soon as I saved it up. I have to work with Zoli and inform the police about it. The whole business scares the shit out of me. My life is a whole heap of shite.'

'You can't inform on your friend, how can they ask that?'

'They offered me a deal. If I inform on him, I can stay, if I don't, they will extradite both of us for stealing.'

'For stealing a bunch of green bananas?'

'They call it fair play. I lost their trust in me, now they treat me as a criminal.'

'Did you accept it?'

'What else could I have done?'

'Samu, we have to hide. What about going to some other place, like Scotland?'

'They can find you anywhere. Scotland Yard, remember?'

'Why put yourself into so much danger? What about Zoli's suppliers? They might be even worse than the police!'

'I know, they'll kill me.'

'If they can find you.' She turned towards the mirror again, 'look!'

Samu looked and looked and then he understood.

'Sofie and Samu. Who is who?'

In the morning, with a fresh brain, they tried it out. Samu put on Sofie's old clothes. The long skirt, the T-shirt. Most of them fitted, but they hung on him ridiculously. He had a flat chest and not even Sofie could change that.

Sofie was positive. 'You just need to put on some make-up every night and start walking with a swing in your steps. It'll work. You should call yourself Simone.'

They went out for a walk together, to see how the camouflage worked. By Sofie's side he walked secure in his new disguise, but not at all confident. On Cromwell Road no passers-by in the street showed any sign of upset or surprise looking at them. He could cheat them, or so it seemed.

On their return they bumped into Mr Whingley, whose first reaction was laughter, but he gave a second look at Samu, which seemed to show disgust. Mrs Ahmed just rushed into her room as if she had seen a ghost, which was her habit of greeting them, anyway.

Samu was less convinced of the idea now, but Sofie was adamant that the people in the house already knew him as a male, while strangers would only know him as a girl. He feared the confrontation with Zoli, for he was frightened of his blood-brother opinion, but he knew that their relationship was over. At least he had the gun, although he was sure that he would never use it. He only bought it off Zoli to prevent him using it – or that was what he kept telling himself.

In their room they opened the letters that they had picked up at the Post Office. One in Samu's name from Amsterdam and one in Sofie's name from London.

When Samu opened his envelope he unwrapped many pieces of cardboard. There were a hundred little squares on the neon orange-coloured sheets, which, according to his quick calculation, meant £2,000 on the street market. He knew that Zoli would turn up soon, requesting his post, which meant that he needed to inform the police so that they could come and catch him, red-handed.

Sofie was reading her letter, stony faced. 'Victor decided to go back to Hungary.'

'What? Is he mad?'

'He says that in Hungary there is still a chance that it will all change, and he wanted to stay there to see it and to influence it.'

'He is running into his grave,' Samu said. 'But he can go back easily. All he has to do is to get on a train, show them his passport, and that's it. He will be punished for having stayed longer than allowed, and he won't get any job as a teacher anymore, but he probably doesn't want that, anyway. It's ridiculous. The great revolutionary. How could we've been so stupid to believe him?'

'We made him into our hero. He'd be nothing without us. I'm sure the ones that stayed will be happy to have him back,' Sofie said bitterly.

'Great friend.'

'What was in your letter, Simone?'

'Don't call me that, at least, not at home.'

'OK. So?'

'Acid for Zoli. I think we should move out from here, Sofie.'

He went down to phone DC Richardson, but when he entered the phone box, he already knew he would not do it. On his return from the futile journey, he found Sofie sitting in the same position, still reading Victor's letter. For a fleeting moment, he thought that Sofie could never cope with change. She was rather stiff, if he thought about it, but who was he to judge her? She shuddered when he started to talk.

'No matter what Zoli has done to me, I cannot just give him up. I'll hang out the black scarf in the window, as we agreed it would be our sign to show that the letter has arrived, and I'll let Zoli collect his stuff. I'll talk to him then.'

Sofie stood up and stepped closer. 'I knew,' she whispered and gave him a big hug.

Chapter 50

Zoli came to collect his consignment the same night while Samu was at work. Zoli sneaked in, as was his custom. Again, he looked exhausted. Sofie had to give him the letter.

'Hi Zoli,' Sofie said, barely getting over her shock at having to deal with him on her own, 'here is your letter. Samu told me to let you know that he is watched by the police, and you should be very careful. As far as I am concerned, I'd prefer if you never came back here.' She looked forcefully into his hazy eyes.

Zoli snatched the envelope out of her hand and peeped inside. His face burnt like a poppy field.

'You stupid bitch!' He sniggered.

'It's not my doing and it isn't Samu's fault either. You should be so lucky to have such a good friend and all you did was use him.'

'Tell Samu that he should better disappear. There can only be one Samu Horvath,' said Zoli, pushing her against the door.

'The police already know your face. They have pictures of you. They know who the real Samu is,' she shouted, struggling, trying to get out of his grip.

Zoli, even though he looked tired, seemed to possess a devilish energy. He pushed Sofie onto the bed and lay with his whole weight on her.

She screamed.

The next minute she heard Mr Whingley's high-pitched voice, 'leave my house, immediately.'

A loud flat noise followed and Zoli wailed, his saliva spraying over Sofie's face. He rolled down from her onto the floor and she could suddenly breathe. Mr Whingley had a cricket bat in his hand. He stood there, in the middle of the room, ready to hit again, like a batsman waiting for the ball.

'Stop there old rastard,' Zoli roared at Mr Whingley, jumping on his feet and grabbing the cricket bat from the old man. Mr Whingley froze with his mouth open, now scared. Zoli turned to Sofie.

'I'm going. But you can tell Samu that he is in big trouble. I have mighty friends.'

With that he threw the bat at the bed and flung his body into the darkness of the corridor. Mr Whingley collapsed onto the bed, panting. Sofie, with a racing heart herself, ran to the toilet to bring some water for him.

'Thank you, Mr Whingley, you saved my life.'

'Of course! A rushed to ya' help th' minute me heard ya' scream, kiddo. Gosh, I hope this not Samu call a friend. He no man. He jerk chicken.'

'No, I don't think they are friends. Not anymore. I hope he won't cause any more trouble for you.'

'Don't ya worry about ma. A just 'ave to get a few youngsters to watch out for ma. The whole neighbourhood gonna look out for us, don't ya worry.'

'Now I understand why you kept the cricket bat under the table in the entrance hall, Mr Whingley.'

'Yeah, and me be still pretty good as a batsman. Me used to play for Jamaica when me was young.'

'Thank you.'

Mr Whingley invited Sofie for a late-night dinner, saying that food and herbs together were the best medicine for a shock like this. So they ate whatever was left over from dinner: a sweet-smelling coconut dish with a rich array of colourful vegetables, and listened to music. After food, Mr Whingley said a quick prayer and lit his pipe. Soon, his eyes started to glow in the soft light and Sofie mellowed. She could feel her muscles getting softer.

'This,' Mr Whingley pointed at the smoke at the end of his pipe, 'come from the holy herb. Bible says: "better is a dinner of herb where love is, than a stalled ox and hatred therewith". Mr Marley teach me this, dear Mr Marley.'

Mr Whingley was still grieving Bob Marley who had died a few months before. Overwhelmed by sadness, Sofie just nodded. It was so true. It was so very true. Bob Marley was singing about equality, and he was singing for her, too. Sofie's limbs became heavy, and a soft layer of shimmer engulfed her body. She smiled. Mr Whingley noticed the effect of marijuana on her.

'The herb will show you who ya are. Listen to it.'

Sofie just wanted to curl up into a ball, a hairy ball. 'I think, I am a rabbit.'

He grinned and pointed at Sofie's dark brown brush of hair. 'Or a mole.'

'What's your first name, Mr Whingley?'

'Todd. Tadeus, Todd.'

Hearing this Sofie burst out in the most imbecile laughter that she had ever produced in her life.

Chapter 51

When he had heard what happened and had enough time to take it all in and weigh the gravity of Zoli's message, Samu decided to try the trick and go to work dressed like a woman. Of course, this was an exaggeration, like everything else in the present circumstances of his life, for he was wearing only a few of Sofie's clothes, but they were good enough to try. He wanted to know whether he could indeed hide in the crowd, changing shape like a shaman. He did not wear a skirt but put his long hair into a ponytail high at the back of his head like Sofie had used to wear hers before chopping it all off. He put on make-up as Sofie taught him, herself an amateur. He coloured his lips pink and painted his eyelids with blue eyeshadow. He wore his own black leggings, being much taller than Sofie, but he had a problem with his chest. Sofie never wore a bra: she had neat little breasts that fitted his palm and found that bras were constricting, so he could not fix any breasts for himself. He put on Tender's black leather jacket that he had picked up in his office the night when it was raining. Tender had just waved him off, generously, like ever. He tried to move with languid steps, throwing his hips from side to side as Sofie had shown him. She said that mannerisms were more important than actual looks nowadays, and she was right. In the tube it all went fine, the crowd sheltered him in a way, but in the streets of Soho he lost his courage and thought that he could not pretend. When he glimpsed his mirror image in a shop window he saw a desperate little gay boy, shockingly vulnerable and clearly gone mad.

Samu walked into the Il Paradiso, feeling dejected, trying to be invisible, but Tender saw him through his glass wall and nipped out of the office to open the door for him as if he was doing it for a diva. They laughed about it. Samu was grateful that he tried to make him feel comfortable.

He did the dishes all night, as was his duty, grateful for the protective steam that made him invisible, listening to the wave-like rhythm of roaring applause from the stage, thinking about Sofie.

She would never believe him again – that he loved her – of this he was sure, even though he did, with an awful pang in his being.

Just the other night he had persuaded her to smoke weed, which was generously supplied by Mr Whingley. Mr Whingley had seen that Sofie was not happy and had told Samu to smoke with her and discuss everything. For Mr Whingley, weed was a medicine for all ailments. He told Samu that he used to have a wife who had given him many children. Now that he was a widower, he still missed his missus, but he could now recognise aspects of her in his grandchildren. According to Mr Whingley, the whole purpose of a relationship was to have a family. If they experienced disharmony, they owed it to each other to discuss it. If it turned into a fight, so be it, at least the devil would be out in the open; however, he assured Samu, if they smoked weed, the fight would lose its edge and it would become something else. Could be lovemaking, or simply intimacy, but much softer.

Sofie had smoked it reluctantly, as prescribed, even though she hated the smell, and they'd melted into each other again, talking and talking. But her eyes had shone like red lights, instead of the green she used to have. He could not get any closer to her. They lay side by side, the skin on their arms touching, like Siamese twins grown into each other, but they could not use their fingers and arms.

He seemed to remember that they had been happy sometime long ago in the past and he could not understand where all that love had gone. This was so much deeper compared to all the fun he had with Tender. With Tender it was a game of power, and they were good friends, with Sofie it was pure love, but now without the sex. He knew that this had never changed from the first moment of their relationship, but if he was honest, pure love could be very dull. When her eyes had been green lights they had sex, everywhere and anywhere: she had never said no to him. Something had changed between them, and he was trying to find the reason for it. *When did this happen?* Then the thought of having been betrayed crept upon him with a sudden doubt that Sofie might be loving someone else. This thought hit him so hard in the belly that he had to bend over the sink, but then the smell of dirty dishwater churned up his stomach so that he nearly vomited into it.

When he left work, he did not try to pretend to be a girl anymore. He was a man on a mission, and he had to find out what stood between him and Sofie. He managed to catch the last tube and noted the presence of his minder, the man in the grey jersey, waiting for him at the entrance, following him from a distance. The guy did not have any illusion about Samu's identity, and this just confirmed to him that he was who he was, no make-up could change the fact that he was a man.

At home, he shook Sofie awake.

'Did you ever have sex with someone else apart from me?'

Sofie's reaction was brutal. First, she seemed shocked then she blushed and finally she buried her face into her palms. But after a few moments of hesitation and hiding, she looked him into the eyes and said, 'Yes, and it was beautiful.'

All the muscles in Samu's body tensed painfully and his fingers curled into a fist. He turned away from Sofie, for he was frightened that he could hurt her. He punched into the door instead.

'So this is why you rejected me. And you did not even bother to tell me.'

'It happened while I was alone, and I did not think I would ever see you again. But don't you ever make yourself believe that I rejected you. You raped me; that is a fact, and nothing will ever change that,' she screamed.

Samu, fully aware of the terrible pain in his right fist, turned his back on her and ran.

Chapter 52

When Sofie went down to Mr Whingley to discuss the terms of moving out, he said that there had been a phone call for her from Hungary.

'They gonna call again. Me don't hear you and Samu coming 'n. A cup a tea?'

Sofie sat down and Mr Whingley poured her a cup of his famous herbal tea. The drink was hot and sweet and it warmed her tired heart. She sipped it slowly, trying to calm her racing mind. Mr Whingley took out a small doll from one of his drawers.

'Take. It wearin' ya hair. It gonna help ya make ya dreams come true, ya'll see.'

Sofie took the rag doll into her hand. It did look like her, her old self, a little bit. It had large brown eyes and long hair. It was smiling.

'It does look like me. And it has an empty head, like me.'

'Ya must never lose her. It be a piece of d'art. Verra valuable.'

'Yes, I paid a high price for it, didn't I? But thank you for giving one to me, I appreciate your kindness.'

'Ya deserve it. Is somethin' wrong? What this dark shadow over ya head?' He started to wave above Sofie's head, as if wanting to sweep away all her worries.

Sofie could not but smile. The telephone rang.

'Budapest want ya,' he said. 'Ya answer it.'

Sofie picked up the receiver. 'Hello, Mum?'

Her mother's voice sounded worn and husky at the other end of the line.

'Hi Sofie, I have bad news. Nan is not well. She had a stroke, Sofie. We have to prepare for the worst. I phoned your uncle. He is on his way here. He's flying this time.'

'Oh, God. I must come and see her.'

'Sofie, darling. Think what you risk if you come home. The police have been asking about you and they will sentence you in your absence.'

The line became distorted, as usual.

'OK, Mum, I will think about it.' Sofie hung up.

Mr Whingley patted her hand. 'Sorrows?'

'Yes.'

'Tell ya doll. Do.'

Sofie just shrugged and left him alone with his dolls. She went for a long walk, thinking about Nan – the last time she saw her. Her wavy white hair, the small blue eyes that had never seen make-up. Her smiling face, the wrinkly cool flesh on her arms that she loved touching when she was a child. She could see her lying on a hospital bed, alone, lingering between life and death, ready to go to meet her maker and her sisters and parents that went before her. Even the baby that she had carried in her arms to the cemetery during the war. Her husbands.

Sofie did not really know where she was. The city rushed around her like a stream, providing instant purification. It started to rain, and she carried on till she was soaked through. Then she took shelter in the British Museum. She wandered around, remembering other times in Budapest when she sat on the steps of the National Museum, the wide stone under her feet, the comforting knowledge of being small compared to the magnitude of space and time: the magnitude of history. She was drawn down the stairs, into the basement, where she found the Mayan department. She was too sad but also transfixed by the limestone lintels that described a story of self-sacrifice: Lady K't sta Xook piercing her own tongue while her husband the king was holding a torch over her head. So, it all started four thousand years ago. The blood sacrifice of a woman. The queen had a long, elongated forehead reaching back into space, as if she had to store a lot in the back of her brain. Sofie could not take her eyes from this revelation, she just stood and stared.

A male falsetto voice woke her from her reverie, lecturing, 'and the sacrificial victims believed that they were fulfilling a holy task in their community.'

She turned toward the source of that strange voice and discovered a tall lanky man, probably an academic, or a guide lecturing a group of young people. They might have been students. They were seemingly transfixed with another lintel she had seen two minutes before. 'The lady queen having a vision of a serpent'. Now Sofie shivered. To the echo of that falsetto voice in her head she transformed into the Lady Queen, the sacrificial victim. Samu had come to her, followed her to England, perhaps with a deep desire to be rescued, but her sacrifice was in vain. Indeed, she had turned him into a homosexual. Now he even had to hide as a transvestite. But not everything was her making. Zoli played a crucial part, too, or it was simply fate. Apprehending the absurd taste of this fate she had to laugh. Samu, the man that raped her, deserved this. Samu, the boy she once loved, was gone now. He was the forger of his own fate.

That night she dreamt about being back in Hungary. Better to say, she was trying to get away from Hungary again. She had to climb a high wire fence and she kept losing her grip, falling back and trying again. At the bottom of the fence two German Shepherds kept jumping up towards her, barking, their huge teeth trying to bite her leg. She could hear people approaching and the reflectors were switched on. Sirens boomed. She woke up panting. She put on the light on the bedside table and looked around the room. Twist Oliver was sleeping in his basket peacefully. She knew that she was safe, even though Samu was not at her side.

Chapter 53

Sofie was alone with her struggle and once again she had to decide to stay or to leave. She phoned Budapest.

'Sofie, you need to think it over,' her father said over the phone. 'You would only get jobs outside Budapest, and you could only dig or clean.' The irony did not escape her: she had to choose between being a cleaner in London or in Hungary.

'I am not sure whether you would have to go to prison, but you can forget the university for once and for all.'

She was torn between her head and her heart and admired Victor, once again, for having had the courage to go back, even though he had left with his blue passport for the West. Samu missed the point when he was angry about that. The truth was that Victor needed to have a purpose in life. He could only fight without violence, but the violence the state applied against him had been too shocking to bear for too long. He had chosen to be a useless member of the socialist society. Instead of teaching children to be good citizens of the state, he chose to look after the leftover kids in the streets and lead them. Jesus told him to do so. He left because Margaret had offered her help and he was tired of the constant threat of work camp imprisonment. However, he could not abandon 'his children' without feeling guilty. Having lived in the free West, he had come to realise that this world was even more violent. She reread the letter. "This is a very, very hard world. No excuses, no charity – but there is "fair play". When I took the mescaline, I broke the rules and Margaret had the right to kick me out, which she did, and I fully accept the consequences. I admire the British for their "fair play". Of course, we know nothing about this in Hungary. Yet, no matter what I suffered there, I have to go back, for there I can still make a difference. Here I am only an immigrant, a tolerated extra without any role to play. Sofie, thank you for believing in me, thank you for bringing my manuscript."

Sofie decided that she could not go back to Hungary. She resigned to the fact that she could not be there for her grandmother and prayed that she would survive the stroke and heal well so that they could meet again. She spent her days fasting, for she forgot to eat, in parks in the city, praying and thinking about all her family at home. She wanted to send all her energy to her Nan, for her safe recovery. She was sitting on a bench in the park. The sunshine beamed through her eyelids, and she could feel the golden light flowing into her, filling her up. She could feel someone sitting down by her side and she immediately knew who it was.

'I am very proud of you,' Nan said in that soothing deep voice of hers. 'You're a strong woman now. Just be yourself and stick to your dream.'

Sofie put her tired head down on her lap. 'Nan, I love you.'

'Isn't it a lovely day? Shall we take a walk on the sunny side?'

Sofie got onto her feet mesmerised by the vision, while Nan carried on: 'Will I just tell you that there is no solution: the world is in constant turmoil and we are here to make it livable with random acts of kindness and caring for each other?'

Sofie's gait was light, but every time her sole touched the ground, the world seemed to reverberate with the words of the booming voice. 'The everyday human behaviour, care and kindness, are the most important things we can give each other. Samu loves you in his own way and he was desperate. Never you mind about that money.'

When she got home after her long walk in the park, Sofie packed her belongings. Samu was in bed, and he woke up. He looked at her sadly.

'It's only sex,' he said.

'There's no such thing. Only sex. You should be honest with yourself. It would be easier for you, too.'

'What do you mean?'

'Samu, you're gay. There's nothing wrong with that. Just we're not compatible.'

Samu looked perplexed.

'I need to live on my own and find out who I am,' she said.

'I miss you already.'

Sofie sighed. 'I want to take Twist Oliver with me.'

'No.'

'I want him. He's my only friend. You have Trevor. I have nobody.'

'He's my friend, too.'

'Why don't we let him decide?'

Samu agreed reluctantly.

Sofie opened the door and, swinging her big bag onto her shoulder, asked Twist Oliver, 'are you coming with me?'

Samu squatted down to the dog and reached his hand out to him. The dog seemed to understand the situation. It sniffed at and licked Samu's hand, but then turned its back on him and followed Sofie.

At the bottom of the stairs the air was heavy with the aroma of chicken fried in coconut oil. When the smell of sweet food reached its nose, the dog started to scratch the kitchen door, which was opened and the dog was duly let in.

Sofie forgave him.

Epilogue

Sofie tentatively climbed the steps in Il Paradiso. The wooden floor creaked under her feet and she saw some glitter wedged into the worn out fibres of the blue carpet. She smelled sour sweat mixed with the sweet smell of talcum or make up, she was not sure. *Body secretions do not lie. But you should not be judgemental.* There was good in every bad as her grandmother used to say and this place was an empire of pleasure, compared to the bleak violent world outside.

She knocked on the door that had a "Lucky Lucy" label, hand drawn but with funky letters, adorned with glitter. She recognised Samu's handwriting and smiled. The door opened.

'So here you are,' he took her into his arms, 'my little Sofie.'

He had some creepy nylon material on his chest, yet she enjoyed the hug, nonetheless. She melted into his arms and felt *home* for a moment.

'Here I am. And you, Lucky Lucy?'

He held her away from him, holding her shoulders and looking sternly into her eyes.

'Don't call me that. That's only my stage name.'

'Sorry. How are you, Samu?' He pulled her into the room and made a sweeping gesture, showing it off to Sofie.

'As you can see, I'm fine, doing well.'

The dressing room seemed to be filled with feathers and headdresses. Two sets of dresses, a white and a black hung on a coat rail, two pairs of oversized, high heeled shoes stood along the wall. The mirror was framed with light bulbs and there were plenty of make-up boxes, all lined up like soldiers in a regiment. An open book lay on the dressing table and on the side, another seemed to be by Anthony Burgess - another one by Saul Bellow. Sofie took the book into her hand, yes Anthony Burgess – *Clockwork Orange*.

'You know the film is banned in this country?' Samu asked her.

She nodded and frowned.

'So much about freedom of expression,' Samu said.

'I never read it. Is it any good?'

'You can have it when I finished.' He put his fingers through her shoulder long hair that she had been growing since that fateful day. It was growing in all directions like a lion's mane. She liked to think, somewhat symbolic of her own power.

'Look at you, you've changed.'

'Didn't you?'

'No, I'm still the same Samu deep in here,' he pointed at his chest. 'How's life in Manchester?'

'Well, I'm studying, you know. English and History.'

'The truth?'

'Yes,' Sofie said pulling away from him. 'I'm so glad you're doing well. We're here to see the show.'

'We?'

'Justin, you know the guy from Manchester.'

'Ah, the salon communist.'

Sofie nodded. Heat rose to her cheeks and she knew she was blushing, but she blurted it out: 'None of my boyfriends want to be genuine.' She missed the target, however. Samu must have been used to such attacks. He just shrugged. 'Do you love him?'

Sofie's eyes wandered over Samu's shoulder. She looked into her own eyes in the mirror behind him.

'I never thought about that,' then she looked into Samu's eyes to finish the sentence: 'We have great sex.'

Samu smiled. 'If you say so, I think, you do love him.'

Sofie was wondering, what she felt. Something touched her. It was not sadness, but some kind of knowing, which had a weight. Samu did not forget who she was, after all. Sex and love were the same thing for her. Samu lightly kissed her hand and said, 'Thank you.'

She did not have to ask what he thanked her for. She knew that for him, she would always remain the same; the girl who had granted him freedom.

In leaving, Sofie passed the office. The lights were on and she saw something bright through the slit of the half-open door, a flash of green, the unforgettable kind. She pushed the door open and stepped into the tiny room. An old leather sofa lay on her left with a low coffee table in front. On it, a piece of colourful plastic.

Examining it from close she saw that it was the painting: Bedroom at Arles by Van Gogh. Sofie admired the printed plastic and entered the room of her dreams. The birds were chirping in the garden and someone, perhaps a maid, was singing, too, in French "*sur le ponte d'Avignon*" and she could smell the scent of lavender. It seemed that the door was slightly ajar, something she had never discovered on this painting before. The floorboard creaked behind her. Trevor stood in the door of his office, observing her face.

'Hi, Sofie. Nice to see you.'

'Oh, Trevor, sorry for intruding. I just could not withstand the pull of this painting. It is my favourite by Van Gogh.'

'And mine. It's so pure and simple, almost naive, and look at that light. I got that placemat in Amsterdam at the Van Gogh Museum.'

'Wow! So this is a placemat!'

She turned around the object and indeed, the logo of the Museum was printed on the back.

'I wouldn't use it for that.'

'Well, you can keep it, if you like. I have a few more at home. Did you come to see Samu in his new number? He's fabulous, I promise you.'

'Yes, I'm looking forward to the show. See you later and thanks.'

She ran down the steps like a whirlwind, clutching Trevor's favourite painting under her arm. *What a gift!*

Justin was waiting for her in the foyer and they found their table in the cabaret. Yes, Samu played the diva very well, and the songs were quite nice. She ate, drank and kept touching Justin's thigh, slightly with her knees under the table, grinning at him from time to time. She felt blessed. She was sitting on God's palm, yes.

ACKNOWLEDGEMENTS

I would like to thank Newry and Mourne Council, who provided me with a bursary to spend time with intensive writing in the Tyrone Guthrie Centre in Annaghmakerrig, and the Arts Council of Northern Ireland for their support with the writing of this novel.

During its long gestation, the novel was long-listed for the Bath Novel Award (with the title Finding Freedom) and extracts were published in The Journal of Transnational Writing (The Crossing). The Prologue appeared in Sixteen Magazine and it was included in Angel Fur and other stories.

I would also like to express my gratitude to Dave Hallsworth's widow Elsie, who provided first-hand background information about the Laurence Scott industrial actions in Openshaw, Manchester.

Many thanks to OCA Bradford, where I was a lecturer for a period and the frequent work journeys to the North made it possible for me to do my research.

Finally, I would like to thank my partner Alistair and my children, Vivien, Daniel and John for their eternal patience with me.